"Jasper writes t̶... ... ...for your keeper shelf and ready for recommendations to your friends."　　—*Romantic Times* (4½ stars)

Eventide

"I had high hopes for the third book in the Dark Ink Chronicles, and I was not disappointed. . . . *Eventide* is an action-packed trip into the heart of Riley's journey, and I can't wait to see where she and Eli go from here."

—Night Owl Reviews (top pick)

"[*Eventide*] will elate fans. . . . The lead couple is at their best, but this is Riley's show."

—Genre Go Round Reviews

"Riley is funky, is comfortable in her own skin, and loves and protects those close to her. . . . Some new characters are thrown into the mix, and I feel that a lot of great things will come of their arrival in future books."

—Urban Fantasy Investigations

continued . . .

Everdark

"You won't be able to put it down."
—Dark Faerie Tales

"Ms. Jasper has a great voice that draws the reader in, and writes a solid paranormal series that adds a fresh perspective on vampires, magic, and the South. I can't wait to see what she comes up with next."   —Night Owl Romance

"The characters are personable and vibrant."
—Smexy Books Romance Reviews

"Add in voodoo, the Gullah culture, and the town of Savannah, and you have the makings for a great paranormal series. . . . This is a must read for all major paranormal fans."
—The Romance Readers Connection

"Serious action sequences—we're talking training, free running, vampire fight club, throwin' knives, etc.—but at the heart of [the story] is the bond between [Riley and Eli]. . . . You will love *Everdark*."   —Vampire Book Club

Afterlight

"Sultry, sexy, spooky Savannah—the perfect setting for hot vampires. . . . Beware of reading *Afterlight* after dark!"
—*New York Times* bestselling author Kerrelyn Sparks

"*Afterlight* is a book every paranormal lover is going to fall in love with. . . . Ms. Jasper penned a winner . . . . This is a must-read paranormal book, and it comes highly recommended."
—Night Owl Romance (5 stars)

The Dark Ink Chronicles
by Elle Jasper

Darklove

The Dark Ink Chronicles

ELLE JASPER

A SIGNET ECLIPSE BOOK

SIGNET ECLIPSE
Published by the Penguin Group
Penguin Group (USA) LLC, 375 Hudson Street,
New York, New York 10014

USA | Canada | UK | Ireland | Australia | New Zealand | India | South Africa | China
penguin.com
A Penguin Random House Company

First published by Signet Eclipse, an imprint of New American Library,
a division of Penguin Group (USA) LLC

First Printing, December 2013

ISBN 978-0-451-24005-7

Printed in the United States of America
10 9 8 7 6 5 4 3 2 1

Part One

***

HALLOWED GROUND

You must be dead, because I don't know how to feel.
I can't feel anything anymore.

—Elliott, *E.T., the Extra-Terrestrial*, 1982

*Riley's not the same since she lost Eli. She's . . .
hardened. Closed down. She lets off just enough
emotion to seem human. I can tell her brain has
given up hope. But her heart hasn't. And that makes
her dangerous and unpredictable. If anything, I can
read a woman. And I'm reading her right. Which
means I'll just have to keep a closer eye on her. She'll
either love me for it or kick my ass. I'm betting on
the latter.*

—Noah Miles

*I*t's cold here. Ice cold. The kind that burrows straight
through your skin and jabs deep into your bones. I
can't shake it. I inhale, and that frigid air rushes down
my windpipe and bangs into my lungs. It clings to
my insides, and I puff it back out. Funny. No frosty
air comes from my mouth. I'm more cold-blooded
than warm-blooded, I think. My core temperature isn't
even human enough to heat my breath. What does
that make me? Hell if I know. I don't even know what
I'm doing here. My eyes drifted shut, and the next
thing I know, I'm here, in this place. Something wants
me. That much I know. I can feel it.

As I jog up the darkened street, I notice how barren
it is here, too. No trees. No grass. No shrubs. Not even
a single bird. Only gray concrete, gray sidewalk, gray
stone, gray sky. Even as I fine-tune my hearing,

nothing happens. No beatings of hearts—not even a rat's. Is there nothing alive here? Am I? Hell if I know.

I let my hands skim the building's stone surface as I turn the corner. My body is pressed close to the stone, and I peer ahead. A heavy mist has crept in, fallen over the ground like some white vaporous blanket. It swirls around my feet as I walk, and the farther I go, the higher it climbs. Soon, it surrounds me. I see nothing. I hear nothing.

Then the stench knocks into me, full force. It's many things, all rolled in one. Rancid old blood. Decay. Rotting human flesh. Scorched tissue. The more steps I take, the stronger the scent becomes. I follow it.

One second I'm on a cobbled road; the next I'm on the river's bank. The mist rolls across the black water like a live thing, and the stench seems to come from below. The loch. I ease down the embankment. I stop at the water's edge, and inhale. That horrible smell of death is coming from beneath the water.

"You're so easy." A voice sounds from behind me. "Too easy."

That voice. I whip around, but the speaker's strong arm has snaked around my throat and pulled me tightly against him. Yeah, a male. Big. Hard. The back of my head presses against his chest. There's no heartbeat. What a shock.

Just as I move to raise my foot, his muscular leg traps mine. He drops his free arm over my breasts and pulls me closer. He thinks I'm thoroughly trapped. I let him think it. His head drops to my ear.

"I can't decide if I want to fuck you, then kill you."

His graveled voice brushes against my cheek. "Or just kill you." He pulls me closer, and I feel his hard cock press into my back. "Difficult decision."

I look down at the arm holding me prisoner. Leather jacket, leather gloves. Vise as tight as iron. My head falls to the side, exposing my neck, and I move my ass seductively against his crotch. "How 'bout now?" I ask, my voice low, teasing. I peer into the loch, but it's cloudy with mist. I can't see his face. I can't see anything.

His laugh against my throat is deep, more like a whisper. Edged with certain . . . hatred. Yet . . . there's something about it. I don't know. "Convince me," he says. His teeth graze my skin. "Tell me what you'll do to me if I let you live." His lips move to the corner of mine, and it's an achingly familiar gesture. "Make me want you."

With slow, rhythmic pressure, I move against his groin, pushing against the thick bulge. His body tenses at my movement, and I know he's turned on. I don't know why, but I am, too. I gotta get my head back in the game. That is, to live.

"I can make you come without laying a hand on you," I whisper, and I press my back into his chest.

His arm that is still banded over my breasts slides, and through the thin silk of my bra, his hand cups me. I press my ass against his crotch, and he hardens. "And how would you do that?" he whispers against my jaw.

"Because you're going to touch me," I answer, and before the words fully leave my mouth, his hand leaves my breast and skims my stomach. "And when you do,

I'll explode." A moan escapes my throat, and my vision blurs. I blink. I gotta get it together. "And you won't be able to help yourself. You'll come."

His gloved hand moves over my hip, over my groin, and I thrust against him. He cups me, his thumb pressing against me through my jeans. Just as the climax starts, his grip relaxes and he starts to turn me around. I go limp, and slide to the ground. In the next second, I leap, and I land, crouched, about ten feet away. Through the mist, I blink. The orgasm still lingers, and I will it away.

I look at my captor.

My breath hitches.

My mouth opens to call his name.

"E—"

Just that fast, he's on me again. His hand encircles my throat, and his face contorts to full-raged vampire. His jaw juts forward, almost broken, and jagged teeth drop from his gums. His eyes turn bloodred, and his scent blends with that in the loch. The air is squeaking from my lungs, so audible I can hear it in the misty air around me. He lifts me, my feet dangling over the water.

"You will die now," he says, and lowers me to the loch. "And watching the life drain out of you is what's going to make me come."

I try to kick, to shout, but I'm paralyzed. Screams not my own pierce the air, and he starts to lower me down. The stench grows stronger. I feel water at my back, and hands upon hands pull at me from below. He holds me there, my face and eyes just beneath the surface of the loch, staring up at him through the wa-

ter. Had he not been squeezing the life out of me, I would have died from just seeing his face. Full of hate. Full of loathing.

A monster.

It's Eli.

As I thrash about, and what little air is left in me seeps out, my lungs explode. Unseen hands grab me from the depths of the loch, and before the blood vessels burst in my eyes, I see the others who have gone in before me. . . .

"Hey, Ri." A familiar voice seeps into my conscience. "What are you doing?"

For a moment, I'm speechless. Slowly, I open my eyes. I can't focus. I can't speak.

He grasps my forearm and squeezes gently. "What the hell's wrong with you, darlin'?"

I blink and focus. It's only Noah. And we're in a cab.

Noah flashes his big white, wolfish smile at me. "Anything I can help you with, babe?"

With a heavy sigh, I push my thumb and forefinger into my eye sockets. "No. Bad dream is all." I shake my head. "Are we there yet?"

"Yeah, we're here. You okay?" he asks.

Weird. I remember driving along on the A-96, looking out across the Moray Firth. That's it. As I glance out the window into the night, I see we've ended up on Montague Row, at the guesthouse Jake Andorra, our boss, rented out for us. Rented the whole damn guesthouse so we wouldn't look so suspicious coming and going like we do.

WUP. Worldwide Unexplained Phenomena.

That's what we do. It's an elite organization Noah and I, and a handful of others, belong to. Weirdly enough, I'm probably the most normal of the group. WUP is made up of vampires, werewolves, ancient Pict immortals with wicked skills and sick fighting abilities. Then there's, well, me. A human with vampiric tendencies. So far, I'm the only one. Jake Andorra, a vampire with lethal skills, asked me to join. Although I'm pretty sure most of my team members would argue my tendencies have gotten way the hell out of control. But damn—I've been bitten by three powerful Strigoi vampires from an old Romanian family, as well as my vampire fiancé, Eli. All of their DNA bound with mine, and I took on a little of each one of their traits. I can now speak French and Romanian fluently. I guess my mind control is the strongest trait I've acquired, and I'd be a big fat liar if I didn't confess to thinking it was cool as shit. Anyway.

WUP members are dispatched and assigned the most difficult of cases involving things humans can't even begin to grasp. Basically, we're hunters. Anything involving supernatural beings vs. humans, we're on it. Vampiric situations are the most common, although there's a pretty big werewolf war going on farther west in the Highlands, which is where the rest of the WUP team is right now.

A werewolf war. Sounds pretty big, right? Apparently, two clans have waged war between themselves, and once again, innocent mortals inevitably get in the way. Werewolves are bat-shit crazy and unpredictable as all holy hell. WUP will need every spare set of hands they can use. But under Jake Andorra's orders, me and Noah have been assigned here, in Inverness. Our mission is simple: Take out the rogue vampire or vampires wreaking havoc on innocent humans. Noah's strength combined with mine is more than enough to wrap up this job. Usually, they're newbloods—humans newly transformed and just coming into their vampirism. And totally fuck-wild with bloodlust. It's not too uncommon, rogues. They travel, hardly ever staying in the same location long. But any time is too long. They kill. Innocents die a horrible death.

So me and Noah will hunt down these rogue vampires and make the humans and city safe again. Shouldn't take long. But there's something else I have to do here. Something I have to do alone. And the selfish part of me says it's more important.

Sometime between the Firth and here, I dreamed. Again of my fiancé, Eli, except this time was different than the others. It was . . . bizarre. That's another thing I do—I have wicked dreams that sometimes place me in real situations, and sometimes in other bodies. I almost experience things others have experienced, and it is intense as hell. I shake it off and finally answer Noah. I give a nod. "I've never been better. Let's go."

Noah stares at me a minute, with those calculating mercury vampiric eyes. Finally, he leans over me and opens the cab door. "After you."

I climb out, and the chilled air bites through the black leather jacket I'm wearing. It's not uncomfortable, the chill. Lately, I welcome it. Seems I'm always hot lately.

"Here, grab these and I'll get the rest. Here are the keys to the back entrance." Noah hands them to me and nods. "Just up the walk there, turn left down that alley."

"Yeah, okay," I answer, and grab the two duffel bags containing our gear.

I could have sworn we got in that taxi over an hour ago. It's only been twenty minutes or so since we landed. Wicked-ass dream that was, and I damn sure don't want to have another like it. It left me not only aching for Eli, but fearing what he may have become. Stepping away from the curb, I sling one pack over my shoulder and head in the direction Noah indicated. It's dark, well after sunset. The old gray stone of our Edwardian-era guesthouse blends in with the pale haze lingering in the air. A sign hangs on an iron post that reads ABER-NANTHE GUESTHOUSE. NO VACANCY. As the breeze catches the metal sign, it creaks back and forth. The typical city sounds surround me, but I tune them all out and listen close as I walk. Every noise ceases except the very, very faint ones. The lapping of the firth against the shoreline. Seabirds cooing as they bed down for the night. Pigeons. Gulls. Rats scuffling along the cobbles.

I turn down the narrow close leading to the

guesthouse's back entrance, and a soft breathy sound reaches my ears. My skin breaks out in goose bumps. The fine hairs on my arms and neck stiffen. I'm on total alert, and my eyes scan. I see nothing, but I hear. Breath, but no heartbeat. Shadows reach, stretch in awkward lengths. It's hard to tell where the stone ends and the shadows begin. Something's here. I feel it.

Out of nowhere, a hand encircles my throat. I drop my bags. My feet leave the ground.

Apparently, there are wily, ballsy vampires afoot in Inverness, Scotland.

"When all is said and done, Ms. Poe, you're nothing more than a glorified human armed with pointy little weapons." The bloodsucker knows my name? He squeezes my throat tighter, lifting me higher off the cobbles. "You can still *die*." His lips pull back, gums recede, and a dozen razor-sharp teeth drop from his top jaw, jagged and lethal as shit. What the hell? I've only been out of the cab for three minutes. He pulls me closer. His breath alone nearly knocks me out. It reeks of old metallic blood, flesh, and decay. Sounds like a cool name for a heavy metal band. *Blood, Flesh, and Decay* . . .

And the smell is familiar. Like from my dream.

"When all is said and done," I repeat his words, gasping for breath at the same time, "you're still nothing more than an asshole." My voice is raspy as it pushes past his fierce grip against my windpipe, and my feet aren't even touching the ground when I rear one leg back and knee this bloodless prick in the groin. His grip loosens, just enough, and his pupils dilate. I see the pain there, in their depths. It's all I need.

From the waist of my jeans I palm my silver blade, flip it, and jam it straight into his heart. All within, no lie, the blink of an eye.

The vampire drops me and falls to the ground. He is seizing, quivering, gurgling. His body starts to smolder, disintegrate, and finally, bubble into that disgusting pile of white junk they become when they meet their end.

He didn't even see it coming. Funny how male vampires are way more male *human* than they like to admit. Target their wieners and wham—on the ground they go.

Glorified human with pointy little weapons? *Kiss my ass.*

"Riley, what the hell?"

I glance behind me. Noah Miles is standing on the street side, scowling down the narrow alley I'm standing in. He swaggers toward me, his gaze lowering to the quivering pile of used-to-be vampire. Mercury eyes flash so angrily, they almost glow in the dark. Ever since Edinburgh, he's smothered the hell out of me. Edgy, watchful, and overly mother hennish. He gets on my fucking nerves. Everybody does, actually.

"I liked you better when you were just a horny, whimsical old vampire," I say under my breath, and then sigh with frustration. "I'm fine."

"Riley. You left me, like, ten seconds ago."

I look at my WUP partner. "I was just . . . walking by. Heading inside." I incline my head to the heap on the ground. "He grabbed me." I shrug. "I let him."

Noah mutters under his breath, something annoyed and unintelligible, and stares at me. "Come on, let's make like a tree and get out of here." He grabs the bags I dropped and shakes his head.

I watch Noah Miles's broad back as he retreats to our guesthouse's back entrance. The way he moves tells me he's waiting on me to follow. Slow, careful, on full alert. One thing I can say about him: When he makes a vow, he damn well means every solemn word of it. A vow to protect me, keep me safe, no matter the cost. This he made to Eli, back in Edinburgh when the very real threat of the Black Fallen killing all of us lingered.

"He knew my name," I say to Noah's back as we stand at the door.

Noah's shoulders rise and fall, as though he's taking in a long, exaggerated breath. "That really doesn't surprise me, Poe." He glances back at me. One eyebrow lifts. "At all."

I move ahead of him and through the door. "Just saying."

Inside, I find the switch on the wall and flip it on. The light illuminates a small kitchen area. I move to the hallway and flip another switch. It shines on a staircase, and I head up. At the top, I find a corridor with doors. I throw open the first one and hit the light. Big bed. Fireplace. Terrace overlooking Montague Row. I throw my pack onto the fluffy pink duvet and open it, withdrawing a leather case. I open it and stare down at my cache of pointy little weapons.

"I'll stay on the first floor," Noah yells up.

"Yeah, okay," I answer absentmindedly. I pull off my leather jacket and toss it on the bed, too, leaving just my black leather vest on. I truly prefer nice soft cotton, but it can't hold my blades like leather can. Swiftly, I remove and secure on my person multiple silver daggers, knives, dirks. In my vest, the waist of my jeans, front and back. Grasping the lightweight leather holster, I push my shoulder through and secure the strap around my waist. I snug it tight. Then I eye the one remaining weapon I have.

Right now the most important.

My scatha.

What's that? you ask. Well, in the wise words of the great Inigo Montoya, let me s'plain. From the beginning.

When I think of who I used to be, it seems as though I'm looking at someone else in an old high school yearbook or old photo album. I barely recognize myself. The line separating my old life and this one is hazy, muddled, and most of the time I don't know if I want either one of them anymore, if given the choice. I feel icy cold inside now. Ever since Eli's death.

In my full-blown human days, I used to be a juvenile delinquent. Then I found my mom murdered, and it set me right. With the help of loving surrogate grandparents, albeit root doctors, I became a successful tattoo artist and business-woman. I raised my baby brother, Seth, to near adulthood. My business thrived.

Then the vampires descended upon first my brother, then me. Some vampires good. Some very, very bad.

One . . . *perfect*. But he's gone now. Eli. My fiancé. He was killed by a Black Fallen—a fallen angel whose soul is darkened by the most evil of magic. My friend Victorian Arcos, a powerful Strigoi vampire, was killed, too, by a Black Fallen. The Fallen were taking over Edinburgh, seeking complete mortal power, and killing a lot of innocents to do it. They sought an ancient book of dark magic, and then, well, WUP got in their way. Eli and Vic especially. God, I've never felt so out of control in my life as when those fuckers took Eli and Vic away from me.

Yet Gawan Conwyk, a thousand-year-old Pictish warrior and swordsman, has given me a shred of hope that maybe, just maybe, they're not so dead after all. Once an Earthbound angel, Gawan earned his mortality by offering himself as a sacrifice to save a mortal's life. Not only is he wicked fast and lethal with the blade, but he knows things the rest of us don't. He knows about Heaven, Hell, and in between. According to his theory, Eli and Victorian might just be suffering in an alternative plane akin to Hell itself. Or purgatory. I'm not sure I believe it just yet. In my heart, I feel emptiness. I don't feel Eli there anymore. I think I'd feel him inside me, were he still alive. Gawan, though, knows it's possible. That the Fallen would have thought it more torturous to send them there, to a realm where they have no control, vs. simply killing them. Yet I can't ignore the emptiness I feel, too.

I feel . . . nothing. Two hours ago, leaving Edinburgh, I had hope. Where did it go? Even Athios, the wrongly accused Black Fallen who saved me and turned out to be not such a bad guy after all, encouraged me. But I feel a hole inside me. A gaping, lifeless, aching hole. Now that I've lost Eli, I only have Seth, my surrogate Gullah grandparents who raised me, Nyx, my friend and coowner of my ink shop, Inksomnia, and, well, Eli's family. And Noah.

With so many to love, why do I feel so cold and empty?

I pick up the scatha. It's an ancient Pict weapon, fashioned sort of like a combination handgun/crossbow. It has cartridges the size of a Chap-Stick container filled with mystical holy water from St. Bueno's Well. Once I'm in that weird, hellish alternative plane of a world, I can obliterate anything that comes near me with it.

And I have to do it alone.

I tuck the scatha into the holster, shrug my leather jacket back on, and zip it up to my neck. Just as I turn to head out, I pull up short. Noah's standing there. Staring.

"Where do you think you're going?" he asks.

I meet his silvery gaze. "Out."

Noah's face hardens. "Ri, it's only me and you here. Not the whole team, just us. We have some rogue vampires to take care of, remember?"

"I already took care of one by myself." I go to move past him. "Your turn."

His muscular arm juts out and braces against the doorjamb, catching me right at the throat. I pull up short, and our faces are inches apart, and I stare into his eyes. Before Noah was a vampire, he was a cunning soldier in the Revolutionary War. He may have the most beautifully carved-from-stone face, mesmerizing mercury eyes, and sun-bleached dreadlocks, but Noah is clever as hell. He misses nothing. And when he's got your back, he's got it.

Even when you don't want him to.

Which means I gotta do what I gotta do, too.

Noah's pupils dilate just before my thoughts reach his.

I give a dismal grin. *Too late, my friend. Paralysis.* I give this command to Noah in my mind. He goes absolutely, rigidly still. Rigor mortis still. His facial muscles freeze. His arm is still braced against the doorjamb. But I know he hears me.

"I have to try this," I tell him. His eyes are focused on me, and he might even see me. But he can't move. Not a solid inch. That's one tendency I've mastered over almost all vampires I come in contact with. Mind control.

Pisses them all off.

"I'm taking the scatha and going to St. Bueno's Well," I tell him. "Gawan said the ground's hallowed there, and old as Heaven and Hell itself. A portal to a place Eli and Vic might be." I stroke his chin with my forefinger. "He said I have to go in alone." I close-mouth kiss him on his lips. "I promise I'll be safe. And back ASAP. Then we'll kick some more vampire ass. Promise."

I stare into Noah's eyes for a few seconds longer. I see them flash a bit, darken to stormy gray, and I know inside, he is boiling friggin' mad as hell. At me for going, and at me for being stronger at mind control than he is. With a final glance, I duck under his arm, jog downstairs, and head out into the night.

I'm in the narrow close behind the guesthouse, where I'd killed the vampire earlier, and I stop a second. Tying my hair up into a ponytail, I take a deep breath and think. It's close to eleven p.m. I fish my cell phone from my rear pocket, pull up Google Maps, and check out my route. St. Bueno's isn't on any map, and it's not in any tourist book, either. But Gawan Conwyk of Castle Grimm told me how to get there. And according to the map, I need to highjack some wheels. I could hike it, but, eh. Why bother when I can drive? It would be a pain in the ass to run with all my blades flapping all over the place anyway. Besides, I'm edgy. Anxious to find Eli, or at least a trace of him. I'd probably fall and impale myself.

I walk out to Montague Row and glance one way, then the other. A dark blue Rover is just pulling up to the curb in front of a guesthouse three homes down. Perfect. I walk over, just as the driver is getting out. A man, midthirties. He leans in and grabs a paper sack of groceries. Mind control time.

Give me the keys to the Rover. Don't report it missing, even if it's gone in the morning. Just call a cab. I'll bring it back when I'm finished. You won't even notice me. Nod once if you got all that.

The guy looks at me but doesn't really see me. His eyes are kinda glassed over. He nods once, and when I hold my hand out, he drops the keys into my palm.

Go inside. Forget you've seen me tonight. Carry on, my wayward son. There'll be peace when you are gone.

The guy turns and crosses to the front entrance of the stone house. He opens the door and closes it behind him. The interior hall light extinguishes, and I can hear his feet moving up the stairs inside his flat.

I waste no time jumping into the Rover, starting the engine. Sweet, the Rover has a GPS. I put in the address Gawan Conwyk had given me, and head out. Jake Andorra gave me U.K. driving lessons before leaving Edinburgh. Even though I drive a manual at home, this one's automatic, and I'm sorta glad. Roads are narrow as hell here. But no sweat. I got this.

The streets are quiet as I pull out of Montague Row and follow the GPS out of the city. I hit a few roundabouts before I take the A-9, cross over the Beauly Firth, and through dense mist head toward the foot of Ben Wyvis and the small villages of Dingwall and Strathpeffer. According to the GPS, they're about fifteen miles out of Inverness. I hit the gas and make myself remember to stay to the right. A few random cars pass, their headlights obscured until close proximity because of the heavy Highland mist. Soon, though, I see no one. All shops are closed up for the night. I speed up.

I'm now weaving through the small village of Strathpeffer. Gawan Conwyk had explained that it had at one time been a Victorian spa town, and that the people of the time had believed the natural spring waters contained magic. Like, life-eternal kind of magic. It is still in existence. Gawan said it wasn't so much a *spa*, and that it was more of a place people brought their crazy relatives in hopes of a miracle cure. A huge insane asylum Victorian-era town. Very Stephen King–ish. And the architects of the spa weren't giving magical therapy. As I drive through the quiet village and notice the tall, dark-stoned Victorian homes set back upon tree-ensconced hills, I can only imagine the creepiness of the times. Ice-water dunkings in the springs, or, nicely put, *hydrotherapy*. Craniotomies. Whatever. Victorians, Gawan said, were a "weird and morbid lot of folk." I believe it, and coming from me, that's sorta hypocritical and funny as shit.

No sooner have I left the village of Strathpeffer than I see a small white sign with black letters for Dingwall. My British-accented GPS speaker directs me pretty easily, and before long I'm winding through the town center. More narrow streets, stone walls, stone buildings. I pass several stores, a few takeouts, a haggis shop, the police department, and a school. Soon I turn at a car dealership and start up a steep, high hill. At the top, I follow it left, and I'm still climbing a bit as I skirt several small farms. The smell of sheep poop and hay, mixed with whatever that nice herby, clovery smell is of the Highlands, wafts through the vents of the Rover. Too bad this whole trip to Scotland is a WUP mission. Too bad I'm headed into some heinous underworld that I may or may not escape alive from with my fiancé and friend. I might actually love it here. There's something breathtaking and mystical about Scotland. Something unexplainable. A feeling, I guess.

Ahead, a small dip in the road, then to the right I see a sign: Ivy Croft and Cottage. It's a narrow paved drive, and I hit the headlights off and turn in. I pass a relatively large two-story house, and at the smaller cottage at the top, I park the Rover and pull the emergency brake. The moment I open the door, the scents assail me. Clover. Floral. Pungent. Perfect. Quietly, I close the car door and scan the shadows. A half-moon hangs over a field, and while it's not totally dark, the mist makes it hard to see more than fifty feet. According to Gawan's directions, I have to travel on foot behind the barn I'm standing in front of, up the hill, and after passing a set of ancient standing stones, cross into the wood. I glance behind me, to the house at the foot of the hill. Lights are out, and all is quiet. Hopefully, I'll be in and out before the family wakes up.

My hands fly across my body, checking all of the blades holstered onto my person. I double-check the scatha, zip my leather jacket, and with a deep breath, take off behind the barn. I leap over the fence, startling a few dozing sheep. They jump up, bleat, and herd away from me. There is a trail close to the fence, and it slopes up the hill. I start off across the spongy, wet ground. Something tells me I should've worn rubber boots vs. my leather ones.

The half-moon light slips through the mist just enough for me to make out the sheep path I'm running on, and as I climb the hill and leap one metal fence, I see the crooked silhouettes of the standing stones ahead. I'm moving fast, and within seconds I'm beside them. The wind howls, and in the distance, a set of wind chimes dong. A feeling overcomes me, starting at my feet and moving up through my body. It's like a small jolt of electricity, a low hum vibrating and attaching to every single nerve ending I have. I almost feel nauseated, but . . . not really. I recognize it. It's holy ground. The ancient, old-as-hell kind of sacred. It's so strong, so powerful, it's almost as though whispers emanate from the stones themselves. Way ahead, a hill, or as the Scots call it, a *pap*. And to the left, a dark, ominous mass of blackness. The wood. According to Gawan, that's where I need to go. Even without his direction now, I can tell it. The same force that lies beneath my feet and hums through the standing stones beckons from the forest. More whispers. They're calling my name . . .

Bounding over stones, dead clumps of heather, and prickly gorse bushes, I make my way to the shadowy edge of the wood. My whole body is humming now with whatever supernatural power lies within this hallowed ground. I stop, unzip my leather jacket, and grasp the scatha. It's loaded with six cartridges. I have six more stored in the pockets of my cargos. Hopefully, I won't have to use them all.

The moment I cross the wood line, a shift in the air hits me in the gut. No longer guided by Gawan's directions, but on pure instinct, I take off, leaving the footpath and weaving through the mammoth Scotch pines. Deeper into the forest I move, branches scraping my face, catching my ankles. My insides are seized with pain caused by the hum of supernatural current. It almost doubles me over. It's like an overdose of déjà vu. I'm close. Close as hell. But I keep pushing, the scatha tightly gripped in my palm.

The moonlight shifts, and a single beam shines through the canopy of trees ahead. I see it. The entrance to St. Bueno's Well. I move closer. Slower now. Cautious.

I feel the sonic boom move through the trees before I see it, and I stiffen and dig my feet into the ground. When the wave hits me, I rock, nearly lose my footing, and teeter for a moment. A raging wind cuts through the trees following the boom, and I'm forced to close my eyes. The wind is so vicious it takes all of my strength to remain upright. My breath catches in my throat. It's harder to breathe now.

Then, as fast as it began, it stops.

Open your eyes. You must move fast.

My eyes open and my head jerks. I know that voice. It's Athios, one of the not so willing Black Fallen who basically saved my ass back in Edinburgh. What the hell?

I focus now, and everything changes. The massive Scotch pines crack, split at their bases, and all begin thundering to the ground. There's nowhere to run as the ancient trees splinter and crash, and I stand rigid, clutching the scatha tightly. I know it's not real, but it goddamn looks and sounds real. I can even smell fresh exposed pine flesh lingering in the air, as if just chopped for firewood. The scent is so heavy it nearly chokes me. I force my eyes to stay open. They sting and begin to water.

All at once, the last tree falls. The mist hovers and swirls over the downed forest, obscuring the browns and greens with a white blanket. In the next second, it begins to recede, and in its wake, darkness. It's almost as if my vision is blurred, and I can't make out figures, forms, or shapes. I even scrub my eyes with my free fist.

Then I blink, and my vision sharpens. I'm

standing at the end of a street. Dark, shadowy, desolate. No cars. No trash cans. No storefronts. Just a street. At the far end, a derelict church. Ruined stone buildings flank me, along with cracked and torn-up sidewalks. Windows are glassless, and rotted two-by-fours crisscross the gaps. The air around me is dead still, yet some of the windows have tattered drapes that flap in a breeze that doesn't exist. My eyes search every angle, every sharp edge, every shadow. I glance down, and at my feet, see a dead raven. Half of it's smashed into the broken pavement, its wings unnaturally bent backward. The eyes have been burned out. Nothing but a singed hole looks up at me.

I step over the dead raven, and it begins to flap its broken wings. Billy Squier's "The Stroke" starts booming from one of the broken windows above me. My eyes scan the gaping holes, and I see nothing. I take a long breath and move forward. I can't let this world get to me. Besides, I love Billy Squier. What the hell?

No sooner do I move five feet than my heart seizes. I feel it thump, heavy, like a chunk of lead, and my first and immediate thought is *Eli*. My eyes latch onto the church at the end of the street. He's in there. I know it. I *feel* it.

My legs react before my brain does, and I start to run. Only then do the cracks in the sidewalk break wider, and distorted, shadowy shrouds writhe out of them and move toward me. Their screams pierce my ears, and I feel like my eardrums will explode. The figures emerge from the cracks and take new forms and charge me. One has a shrunken cat's head on a long, willowy body and long, jagged fangs. It hurls itself at me, and I point my scatha directly at its head and fire off one cartridge. The body drops in midair. The head is obliterated. Another one from the left lunges, and I fire. It drops, too. I'm closer to the church. Closer to Eli. I feel him there. Waiting for me.

I'm hit from behind and taken to the ground. Something sharp, cold, jabs into my back and straight through to the pavement beneath me. The pain is white-hot, almost blinding me. I gather all of my strength and explode upward, the thing still attached to my back. I flip, my back facing the ground, and we crash down. Quickly I roll, jump, and fire the scatha. Obliterated. I don't bother looking around me. I take off. The church is ahead, maybe fifty feet. One of the double doors is caved in. The stone is charred, as though it's been burned. The screams of the shadow creatures surround me, calling my name in such deafening tones I think I'll lose my fucking mind. I push it all aside and speed up. With the dark shrouds all around me, with their little shrunken cat heads and distorted bodies grabbing for me, I leap the last fifteen feet in midair and crash through the double doors. One roll and I land in a crouch. The cat heads stop screaming my name. Even Billy Squier quiets. All is silent for a few seconds, and I search the inside of the decaying remains of the kirk. It smells like rotting flesh, death, and moldy wood. A creaking sound above me makes me look up. My heart crams into my throat. My body is paralyzed. My mouth moves, but no sound comes out. *Eli! Vic!* I say in my mind. No answer.

My vampire fiancé, Eligius Dupré, and vampire friend and WUP team member Victorian Arcos are hanging from the rotted rafters above. Tied at the wrists, they're both completely naked. Their pale bodies are so covered by scorched whip marks that the stark slashes make it nearly impossible to tell their limbs apart. Some of the slashes are gaping. Made by blades. *Holy hell . . .*

The moment I decide to move, the sound of beating wings makes me pause. From a rafter close to Eli, a giant black gargoyle sweeps toward me. Its screaming talons and fangs are aimed for my head. I drop to my knee and fire the scatha, and the moment the cartridge hits, its body flies backward and crashes against the derelict stone wall. Black ashes fall to the floor.

Another one comes at me, from Victorian's side, and it's close, moving fast, and I have to free-run over broken pews and crumbling stone to get a good shot at it. I leap, half twist, and aim the scatha at the screaming thing. The cartridge knocks it back, too, and turns the creature to ashes. I've got eight cartridges left, and I'll need every one of them to get us all out of here. I waste no time free-running, leaping off whatever solid thing my feet can find hold of, to reach the rafters above. I reach Eli first.

Hanging by one hand, I have no choice but to holster my scatha. I do so quickly, and gently grasp Eli's jaw with my now-free hand. "Eli?" I say, and my vision is blurred by the tears that are filling my eyes. I can't believe I'm looking at his face. His *live* face. I didn't think I'd ever see him again. "Eli! Can you hear me?"

A low groan emits from his throat, and that's all I need. All in one motion, I wrap my legs around his waist, grab a blade from the back of my jeans, and cut the rope binding his wrists to the rafter. We start to fall, and I notice his body is colder than usual. We drop twenty feet to the floor, and I swing under him just before we hit, landing on my feet. He's heavy as hell, but I've got him. I crouch with him and lay his head gently down, his dark hair falling over his still-closed eyes. But he's alive. *My love is alive!*

"I'll be right back and we'll get the hell out of here," I whisper to him, and graze his lips with a kiss. They're cold, too, and I shake the chill off and gather my strength. Finding a foothold on an overturned pew, I free-run up the wall and leap over to Victorian. Mimicking my movements from before, I wrap my legs around Vic's naked body.

"Arcos? Can you hear me?" I say close to his ear.

A faint grunt comes from deep within him. Again, that's all I need for now.

Letting go of the rafter with one hand, I hold Vic tightly, and with one swipe, I cut through his binds with my blade. We fall, and I land, laying him beside Eli. God Almighty, they're both covered in cuts and slashes. No blood, just dark, sooty marks on every limb, their faces, their chests, almost as if burned with some fiery weapon. Although their flesh is bloodless, it's filleted open in places. *What the hell happened to them?*

The sound of beating wings begins, inaudible whispers colliding, but I know what they're saying. *Riley . . .*

Time to get out. Now.

I've got no alternative but to drag Eli and Vic out by their bound wrists.

A loud beating of wings erupts from outside, and I know when I, dragging two six-foot-plus, hundred-and-eighty-pound naked vampires, explode through what once was the doorway of the church, I will have to have one free hand to fire the scatha. Quickly, I check the bindings on Eli's and Vic's wrists, and I cringe at what the paved cracked street will do to their flesh. But I can't help it. I have to have a free firing arm.

With the screams filling the church, I load the scatha's ammo chamber with four more cartridges, making it completely full. I then take the long piece of rope hanging from Eli's bound wrists, and the one from Vic's, and grasp them in my left hand, then wrap it around several times until they're snug together. With the scatha gripped in my palm, forefinger on the trigger, I take a deep breath and, using all of my strength, run full force at the doorway. The guys are heavy as mother hell, but we're moving fast. The moment we clear the kirk, there are tiny-headed, fanged cat creatures all over the street. They're still as death, just staring at me with vertical pupils, and three lunge at once. I rapid-fire three rounds off, and three headless creatures fall to the ground. I take off, ignoring the groans I hear coming from both Eli and Vic. I have no idea what kind of condition they're in. I don't care. They're alive and that's all the info I need for now. I just need to get us the fuck out of here.

The street seems to have grown longer, and I don't know what to do except keep running toward the end of it, away from the kirk. There are more shrouded creatures writhing up from the sidewalk cracks—too many for the number of cartridges I have left. I keep running, only firing at the ones who get too close. My arm feels like it's being torn off, and I glance back to make sure both Eli and Vic are still there. A cat creature has landed on Eli's back and is gnawing on his ribs. I stop, drop to one knee, and fire the scatha, blowing it off Eli. Quickly, I load the remaining cartridges. I have three more left.

Shit.

Frustration clouds my judgment. What the hell do I do? I run toward the end of the street, but it stretches out long before me, like it's never going to end, and distorted shadows grab at me, folding the darkness in on me. It's now pitch-black, and I can only see the glowing eyes of the creatures hiding, preying, stalking us. I keep running, Eli's and Vic's bodies bounding limply behind me. They are heavy as shit, too. Like a ton of bricks. I fire another shot at something that flies at me from the shadows. Sparks flutter. I haul ass. One more cartridge left.

Then darkness settles at the end of the street. A pitch cloud, clustering together. First one pine tree, then another emerges. The woods! The god-damn woods! I draw every ounce of speed and strength I have and make my way there. One more creature leaps out at me, and I fire just before it knocks into me. I'm out of ammo. Almost there . . .

The moment my feet hit the spongy forest floor, that sonic boom wave flashes through the pines and knocks me backward. The rope en-twining my wrist to Eli's and Vic's breaks, we all separate, and I fly hard through the air until a tree trunk stops my body. My shoulder pops, and I fall to the ground. Shaking my head, I try to stand, fall back down, stand again. Everything looks blurry, and my knees feel like rubber, and the pain in my shoulder screams as I lift my free hand to my eyes and scrub them. My other hand still grips tightly the scatha. I shake my head again.

Something's wrong.

My frantic eyes search the forest floor.

Eli and Vic are gone.

A cold, sick wave of nausea sweeps over me, and I run, fall, get up, and run some more. I search everywhere, and I'm going in a big circle. Finally, I'm at the opening to St. Bueno's.

Eli and Vic are nowhere in sight. I know they came with me through the boom. Where the hell did they go?

I sink to the ground. I can't catch my breath, almost like I'm hyperventilating. I try to inhale deeply, and I can't. After several tries, I realize it's because I'm sobbing hysterically.

Finally, I lean back on my heels, draw a long, deep breath, and my lungs allow it.

"Eli!" I call out.

The sound resonates off the trees. Bounces off St. Bueno's caved walls. Smacks right back into me.

It doesn't even sound like my voice.

All is quiet. Not even a single rustling leaf cracks the silence.

When no answer follows, I slump against the tree trunk, drop the scatha, and close my eyes.

Part Two

PLAGUED OBSESSION

You don't die from a broken heart. You only wish you did.

—Unknown

I miss my sister. I know we aren't twins or anything, but I guess I still feel some sort of weird connection to her. And I can feel it—something ain't right. It's a sense that makes my stomach hurt. Like something's coming and this time, she won't be able to stop it. That's the thing about Riley. She always thinks she's got everything under control, no matter what it is. Drugs. Bully cops. Gangs. Vampires. Well, I'm not a kid anymore. And I won't let her fall alone.

—Seth Poe

My body jerks. My eyes fly open. Everything's dark. The air is sickening, still.

Eli. Vic. With a burst of energy I leap to my feet. Instinct makes me grab my left arm. Pain singes the shoulder joint. Where the hell is my scatha? I scan the ground. It's nowhere.

Doesn't matter. *I have to go back in. . . .*

My feet move first, and after two steps I'm snatched to a halt. Pain shoots from my shoulder and I hiss.

"No, you don't," a raspy voice says to me. A vise squeezes my good arm.

Dazed, I turn to my captor. Dreads. Crooked smile.

My partner. "Let me go, Noah," I say evenly. My eyes are locked with his.

"Don't do it, girl," he says, and pulls me close. "This time, that mind shit won't work." From his fingers dangles the leather cord he wears around his neck, with a sachet of herbs concocted by my surrogate root doctor grandfather. It keeps his intoxicating sensual vampire scent, irrefutable by any and all species, at bay. He throws it over his head, away from the both of us. It lands at least twenty feet away. My eyes widen.

I feel my pupils dilate, and my body relaxes. I fixate on Noah's lips. Full. Curved at the corners. Sexy as hell. Inviting. I gotta taste them. . . .

My body's hot now, flashes of sensory fire scattering all over my flesh in patches. Stomach. Neck. Thighs. Crotch. Nothing makes sense to me except getting as physically close to Noah Miles as possible. I have to have him. Both of my hands reach for Noah's head, he dips back, and all I touch are a few dreads. That'll do. Wrapping my fingers tightly around them, I yank his head toward my mouth. At the same time, I leap onto him, curling my legs around his waist. One of his large hands separates us, and it's pressing against my chest, pushing me away. My eyes dilate wider. I lean toward him, mouth open, the pain in my left shoulder forgotten. . . .

"Whoa, my little horny toad, take it easy," Noah commands, and pushes me off his body. He chuckles, and the sound excites me. "I can't wait to tell you about this later," he says. He scoops me up in his arms. Runs. Picks something up. "Damn, Poe," he mutters.

I'm barely hearing him, so deafening is my heartbeat roaring within me. Pounding in my groin. Sex. That's all I want from Noah Miles. Sex. *Now*. With my good hand I grab a fistful of dreads and yank his head toward me. His mouth, so close, my teeth nip at his jaw. I want his tongue. . . .

A flash of light goes off in my face, but I don't care. It could be a pair of headlights on a truck barreling at me full speed for all I care. As long as I get these goddamn clothes off. . . .

"Riley, damn it," Noah mutters, and his hand stills mine as I find his crotch.

I feel as though I'm flying through the air, Noah carrying me, and I have not a care in the world except crawling as close to him as I physically can. The wind pushes at my face, and I bury it against his neck. I kiss him there, taking small nips, licks, and I find his earlobe with the silver stud he wears. I pull it into my mouth and groan.

"Jesus H. Christ Almighty, girl," Noah groans, and pulls his head away. "Riley, give me a break, darlin'."

We're moving so fast I can't make my legs creep up his body any higher. I'm nearly out of my mind with lust, the scent of Noah an addicting drug. He keeps pushing me away, and it's pissing me the fuck off. "Please," I beg.

The next instant happens so fast my head spins. I'm flung onto a leather seat, my right wrist is tied to the leather door pull, and I'm crammed inside, door shut. My brain is fuzzy. I feel light-headed. Dizzy. The pain in my left shoulder begins to throb.

The driver's-side door opens, closes. I shake my head and look up. Noah's staring at me, his eyebrows lifted in amusement. One corner of his mouth is tilted upward. Yet a pained look lingers in his eyes.

He cocks his head. "You okay?"

I shake my head again. The fog is clearing, and I glance around. "What happened?" Peering through the Rover's windshield, I notice I'm back at the cottage. I turn my stare on Noah. "I've got to go back—" I move to open the Rover's door, but my hand is tied. "What the hell?"

"You can't go back, darlin'," he says. "You're out of ammo. You'll get yourself killed. There's nothing more you can do."

I try to lift my left hand to untie my right, and pain shoots through me. "Son of a bitch . . ." I look at my shoulder. It's hanging lower than it should. "You gonna help me with this, Miles?"

Noah shakes his head, starts up the motor, and puts the Rover in reverse. "Hell no," he replies. "Not until you calm down."

Anger boils inside me, and my eyes dart to his neck. His antisexual attraction sachet is hanging there. I know exactly what happened. I lift a furious gaze at Noah. "You actually used that on me?" It's getting light now, and I see more than just the shadow of Noah's face.

He smirks. "Had no choice. You were being stubborn." He stops, puts the Rover in drive, and we start down the lane. I glance across the field and notice a man walking toward us with long, purposeful strides. A black-and-white sheepdog jogs at his side. He lifts his hand, and Noah stops.

"Can I help you two this mornin'?" he asks. His eyes light on my shoulder.

He's a handsome guy, great accent, late thirties, early forties. The slightest touch of silver tinges his temples. Hazel eyes. Broad shoulders.

"Ah, no, we were just out for a hike," Noah explains. "Nice standing stones."

"Och, yeah," the man says. "Thousand years old or better, those." He glances at me again briefly. I can tell he sees something's not right. I smile at him.

"All right, then, I best get to my chores. Enjoy your day," the man says, then turns and finds his dog chasing the sheep in the field. "Och, Shep, you wicked dog. Get back here!" He grins and waves, and Noah continues on.

"Tell me what happened," Noah asks. "I know you went in after Eli and Arcos." He shoots me a mercurial glare. "What you did to me at the guesthouse? Shitty."

"You're leaving me with a dislocated shoulder," I answer.

"Just until we get back to the flat," Noah says.

I tell him what happened back in . . . wherever in Hell that place was. "Weird, lanky shadow bodies with tiny cat heads and sharp fangs and claws. Gargoylish-things guarding Eli and Vic in that old church, and Eli and Vic were suspended

by their wrists, and naked, from the rafters." I
look at Noah, and I'm not mad at him anymore.
I know whatever he does, he does to protect me.
That vow he promised to uphold to Eli? I have a
feeling it's going to interfere. A lot. "Noah, they
were both alive. They groaned. I dragged them
all the way out of that hellhole by their wrists."

He gave me a sideways glance. "Then what?"

I shrug. "Once we hit the forest, I don't
know . . . the same kind of sonic boom swept
over us. Knocked my ass at least twenty, thirty
feet through the air. Broke the rope I had bound
all three of us together with." I try to lift my
shoulder. No go. "I hit the tree, tried to get up,
fell, tried again. And again." I shook my head.
"They just . . . disappeared." I look at my partner. "But they were both alive. Swear to God
they were."

At the foot of the long steep hill leading away
from Ivy Cottage and St. Bueno's, Noah puts the
Rover in park. He half turns in his seat and looks
at me. "I believe you. We'll figure something
out." Lightning fast, he reaches over my body,
places his large hand on my left shoulder, and
snaps it back into place. I suck in a quick breath
of pain; then it's over. With a much more tender
touch, he grazes my chin. "Next time, trust me,
okay? Don't use your mind power on me again,
Riley. I want Eli as alive as you do." He then un-
ties my right wrist, puts the Rover in drive; we
head back through Dingwall, Strathpeffer, and
before long we're on the A-9.

We are both silent for several miles, and I try to take in, then shake off, everything that's happened to me since arriving in Inverness. For the first time, I feel lost. Before, I had direction. I had loaded cartridges for the scatha. I had a plan.

To save Eli and Vic.

Now that's all blown to hell.

Where did they go?

"We have work to do, Ri," Noah says, staring forward. The bridge over the Beauly Firth looms ahead, and the heavy scent of sea life seeps through the vents of the Rover. "Get your head in the game."

We are in the middle of the bridge when my cell phone rings from the center console. Immediately, my heart jerks in my chest.

It's AC/DC's "Highway to Hell."

That's Victorian Arcos's ring tone.

Throwing open the console, I grab my iPhone and answer, "Victorian?"

There is nothing but silence for more seconds than I can almost stand.

"Riley? Is it you?" Vic says. His voice is hoarse, quieter than usual. But it's him.

I can barely speak. "Where are you? Are you okay? What happened to you back—"

Victorian lets out a low, weak laugh. "I thought you said you could barely speak, love."

I lean against the headrest of my seat and close my eyes. "Oh my God, you're alive." I sit straight up. I feel sweat pop out at my forehead, and my breath catches in my throat. "Is Eli with you?"

"*Nu, dragostea mea,*" Vic answers in his native Romanian. *No, my love.* "What happened to me? How did I get home?" he asks.

From the corner of my eye I see Noah mutter into his cell phone. He's calling the States. Eli's family.

"Home? As in Romania?" I continue, but my mind is screaming, *Where the hell is Eli?*

"*Da,* Romania. And I know you wish to hear more of your fiancé, Riley," he says in a low voice. "I can still hear your thoughts, love, and I wish I had more to offer. I . . . just don't remember much at all. Except . . . pain. Excruciating pain."

"It's okay, Vic," I say, yet my skin prickles at the thought. I don't want to sound cold, but hell *yeah*, I want to know more of Eli. "Do you remember being in the church with Eli? Me dragging you through the streets? The forest?"

"Yes, in the church with Eli. It happened almost as instantaneously as I appeared back home. In . . . a flash." He sighs into the receiver. "We were strung up by our wrists. Beaten with . . . something not natural. We don't bleed, Riley. But yet . . . it drained us. Then the beatings simply stopped. And we hung. We spoke until neither of us could speak any longer."

"Beaten by who? And why?" I ask.

Vic sighs into the phone. "I never saw a face, only shadow. But I got the same sense I had when Jake Andorra hit me with his sword. I think it was one of the Fallen."

"And the beatings stopped because the Fallen were killed," I offer. "Why, do you think?"

"I haven't a clue, other than pure torture brought pleasure to them," he says. "Or to bring pain to you, which seems more likely."

"Well, that was a success," I say. "I've been out of my fucking mind, Victorian. Anything else?"

"A warm body, wrapped around mine—I pray that it was yours. A fall. More pain, I think I was being dragged down the street. Something . . . knocked me hard. Had I breath within me, it would have been gone. A strange language I didn't understand, muttering something unintelligible. Then . . . nothing. I woke up here, with my papa staring down at me. Who's with you? Miles? I'll join you two—"

"Slow down, Arcos, and no, you won't," I insist. "I've got to call Jake and let him know about this. He's got to be told. You stay away from here, Vic. For now. Okay?"

Silence on the other end.

"Victorian. I. Mean. It."

"For now," he agrees. "But only because you ask it. Riley?"

"Yeah, Vic," I respond.

"Stay close to Miles. Do not try stupid things alone. And I will come right away, if you desire. All you have to do is ask."

I exhale. "I know you will. Thanks. I'll be in touch. And hey," I say quickly, before he ends the call.

"Da?" Yes.

"I'm really glad you're alive."

Victorian softly chuckles. "I haven't been that, love, in centuries. But I know what you mean. I am glad, also. Thank you. I know 'twas you who saved me, even if I couldn't see your face."

We end the call, and I glance at Noah.

He shakes his head. "I spoke with Gilles. Eli isn't there."

My heart drops to my stomach. "How can that be? How does Victorian go from a forest in Scotland to Romania in a blink, but no sign of Eli?" My eyes search the gray waters of the Beauly Firth. Cars are on the road now, people in their ordinary lives going about their ordinary business. Shoppers. Tourists. Locals. Fishermen. Suits.

Yet there is a true Hell, right here on Earth. And none of them even know it.

Noah's cell rings, and my heart leaps as I look at him.

"It's Jake," he says. "Andorra," Noah answers the phone. "Okay, hold." He pushes something, and Jake's voice booms out of the speaker.

"Riley, are you hurt?" Jake asks. His unusual accent is something I'm finally used to. A mixture of Scots brogue and something indefinable. Something ancient.

"No," I answer. "Jake, what's going on?"

"You tell me," he says.

So I do. I give him full details of everything, starting with me arriving at Ivy Cottage, my trek up to the stones, then the woods and St. Bueno's.

Everything from the moment I entered that alternative world filled with weird tiny cat-headed demons, to pulling Eli and Vic out of the rafters. I end with the sonic boom that separated us all, and then I tell him of Vic's phone call from Romania.

"Are you sure that was Arcos on the phone?" Jake asks.

The question catches me so off guard words fail me.

"Riley, I took his head myself," Jake reminds me. "You saw it happen."

I shake my head. "No way is it not him, Jake. I refuse to believe it." I glance at Noah, and he's looking ahead in traffic and pulls onto Montague Row. "No freaking way. Besides, Jake. I saw your sword flash, and then Victorian disappear. So I can't vouch for the beheading. I mean, it looked like you'd done it. But I don't know. Shit."

"I'll call his father," Jake says. "You two get your heads in the game and wrap up Inverness. We need you here. Fucking wolves."

The line goes dead. Just like Jake Andorra. Business finished, hang up.

Meanwhile, all I can think about is Eli. He's *got* to be alive.

And I don't care if it kills me, I'll find him.

When Noah parks the Rover, the owner is standing on the sidewalk, briefcase in hand. Poor guy. I hope he doesn't get canned because he's late to work. We hop out, I holster my scatha, and Noah leaves the Rover's engine running.

"Hey, nice ride," Noah says to the guy. His eyes are glassed over, but he nods.

"Aye," he answers, and focuses on his car. He scratches his forehead, confused.

"Have a nice day," I add.

The guy walks to the driver's-side door, still open. "Right, then," he says. "Cheers." Then he climbs in and takes off down the street.

I glance up, toward the sky. There's no sun out, but it's daylight. A dull gray haze surrounds the city. Car horns, voices, doors opening and closing, dogs barking. All the sounds collide at once, and I force myself not to cover my ears like a little kid. Suddenly, I'm drained, no energy, and all I want to do is close my eyes.

"Damn, I know that look," Noah says, and grabs my arm. He pulls me to the guesthouse posing as our hideout. "Let's go, Sleeping Beauty, before you make a bed on the sidewalk."

I can sometimes go days without sleep now, but when it hits, it's narcoleptic hell. It's coming over me now, a wash of weary indescribable, almost as if I've had a long day at the beach in ninety-degree breezes and salty waves. Just . . . exhausting. I feel my feet leave the ground, and my nose scrapes Noah's neck. He chuckles, mutters something. He's carrying me, putting me down. My body's against something soft, smells nice. Everything's dark now, all is silent, and I'm going out. . . .

The river. Brine. Marsh grass. Not the river Ness. Home. I inhale deeply, until the air singes my lungs.

The blow of a porpoise in the harbor hisses through the night air.

My eyes flutter open, and I'm in my bedroom, upstairs from my shop. Inksomnia. Seems like it's been forever since I've been home. Everything's hazy, and I scrub my eyes to clear my vision. The French doors leading out to the small balcony are open, and the gauzy drapes are fluttering in a barely there breeze. I can feel it on my face, my bare arms, and with it carries the scent of something other than brine. . . .

Rising from my bed, I glance down at my body. A sheer champagne-silk slip clings to my skin, grazes my breasts, and the material shifts with the sea breeze. It barely covers my thighs. My long straight hair falls over one shoulder, and I push it back. The wooden floor is cool beneath my bare feet as I make my way to the open door. I pause and place my palm against the wooden French frame. The lights glow an amber hue against the aged cobbles of River Street below, and the sound of the river washing against the marshy shore on the opposite bank lulls me into a calming trance. I inhale again, and close my eyes. . . .

I sense him before I feel him, and when he moves behind me, my body reacts, a thousand nerve endings snapping fire at once. His hand skims my arm, over my hip, my thigh. With his other hand, he pushes back my hair and exposes my neck. Soft, firm lips drag with erotic, painful slowness across my skin, lingering on my shoulder. His scent, so familiar, makes my heart slam against my ribs with anticipation. My joints weaken at the knees. I'd know his touch, the feel of his mouth against me, anywhere. He's mine. He's back. . . .

Eli. . . .

He turns me in his arms, and grasps my face with both hands. My fingers find his chest bare, and my eyes drink him in. I never thought I'd see him again, and a feeling greater than joy seizes my heart. My lips part to speak, but he hushes me with one finger across my mouth, silencing me. Slowly, he shakes his head, and I swallow whatever crazy words I had. I don't want to break this spell. Is it really happening? Is he really here, under my touch? Am I really looking into the face that I love?

A hank of pitch-dark hair falls over one of his trademark cerulean Dupré eyes, and he searches my face as though seeking some fine, minor detail he'd earlier missed. I allow him this, but impatience is biting at me. I want him, his lips, his tongue—I'd crawl into his skin if I could. I can't get close enough. And I'm not sure how much longer I can wait, but I let him take his time. Slowly, he explores every small detail. I'm dying. . . .

Tilting my head to the right, he lowers his head toward me. Something flashes in his eyes, just a fraction of a spark, just before his lips, those sensual, full, erotic lips, graze mine. And I'm lost. . . .

His hand cups the back of my head as he leans into the kiss, and he leaves nothing unloved. His mouth caresses mine, at first, gentle, searching, testing. Then he tastes me, and as if a firecracker has exploded, his free hand presses against the small of my back and yanks me against him, and my arms slip around his neck, entwine through his hair. I kiss him back with fervor, and when his hand lowers to my backside, he pulls me harder to him. A rock-hard bulge is between us, pressing against me, and I can't stop the smile on my mouth that he's kissing right now. My hands drop from his hair, my fingertips trailing over his chest, and I find his waistband. Undoing one button, then two, then three, I feel Eli's kiss deepening as my palm finds the erection straining against his jeans. I release him, and the feel of him is so familiar, so right, I can't help the vulnerable groan that escapes me. Eli catches me behind my knees and picks me up, our lips never parting, and carries me to my bed. We fall together, and he stretches over me. Then he breaks our kiss and looks at me through his fall of lush black hair. His face is half cast in shadow, and it's nothing but a straight-up turn-on. He studies me long, hard, and I writhe with anticipation beneath him. Bracing his weight with one arm, he caresses my face with one knuckle, drags it across my lips, then down the column of my throat. Neither of us breathes a word. I'm afraid to. I don't want this to not be real. . . .

"Do it now, Eli," a strange female voice echoes from the shadows.

Eli goes totally still above me. Who the hell's voice is that? Eli's strength radiates through his body, making him quiver.

"Do not make me say it again," the female voice commands. "Now."

A single headlight beam flashes across the interior of my room, and illuminates Eli's face for one half

*split second. But I see it. I see it clearly. I see him
clearly.*

*His face and body are marred by singed slashes. His
jaw is extended, a row of sharp teeth dropped to jagged points. His eyes are . . . black as pitch.*

*He knows I know. He grabs my throat with his free
hand and jerks his face to mine. I scream. Grab his
hair from the back and yank his head away. I flip him,
now straddling him. He screams, his head rolling side
to side so fast it blurs. And it's a bloodcurdling sound
I've never heard before. I scream, too. . . .*

"Riley!"

I'm flipped onto my back, and the harsh im-
pact of my shoulder blades on the floor makes
my breath wheeze out. A sharp slap against my
cheek burns and makes my foggy vision begin to
clear. The light from a swag lamp above me makes
me squint. I see clearly now. Noah is on top of
me, holding me down.

"Are you back?" he asks. His voice is raspy,
tinged with concern.

"Yeah," I answer. "Get off me." I give Noah a
shove. He jumps up and extends a hand. I take
it, and he pulls me up. I'm groggy, as though I've
been sleeping for days. With the pads of my fingertips, I rub my eyes.

"Twenty-eight hours to be exact," Noah says.
Never does he miss an opportunity to read my
mind. I'm most vulnerable when I just awaken
from one of my fallout sleeps. Jesus, twenty-
eight hours. Wasted. "And a lot's happened since
you passed out."

I look at him. "Like what?"

Noah shakes his head. "First, what'd you see?"

I notice that I'm still fully dressed, minus the leather jacket and boots. We're standing in the small living room, finished in blue-and-black plaid. I walk toward what I hope is the kitchen, find the fridge, and thankfully, Noah's bought a gallon of milk. I twist off the plastic cap and raise the jug to my mouth. Ice-cold whole milk pours down my throat, and I'm a half gallon down by the time I pull it away.

"I was with Eli, back home," I begin after wiping my mouth with the back of my hand. "He was . . . perfect. Unmarred." I shrug. "He was my Eli. Then he changed. His skin was slashed with those blackened singe marks, like he had in the church when I pulled him out. He morphed, full-vamp changed on me." I meet Noah's gaze. "Someone commanded him to hurt me. A female. After that, he did try to kill me."

"It was a dream, Riley," Noah says. "Nothing more."

I take another gulp of milk, screw the lid back on, and put it back in the fridge. Turning, I lean against the counter and cross my arms over my chest. "I don't think so. He's alive, Noah. Vic's alive. He somehow zapped clear over to Romania once I cleared him of that alternative world. Eli is . . . somewhere else."

"Where?" Noah asks. "Any clue who the female is?"

I press my fingertips to my temples and rub hard. Woke up too fast. Head is splitting. "Hell if I know."

"So you think he put that dream in your head?"

My eyes flash open and I stare at my partner. My friend, too. Noah Miles would lay down his immortal life for me. Without a doubt, he would. I don't believe there's anyone or anything that could stop him. And that's a little frightening. "Or the female. I just don't know."

Noah's face tenses, and I can tell my words trouble him. Troubles me, too. "Let's get Inverness handled," he says, turns me around, and takes over rubbing my temples. So easily, he could squash straight through my skull and into my brain. But he won't.

"That's really, truly gross and disgusting," he says, and turns me back around to face him. "But it's nice you trust me." He gives me a somber look. "We'll get all this figured out," he says. Surprisingly, I'm comforted by that. "Until then, we've got work to do. You've taken one rogue out. I've taken another two."

"Two?" I repeat.

"Yeah, they seem to be unrelated, and both newbloods. One of them crazy and big as shit," he says, shaking his head. "No pattern with their targets, except all hits at night." He eyes me. "Could be an older one transformed a handful of newbloods, and they've all just struck out on their own. Like I said, no pattern to their kills, and they've all been alone. We'll have to hunt like hell until we get them all."

"We'll have to split up," I add.

"Not happening," Noah says. "No way in hell."

"No choice," I say. "Besides, do you realize I can hear your footfall from a mile away? I can call your name and you're at my side within seconds."

"Not seconds," he counters. "Only if I'm close enough is it seconds. Might take a few minutes if we're on opposite ends of the city. And that might be a few minutes too long." He shakes his head, one long dread falling from the clip he has gathered at the nape of his neck. "No way, Riley. Get over it."

"We'll hunt together tonight," I offer. Besides, I can tell nothing will change Noah's mind right now. No sense in wasting time arguing when there's work to be done. "The city's not too big. Let's just get tonight over with, see what we find, and go from there." It is a little hard being all WUP business, when all that's on my mind is Eli, where he is, the condition he's in, and how in hell he put that dream into my head.

"All right," Noah agrees, but his dark blond eyebrows are furrowed into a frown. Those silvery eyes hold mine. "There's takeout in the fridge. Unless you're good to go on all that milk you guzzled."

I grab the fridge door, open it, push past my partner's specially bagged blood products, and find the white foam container of . . . whatever. I grab it and carry it to the microwave. After it heats, I sit down at the kitchen table and Noah watches me closely as I devour two slabs of batter-fried haddock, a pile of thick chips, and a beef pie. At least, I think it was a beef pie. It all went down so fast I barely tasted the glob of brown sauce and malt vinegar Noah had covered the chips in.

Like my narcoleptic hell, the appetite I wake up to is something uncontrolled, and pretty impressive for a girl. I guess it's my body's way of keeping me in good functioning condition. I honestly can't help it. But my thoughts remain on Eli. Always.

I rise and toss my empty container in the trash, down a warm soda, and throw it away, too. I glance at Noah.

"Give me ten minutes," I say. "I need to shower."

"Ten," he agrees. "I threw your bag in the first room."

I leave the kitchen without another word, hurry to the first guest room, and toss my duffel onto the bed. Riffling through what small amount of belongings I packed, I pull out a clean pair of black skinny jeans, a long-sleeved black Under Armour shirt, panties and socks, and a clean sports bra. Grabbing the smaller bag containing bathroom stuff, I head to the room's en suite bath. Within seconds I'm stripped and standing beneath a steaming waterfall. Soapy water runs down my body, my arms, and for a moment, I stare at the dragon's tail that's wrapped around one of them. I skim my hand over it, remembering the day my best friend, Nyx, inked it there. Starting at my lower spine, the dragon winds up and over my shoulder. The tail curls around my index finger. It was the last part to be colored in. Hurt like a mother, right there over my bony knuckle. And it seems so long ago. A whole life ago.

Rinsing the conditioner from my hair, I turn the water off, wrap my hair in a towel, and climb out. Just as I turn my head to close the shower door, the window catches my eye in the mirror. A face. My heart stops.

I whip around and stare at the window.

Nothing's there.

There's a ledge above the toilet, just beneath the window. I leap up and crouch, tilting my head sideways and peering out. I see nothing but a streetlight, the sidewalk, and the Rover I hijacked. Nothing else.

"What the hell, Riley?"

I turn and glance at Noah, standing just inside the bathroom door. "I thought I saw something. A face." I peer back outside. Still nothing but darkness and shadows. I fine-tune my hearing, and everything normal screeches to a halt. The sounds I hear now are that of a mouse's heartbeat. The scratching of some small animal against the bark of a tree. A human's breath easing in and out of lungs.

Nothing else.

I look at Noah and jump down, clutching my towel to my body. I land on the white cotton bath rug. "It was Eli."

"Come on, darlin'," Noah says in his Charleston drawl. "That fast and you know it was Eli?"

My head spins. "I don't know anymore. Get out so I can get dressed and we can get the hell out of here," I say, frustrated. I look at Noah. "It'll only take a sec."

Noah says nothing and backs out of the bathroom.

I drop the towel and throw on my clothes. Quickly, I pull my wet hair back and secure it with a silver clip. In my room, I yank on my boots and jacket and pass Noah in the hall.

The night air is chilled; it's early November in the Highlands. Funny, I can *tell* it's chilly out—probably more than chilly. Air is crisp. I feel the cold, feel the wind. My breath puffs out before me as warm meets cold. But it doesn't affect me as it did when I was solely human. My eyes search the dark, the shadows. I sniff the air. I listen.

Many things assault my senses.

None of them scream *Eli*.

"Shake it off," Noah says. "And get your head in the game." He glances at his watch. "Twenty minutes till midnight. Let's get moving." One final glare, his gaze levels mine. "Don't take off away from me, Riley Poe. Swear to God, I'll kick your ass."

With one more glance around our guesthouse, we head out to Montague Row and follow it along, side by side, at a fairly brisk human walk. It's still early, and there are people moving about. Not many, but enough that I have to tune back my hearing. Too many human heartbeats, voices, whispers at once. Almost makes me dizzy. It's become so easy for me now. I just . . . think it, and it happens. Kinda scary, and I believe that particular trait came from Vic's father, Senior Arcos. In times of extreme adrenaline, though, I have to concentrate. Probably a good thing, or else people would be slapping one another in the face, pulling hair, and tripping pedestrians.

We walk down to the river Ness, and follow the walkway hugging the shore. Even at midnight on a Thursday night, it's pretty lively on the riverfront. Several pubs and eating establishments line the river, and I have to stop and take it in. The moment I halt, Noah does, too, and he looks at me. I close out the drone of human conversation, and listen for minor details. A single racing heart. A whimper. A cry of fright, of disbelief. The air catching in a throat.

Fast footfall.

Heavy, a human male. Not used to running. Heart rate around one hundred and seventy now. I cock my head, listening.

"He's two streets over, heading upriver, toward the bridge," I say.

We both take off fast, slipping closer into the shadows of the buildings, leaping over anything that's in our way. I'm a head and neck in front of Noah, and as we hit the walkway down to the river, I see him. I can't tell his age, but I'm guessing midthirties. Not used to a lot of exercise, and he's winded as hell. Dark clothes, gray woolen coat. He's got a black skully on. I scan the darkness. "What's spooking him?"

Noah and I are nearly on top of him, and we Y off from each other. I take the human, and with one leap I take him to the ground. His grunt resonates against my chest. Quickly, I roll off him and briefly glance up. Behind and above me, I see Noah leap into an ancient tree with long, heavy branches. I turn my attention to the man.

"You okay?" I ask, and jump to my feet. I extend a hand.

His face is stark white against the black skully pulled over his ears. He doesn't accept my hand, instead stares at me. Blank faced. "I dunno—"

It happens so fast my mind spins a little as I react. Noah and another—completely morphed and fanged—drop from the canopy of the tree above. The vampire swings at Noah, who has him by the neck, then builds strength and lunges directly toward the human. I find my blade in the back of my jeans and hurl it at the vampire's heart. It sinks a solid inch over the hilt. The vampire drops to the ground, inches from the human. The moment his body crumples, he begins to convulse.

The man stares wide-eyed at the seizing form on the ground. Stepping closer, I place my hand

on his arm and pull him away. He doesn't resist.
I turn him around and force him to look at me.
The whites of his eyes take up nearly the entire
orb. *Go straight home now. Forget you were chased.
Forget what you've seen. And for a while, stay home
after dark, if you can. Hurry.*

His stare vacant, the guy turns, shoves his
hands into his woolen coat pockets, and starts
up the sidewalk at a brisk walk. I watch him until he turns up a street and disappears.

"One more down," Noah says.

"One more saved," I reply, glancing in the direction of the frightened guy. I look at Noah.
"Did you get anything?"

Noah shakes his head. "Late twenties. Not a
newblood, not old, either." He shrugs. "Again,
totally random."

We continue on throughout the night, but find
nothing more than a handful of drunken college
students celebrating a birthday by pub crawling,
a few domestic fights, and a guy out looking for
his runaway dog.

My hearing picks up a female gasp. It's a
scared, surprised sound. I jerk my head and stare
downriver, toward a row of restaurants and
pubs. No. Beyond that. A park. I hear her whispered plea. *"No, please."* "Let's go," I say to Noah.
I take off. He's right behind me.

The rows we're running down are relatively
even, and I think we'd make better time going
rooftop. I turn down a close, leap from car, wall

to wall, and climb the chimney until I reach the top. Noah's a step behind me. We take off.

Across the rooftops we fly, bounding off chimneys and gutters. I'm following the young woman's heartbeat. Thank God there's still one to follow. Might not be for long.

We haul over four buildings before the park is in sight. I make one final lunge and land in the branches of an old oak. Quickly I find solid footing, and I swing down.

When I land, it's just in time to see a dark head lift from the woman's neck. Her body is limp in his arms. She's blond, petite, maybe midtwenties. Wearing a pub T-shirt and jeans. The light from the streetlamp perched on the sidewalk close to the grass illuminates her face. Terror is frozen in her dead expression. Eyes wide. Eyebrows pinched. Mouth wide open in a silent scream.

The vampire holding her is in shadows. Slowly, he turns his head toward me. I see nothing but one corner of a fanged mouth tip upward into a smile.

A heavy, sickening wash of familiarity comes over me, and before I blink, he drops the dead girl and takes off into the darkness. I don't even hesitate. I follow.

"Riley!" Noah calls, and starts off behind me. The one I'm chasing is fast, and I'm having to kick in the extra energy to keep up. I can hear Noah's footfalls fade a little with each step.

The park is deserted, and I'm chasing this

vampire into the shadows at the far end when suddenly, he has stopped, turned, and is facing me. I stop, too, and stare, peering into the shadows obscuring his features. I see his silhouette, though, and my insides feel sickened. Six feet. Broad shoulders. Muscular thighs. Arrogant stance.

The grass crunches behind me, and I turn my head. It's Noah.

"Riley, I asked you not to take off alone," he says, distracting me for a half second.

I glance back at the figure. The vampire that has just killed a young girl.

He's gone.

I feel my knees go weak, and I want to sink to the ground, maybe even scream. I inhale instead and take off in the direction the vampire disappeared. Vampire. Killer. Bloodsucker who'd just stolen a life, ruined others because of it. That girl's family will never be the same, always a hole ripped in their lives. I hate it so much it makes my insides roil with rage. I hear Noah swear and he's right behind me again.

Without thinking, I crank up the speed, and I'm bounding over parked cars, rebounding off buildings, and next I'm leaping rooftops again. I scan the shadows, searching for the least amount of movement. I startle a flock of roosting ravens, and their wings sound like drums going off in my head. They slow me just enough for Noah to get his hands on me and yank me to a halt.

"Riley!" he says harshly, and snatches me toward him. Both of his hands grip my shoulders. "Stop!"

I look at my partner's face, and shadows fall across most of it. It's Noah, though. I know that. For a second, I'm dazed. What the hell's wrong with me?

Who was I just chasing?

I shift my gaze across the city's skyline. Down the river, the castle lights are still on. Dawn is close to breaking, and I see the river Ness moving like a black eel below me. I look at Noah, who is studying me with a cautious look.

"I'm losing my mind," I say, barely above a whisper. "It has to be residual from entering that alternative plane." I shake my head and lift my gaze to meet Noah's. "Why do I keep seeing Eli?"

Noah's brow furrows. "You thought that vampire back there was Eli?" He shook his head. "Come on, Riley. Eli Dupré? Your fiancé? My closest friend? Original guardian of Savannah? Entrusted by Preacher and Estelle? Forsake his parents? Eli, turned dark?" Again, he shakes his head and lets go of my shoulders. "No fucking way, Riley. It wasn't him. Your mind's playing tricks on you."

"Then what's wrong with me?" I ask. "Why, ever since St. Bueno's, am I seeing him, Noah? Am I crazy? Am I being tormented?"

Noah looks down at me, his silvery eyes soft. "I don't think you are seeing him, darlin'. I think . . . ," He grabs my chin and lifts it closer to him. "I think he is consuming your mind right now. You know Arcos made it out alive, and you want more than anything for the same to happen to Eli. I get that. And he may have. But he's not killing innocents." Noah's eyes hold mine. "He's just not."

The sun is just cracking the horizon. What were shadows and darkness are now haze and fuzzy light. I see Noah's face clearly. He's probably the most sincere soul I know. "Then why," I say to him, "am I seeing him in a bad way? Killing people?"

One corner of Noah's mouth lifts. "Now, that I can't explain, Ms. Poe. But you need to relax. Concentrate. And let's get this job done. Then we'll work on Eli." He taps my nose. "Together. With Andorra."

I heave a sigh. "Yeah. Okay."

Noah inclines his head toward the ground. "You ready to hop off this rooftop before we draw a crowd?"

"Guess we'd better," I say, and leap the two and a half stories to a side alley. Noah lands beside me, and we walk toward the river. Early-morning businesses are opening up. Bakers, butchers, tourist shops. It's Friday morning, and there's a certain feel in the wind. Maybe it's coming from the youth, looking forward to a little fun? Kids out of school? Whatever it is, I know the streets of Inverness are no longer safe. Three rouge vampires killed already. One on the loose, and I have no idea who that one is.

Despite Noah's insistence that it wasn't Eli, I pray for it to not be.

It's only a matter of time before the local police discover the bodies being drained of blood, or minus a very important organ, are more than a fluke. Nothing screams *serial killer* more than a few dead bodies piling up.

Makes me wonder if that guy, before I put the mind whammy on him, knows just how lucky he is. That he was a half second away from having his blood sucked from his body. Maybe it's best that he doesn't know. Sometimes I wish I didn't.

"Let's walk the city today, in the daylight," Noah suggests. "Arriving here after dark, taking off on a blind hunt." He shakes his head. "I don't like to work that way. Inverness isn't too big. Let's head back to the guesthouse, get the maps Andorra gave us, and hit the streets." He drapes an arm over one of my shoulders. "Come on."

I meet Noah Miles's encouraging gaze. If anyone can make you believe in yourself, or a cause, it's Noah Freaking Miles. Must be left over in his human DNA from the Revolutionary War.

"Damn straight it is," he says, reading my mind. "Let's go."

We slip into the streets of Inverness, mingling with the mortals walking to work, to school, tourists checking out St. Andrew's Cathedral, Inverness Castle.

All completely incoherent to the fact that an immortal killer, the very top of the food chain, stalks them. Probably more than one.

Police sirens echo close by, resonating off the stone and brick of the buildings. I can tell where it's headed. The park. To that poor dead girl we left there.

Yeah. No matter who is responsible. They have to be stopped.

Even if it kills me.

Part Three

‧—✦—✦—‧

OLDE BLOOD

A storm's coming.

—James Bond, Skyfall, 2012

*I don't usually worry overmuch about Riley any-
more, but after Miles's mobile call, even I admit it.
She's worrying me. 'Tis a dangerous chance, entering that alternative world like she did. Victorian
Arcos, well, I haven't seen him myself, but I have
spoken with him. He seems stable. Seems himself.
I've reached into his mind, and I don't sense anything sinister that wasn't already there before. But
one thing I do know about alternative realms. Sometimes what comes out isn't always what went in.
Riley Poe could be in more danger than she thinks.
That doesn't sit verra well with me.*

—Jake Andorra

The rest of the morning is spent first going
over the map of Inverness, spread out on the
kitchen table. Noah and I hunch over the creased,
new map, shoulder to shoulder, studying. Inverness isn't very large, so we then head out into
the city itself. We hit every main artery road,
close, and dead-end street in the City Centre on
foot, and fan out to the river and industrial park
by cab. I suspect to most onlookers, Noah and I
are just another touring couple on vacay. What
they don't know won't hurt, as the saying goes.
Rather, possibly, won't kill.

Yet despite Noah's encouraging words to get
my mind in the game, my thoughts stray to Eli. I

just can't help it. He was taken from me, and I want him back. Badly. Why can't he be here now? Why did Vic make it home, but not Eli?

As my eyes take in the Scottish city, I daydream about what it'd be like to be here just as a regular couple in love, touring the city. The Highlands. Taking a boat out onto Loch Ness and searching for Nessie. Walking the hillsides, and traipsing through ancient castle ruins. A ping of jealousy roils inside me at all the regular people living regular lives. Wake up, eat breakfast, go to work, socialize, come home. Normal stuff. Jesus Christ, I'm about as far from normal as I can possibly fucking be.

I want my goddamn life back.

"Hey," Noah says, and I look at him. His eyes soften. "Stop that."

I heave a sigh. "I swear, I'll try."

He pulls me into a side hug, kisses the top of my head, and we continue on.

The Scots are a friendly people whom I find I like more and more as I spend time here. I wish so much of this time wasn't spent on killing and death. It's inevitable, though, and the more I stop complaining about it, the faster I'll accept it. It's what we're here to do. Stop a killer. Apparently, more than one. Wanna know something weird? Sometimes, even though I know it has to be done, somewhere far in the recesses of my brain, I'm saddened that I reduce bloodsuckers to a shimmering puddle of white goop. They used to be people. Sons. Daughters. Sisters.

Brothers. Friends. Lovers. Who would ever look at a vampire, whether on TV, or in a movie, or like me, in life, and give him or her a soul? I guess it has to do with the fact that my family now is made up of age-old vampires who care not only about me, my brother, Seth, and other humans, but about one another. Makes me wonder how it's possible they—Noah, Eli, and his family—can do it. How they can care, but others can't. Or won't. I'm doing a lot of reflecting lately. Whatever that means.

Noah stops a few people on the street, locals at the university, maybe. The early-twenties crowd. They tell us where the best clubs are, best cafés, best pubs. We find our way to some of the seedier parts of the city. Inverness is friendly and welcoming, so what's seedy isn't very noticeable to any ordinary eye. But Noah can sniff out a punk, and we find a group of four huddled against a building near the industrial park. Late teens, early twenties, trying their best to look tough as hell. Doing a good job of it, too. Every one of them is dragging on a cigarette. We walk up, and one kid, wearing a thick, ratty-looking gray woolen sweater and a black skully, pushes off the wall he's leaning on and pulls long on his smoke. His eyes are locked on to mine. They shift momentarily to the black wing inked at the corner of my cheekbone.

"Aye?" he says in a thick accent. He moves his gaze to Noah.

"Where can we score some shit?" Noah asks.

The kid laughs, and the others chuckle with him. "Wha' makes ya think I know where tae get shit?" the kid asks, then looks at me. "Americans. On holiday, aye? This your brother, love?" He inclines his head toward Noah.

A sharp sparkle lights his gaze as he studies Noah. Intelligent guy, maybe nineteen, and he's pretty cute. Green eyes, along with a flawless complexion and strong jaw. Dark eyebrows, nicely shaped, so he must have dark hair beneath the skully. Makes me freaking sick that he's such a dumb-ass, wasting his life on drugs. He must be early on in the game because his eyes are too quick for him to have been doing it for too long. They make easy prey for vampires, the druggies. It's why we find them, find out where they hang, sell, buy. There's a chance we might just save their sorry lives.

"How'd you guess?" I say to him.

"Hopin'," he answers, and grins. Bright white, wide smile. Wicked-strong accent. Maybe we got these kids all wrong. He's tall, stands eye to eye with Noah.

I just stare at him.

"I never fook wi' the stuff," he says to Noah, and studies him. "You dunna, either." He glances at me, then back to Noah. "Cops?" His eyes drift from my feet to my eyes. "Nah. No' cops. But somethin' else."

Yeah. Smart kid all right. "Clubs?" I ask. You got clubs people go to for a good time, drink, dance, and hook up. Then you have the ones notorious for . . . other stuff. Both are hunting grounds for a rogue vampire. But the one with high-traffic lawlessness instinctively draws the worst kinds. People and vamps.

"Boyo's," one of the other guys offers. He draws on his cigarette and points with it. "Four streets over, one up."

"Cost ya eight quid tae get in," another claims. "Worth every pence."

"But if ya fancy a good tune or two, try Hush 51. Just up the river a ways," the leader claims with a grin. "They've a fine live band this weekend."

"Aye," the other added. "finest in the bloody Highlands."

I lift an eyebrow. Sassy little shits. We're talking to the whole band.

Noah chuckles. "What time do you start?"

The leader blows smoke. "Nine." He inclines his head. "Gerry. Tate. Pete. Drums, keyboard, electric fiddle." He jabs his hand out to Noah. "Rhine," he says, and winks at me. "Bass and vocals, love."

What a hot dog.

"Noah, Riley," Noah introduces. "Sorry for the mix-up."

Rhine shrugs. "Happens," he claims, and glances at his band. "We do look a wee bit thuggish, aye?"

The others all chuckle.

"Oy, are ya here, then, because o' the murders?" Tate asks. He's got wavy auburn hair that curls over his ears.

"Why would American cops be here investigatin' Scottish murders, you horse's arse?" Pete says.

"Shut the fook up," Tate says with a laugh. "Just askin'."

"Just passing through," Noah says. "What murders?"

"Serial killer, mayhap," Rhine claims. "Three killed so far." He shakes his head. "Fookin' gruesome."

"Aye," Gerry the drummer adds. "Girl just found this mornin', all of her blood drained."

"Unusual for Inverness," Rhine says. "Take care where you go after dark."

I look at the guys that Noah and I both had misjudged. I guess I'll have to dip into minds a little more often before assuming. And on that note, I decide something before leaving. I give Rhine a smile. "Thanks. See ya round, maybe."

He smiles back.

And I level my gaze at all four band members, ending with Rhine. *Take the cigarettes out of your mouths, drop them onto the ground, and crush them.*

Rhine immediately takes his cigarette out, drops it, and smashes it with his boot. The others, in sync, do the same.

Don't smoke. Anything. Ever again. Cold-turkey quit. Nod if you understand.

All four guys nod at once.

Noah shakes his head and stares at me with

admiration. Probably a little envy, too. He inclines his head, we say good-bye to the guys,
and leave. When we round the block, he glances
over at me. "So now you're the poster child for
the quit-smoking club, huh?"

I shrug. "Yeah, I guess. Just thought I'd throw
it in. Wish some noble mind reader would've
stopped my smoking habit when I was a little
younger."

"You stopped it yourself," Noah says.

"Not really. I think Preacher and Estelle put
some root doctor whammy on me."

Noah chuckles, and we continue up the street.
Surrounded by gray stone buildings, we draw
closer to the touristy city center. We pass a
chippy, a Celtic jeweler, and a kilt maker. As I
glance into the large picture window of the kilt
maker, an image catches my eye. *Eli*. My heart
leaps.

In the middle of the walkway I snap my head
to stare across the street. Passersby walk up and
down the sidewalk. No Eli. No one out of the
ordinary. Grabbing the door handle, I enter Mac-
Clennon's Fine Kilts.

A wave of spice and lavender hits me in the
nose as I walk into the small shop. Racks display
finely pressed kilts of all sizes. An open oak closet
exhibits woolen gloves, mittens, and hats. A thick
iron-legged table presents rows of fingerless
gloves of all colors, made of lamb's wool. In the
corner, my eyes light on the cashier. She's wearing her graying hair in a high bun and sporting a

dark green vest, a white cotton shirt, and a blue-and-black-plaid tie. She smiles broadly.

"Good afternoon," she says. "May I help you?"

I smile back as my eyes scan the room. "No, thank you. Just looking." I mull through the store, notice a few tourists sorting through the various sizes of kilts. One woman sifts through the gloves.

No sign of Eli. Or anyone who even remotely looks anything like him.

I wave at the graying woman, and turn to leave. I almost knock into Noah.

We both head outside. "What's up?" he asks.

I stare across the street, then up and down the sidewalk. I shrug and walk on. "Nothing. Thought I saw something."

We're moving through the afternoon crowd now, and Noah is a half step behind me. Kids in school black-and-white uniforms are weaving with us, as well as a few tourists and locals. I wish I could send out one big mental warning, a juju heads-up, saying *Everyone stay inside after dark!* so that no one here gets butchered. I don't like not knowing what's what. And I seriously don't like having the cold sensation of sensing Eli's presence in a threatening way. It's leaving an aftertaste in my mouth that's beyond hideous.

"Riley?"

I glance up at Noah, then back to the sidewalk. "What?"

When we round the corner, he pulls me to a stop. "You thought you saw Eli again."

A man passes by, and his eyes are level with mine. He spares Noah a brief glance and almost pauses, as though worried we're having a domestic dispute. I can see it in his aging blue eyes. I smile at him and nod, and he returns the gesture and moves on. Nice to know chivalry exists still in humans.

I sigh and meet Noah's penetrating gaze. "First, you have to stop glaring at me like that in public. And stop grabbing me, too. That old guy was an inch from busting your ass right here on the sidewalk."

Noah's body relaxes, and his eyes soften, just a little.

"Yes, I thought I saw Eli again," I answer him. I shove my hands deep into the pockets of my jacket. "When I glanced at the store window as we passed that kilt maker's store, I saw his reflection in the glass." I looked up at him. "The second I turned my head to search the street, he wasn't there. I think I'm losing my mind," I finish.

Noah studies me for a second or two. His jaw muscle tightens. "I wish you were. That's fixable." He glances out over the cobbled street, and his gaze scales the building in front of us. He studies the skyline for a moment longer. "What scares me"—Noah looks back at me—"is that you're not losing your mind." With a nod, he inclines his head. "Let's get back to the map. We've got about an hour and a half before nightfall."

We start back up the street and head to the guesthouse. Noah's words have bugged the hell out of me. He left his meaning unanswered, but I knew it, no matter how hard he disputed it. Knew it just as my body knows how to breathe without conscious thought. Yet his words claw at me the whole way back, and even while we're sitting at the kitchen table, hunched over the map and planning our route for the night's hunt, it bothers me.

He's scared Eli is back from that alternative realm.

And that he's not the same Eli.

A cold shiver runs down my spine at the thought. I try to push it aside, that thought, but it lingers, and soon it feels like fire ants are pinching and biting my insides. I need to get out. Get some fresh air. Just be alone for a few minutes.

I push away from the table and stand. "I'll be back in a few."

"Riley," Noah warns, and rises with me.

"Don't even," I warn in return. "I have to get some air. Clear my head." I frown at him. "Alone. Kinda like peeing without someone standing there, watching. I need a little alone time, Miles. Seriously."

Emotion flutters across his handsome features, and I know he's struggling with letting me out by myself. He wants to protect me, be by my side continuously to make sure nothing happens.

Well, that's all great, but I gotta have a breather.

"Half an hour," I say. "I'm just walking up the street to the market and back." When his face still pinches with confliction, I force a small smile. "Promise. Back before dark."

It's almost funny to see a vampire imitate a sigh. It's breathless, only going through the human motion he did for so long. Noah rubs his eyes and nods. "It's not that I don't think you can handle yourself. There's something out there, Riley. And we don't know exactly what yet."

"Vampires," I offer. "We knew that coming here."

He frowns. "Smart-ass. It's more than that and you know it." He stares at me. "Call me if anything goes on. And I don't mean on my cell phone."

Pushing my arm through the sleeve of my leather jacket, I nod. "Will do."

"Back in thirty," Noah reminds me.

"Yep," I agree, and close the door.

Outside, the shades of late-afternoon drift over the cobbles. It's crazy here in the winter months. November, and it gets full-on dark at four thirty in the afternoon.

As I walk, it starts to drizzle a freezing, misting rain. I briefly meet the friendly gazes of passersby, young and old, as they hurry home, hurry to the pubs, to the market. A gray haze hangs in the air, so thick I have to fight not to swipe it away with my hand.

Suddenly, memories of home, of before Edinburgh and Eli's . . . whatever that was . . . happened. I miss home. I miss Preacher and Estelle, my wonderful surrogate grandparents. I miss

Nyx, my best friend. Seth, my baby brother. Eli's family.

I miss that time. Living on the salt water surrounded by oaks and Spanish moss, tattooing people for a living. Eating Krystal hamburgers until I thought I'd puke. The pungent scent of the marsh at low tide. Having tea with Preacher and Estelle every morning.

And when I first fell in love with a vampire. When Eli was well, strong, and determined to guard the lives of Savannah's mortals. I miss my tattoo shop, Inksomnia, and I miss creating, the artwork, the hum of my ink gun. How life has changed since then.

If I could only have Eli back, the rest I could deal with.

Almost finished with my self–pity party, I turn the corner and the open market is before me. Although the shadows from the building and pending nightfall stretch long over the row of flower bouquets and fruit containers, people mill about making their choices. I look out of place, dressed in all black with a wing inked at the corner of my eye. Long dark hair with a few random fuchsia chunks added in. And although people can't see them, I have just under a half dozen blades sheathed beneath my clothes. Yeah. I love open markets, too. Flowers, food, and random stuff. Takes my mind off all the bullshit. . . .

Then, as I'm sifting through the hoards of gorgeous flowers, a sensation crawls over me. Without much thought, I glance over my shoulder.

Through the crowd, his height and stature rises above everyone else. Everyone mortal. His gaze locks on to mine.

My slow-beating heart plummets to my stomach, and I drop the flowers back into the bin and move toward him. *Don't take your eyes off him this time, Poe. Keep staring.*

I stare as long as I can. My eyes start to water, burn. Then I can't help it—I blink.

And he's not in the same place. *Shit!*

My eyes search the crowd frantically as I weave through them, dodging shoppers and market workers packing up for the evening. Then I see him again. He's standing beneath an awning, and I hurry toward him. *Eli!* I scream his name in my head. *Eligius Dupré, goddamn it!* I see him. I see people stepping around him to pass by. I'm not imagining this. He's not a mirage. He's really here. And I'm not losing my fucking mind.

A slight smile touches his mouth. At first, my heart melts at the sight of it. The memories. The familiarity.

Then it changes. Something snaps in his eyes, and his smile contorts.

The absolute coldness of it sends a feeling of dread clear to my bones. It chills me.

I'm moving fast now, my eyes glued to Eli. When he turns, he fades into the crowd, but I still see his broad shoulders. He's wearing a black leather jacket. Dark jeans. I'm not losing him this time. As we move out of the market area, the crowd thins, and Eli turns up the street toward the river Ness. High above the city center, the castle lights flicker on ahead, illuminating the red sandstone fortress of Inverness Castle through the wintry haze. Eli's stride is long. Purposeful. He knows where he's going. Whether he knows I'm following him, I can't tell. But he doesn't look back when he turns off Union and onto Church Street.

He's barely out of sight when I break into a run. I turn the same corner and pull up short, searching the darkness cast in streetlights and shadows. Few people are on the sidewalk. Not one of them is Eli.

Shit! I break into a run and make it to the end of the street. Looking both ways, I can't find him. I can't even sense him. And just as I'm about to take off running again, I'm grabbed by the shoulder and jerked back. My feet almost leave the ground, and I'm knocked against the closed storefront's double oak doors. My eyes are wide as I stare up at Noah. The streetlight shines on only half his face.

He's pissed.

"What the fuck, Riley?" he says angrily, in a low voice. "What are you doing?"

Snatched out of my crazed momentary stupor, I shake Noah off and push away from the door. "I'm not losing my mind. I just followed Eli from the market. I saw him totally clear, Noah," I say. I wait for a couple to pass us, and I glance in their direction and lower my voice. "He's wearing a black leather jacket, dark jeans. People dodged him. He looked me dead in the eye and I saw his face." I think about the chilling smile that sent shivers down my spine. "He's not right, just like you thought. But I saw him. And he saw me. And for a second, I don't know. He did look like himself." I look at Noah, pleading for him to understand. "Then it changed. He changed. And when he smiled at me, I felt cold as hell. It was him, Noah. Swear to God."

Noah's staring at me. "You're sure?"

"Yes," I answer. No hesitation. "Dead sure."

Noah grabs his cell phone and makes a call. He stares at me as he speaks, and I can hear every word exchanged between him and Jake Andorra.

"She's sure," Noah says.

"Jesus. You canna let her off alone," Andorra says. "He's unpredictable now."

That makes my insides ache.

Noah lifts an eyebrow. "What do you want me to do, Jake? Cuff her to me?"

"If you have to."

Noah swears. "Right."

"Let me talk to her," Jake says. Noah hands the phone to me.

"Jake," I say, "what's going on?" I figure an age-old vampire like Jake Andorra, plus someone who has known Eli for too long to count in years, would know *something*. Give me some sort of clue as to what the hell is happening.

"I'm not entirely sure," he answers.

Give me a freaking break.

Jake reads my thoughts, and chuckles. I don't think it's too damn funny.

"Riley, something's happened to Eli and I don't know what yet. The fact that he's appearing to you, although eluding you at the same time, means something. Almost as if he remembers you, and wants to connect. But he's dangerous. We canna trust him. You canna trust him. Not now. Maybe not ever again."

My heart sinks. "That's not going to happen, Jake."

"Listen to me, Riley," Jake says. His tone is stern, his accent heavier than usual. That means he's not only pissed, but worried. And I hate it. "You canna abandon your mission for the sake of Eli. He may verra well be causing the bloodbath there in Inverness. Do you want innocents to die?"

"Of course not," I answer angrily. "And I'm not abandoning anything. I saw him. I followed him. I want to find out what the hell is wrong with him, Jake. Why Victorian can pop home to Romania safe and sound, and Eli just . . . disappears." I'm so exasperated talking about this, I almost growl. "And now he has reappeared. And I want him *back*, Jake. I won't give up on him, either. He's my fiancé. Or don't you remember that?"

"Aye, girl, I remember," he answers. "But

dunna you forget that I know what he is." His voice is low, edgy. "What we all are. And I know his full potential. You won't go anywhere alone again. No' a breath o' fresh air. No' a run to the chippy. Nothing. Nowhere without Miles. If I have this problem wi' you again, I'll pull you from the mission and fly your arse back to Savannah. Ya ken?"

Noah's staring a hole through my head. His mercury eyes are all but illuminated in the shadows of the awning we're standing beneath. My blood is boiling, but what's left to do?

"Riley?"

"I ken, I ken," I answer Jake. Meaning, in Scot's terms, that I get it. I understand.

"Good. And dunna try your mind warpin' on Miles again. He cares about what happens to you. As do I. And I promise we'll do everything we can to fix this."

"Will you come here?" I ask.

"I can't now. Ginger isn't stable enough to leave. As soon as I can, though, I will."

Ginger Slater is one of my WUP team members. She recently transitioned from human trainee to werewolf elite. She's as unpredictable right now as Eli, I guess, and in the midst of a werewolf war.

"You guessed right," Jake says, using his capabilities to read my thoughts. "Take care, Riley. And stay close to Miles. He's the best chance you've got right now."

"I will," I answer. Jake hangs up, and I hand the phone back to Noah. "I'm sorry," I say. And I mean it. "I . . . panicked, I guess. I saw Eli. He moved. I followed. I didn't think."

Noah jams his cell phone in the inside pocket of his jacket. "Yeah. You just don't want me to cuff you." He grins. "To me."

I like that there's still some small part of Noah, post vow-making to keep me safe, that is still lighthearted enough to joke around. If anyone wanted to be cuffed to me, it'd be Noah Miles, perverted vampire extraordinaire. I miss the old Noah. Nasty as hell, but fun.

His grin widens as he, too, reads my mind. "Let's go."

I guess nothing's fun anymore. Definitely nothing normal. And none of it will be until all of this crazy shit is fixed.

And Eli is back with me. Safe.

We then hit the streets. I have a sense of unsettledness. It's hard to explain. I'm on edge, like I feel something is so very not right. Something besides Eli's unpredictability. With Noah on one side of the street, and me on the other, we search. Listen. Smell the air. Neither of us catches the first sign of a predator. Or a victim.

By nine, Noah holds the door for me as we enter Hush 51. It's Friday night, and while not many tourists are lingering in Inverness, the local crowd—especially the college crowd—has packed the club. There's alcohol. Maybe light drugs. Either way, it makes a human vulnerable, as well as an easy target for a vampire on the prowl. Noah had suggested we hit the club, and I'd agreed. Plus, I was a little curious about Rhine and his bandmates.

The dark wood interior of Hush 51 is polished and shining, and the low lights cast an amber hue over the crowd standing and sitting before the band. Rhine sees us enter, and he grins widely and gives us a nod.

"Aye, aye, settle down, ye feisty wicked pub jumpers," a man with a Hush 51 T-shirt announces at the mic. "Hard Knox, if ye fancy—"

The locals cheer and yell, and Rhine and the guys start up. So their band is called Hard Knox. Pretty cool. The pub is quaking and humming with music, and for a second I'm distracted by Rhine's voice. It's pretty goddamn good. I listen to him as my gaze slides over the crowd. I'm now at the bar, and I nod at the bartender. "Aye, lass?" he says with a smile. The gap between his front teeth is endearing.

"Pint," I respond, and he serves me one. I take a sip. Noah's right next to me.

Then all at once, everything happens. It's as if, without my permission, my own tendencies turn on at the same time. Rhine's voice fades. The patrons' voices fine-tune, and all their words are going off at once in my head. A cold, icy sensation washes over me, and instinctively, I turn around on my barstool and glance toward the far corner.

Noah's leather jacket creaks from the motion of him turning, too.

Eli's there. A woman's beside him. Tall. Almost as tall as he is. Dark, long auburn hair that falls in waves to her waist. Flawless alabaster skin and pouty full lips. Who the hell is she?

At the same moment my brain sends a message to my legs, I slide off the barstool. My heart feels like it's beating out of my chest. They're both looking at me, Eli and the woman, and just as I'm about to start making my way through the crowd, the woman reaches up and grazes Eli's jaw with her hand. She smiles at me. My eyes lock with Eli's.

He knows me. I can see it. And I can also see his eyes flash with . . . something. Regret? Struggle? What the hell?

Then a darkness clouds Eli's eyes, and he lowers his head, presses his mouth to hers, and kisses her.

I'm frozen to the floor, unable to breathe, much less move. I actually wheeze as my breath leaves my lungs. It's painful, and a little dizzying. The crowd seems oblivious of me as I stare, paralyzed, while Eli seductively makes out with the redhead. Emotions run through me fast, and before I finish with pain and sorrow, fury takes over. I feel a hand on my shoulder. It's Noah, and I reach behind me and grab his hand. My eyes are locked on to Eli and the woman. I start to move toward them. The overwhelming urge to kick her ass takes over me. My body tenses. Noah squeezes my hand.

And that's when the woman breaks Eli's kiss and looks dead at me.

Her tongue runs across her lips. And then she smiles and beckons to me with a long, delicate finger. I hear her voice, melodic tinged with an ancient accent, in my head.

Come here, Riley Poe. I've got something to show you. Something that's mine. . . .

I hear Rhine's voice over the mic, his sexy sound crooning over the crowd. Drums. Keyboard. Fiddle. Bass. My feet start to move, as if they've been instructed to do so against my will, and my hand drops Noah's as I weave through the crowd.

Toward the woman and Eli.

The music almost lulls me into a trance as I ease through the crowd. I don't understand why my body is complying, and why I'm not running full force at the woman, knocking her back, and grabbing and shaking Eli until he snaps out of whatever weird zombie state he's in. But I can't. I just keep walking toward them. The woman continues to beckon me, and she slips her hand inside Eli's jacket. She places her head against his chest, and Eli's arm drapes around her shoulders and pulls her tightly against him. He's not looking at me. Not meeting my gaze now.

Even with my eyes glued to the chilling smile on the woman's face, I can't stop.

When I step through the last couple, dancing and singing along with Rhine's band, the lights are now flickering to keep with the beat. The music hums just under the surface of my skin, a fierce vibration that keeps me fixated on only what's in front of me. Eli and this new woman. I'm now less than two feet from them both, and the woman looks at me with icy blue eyes. Her full lips tip upward, and her tongue darts out to lick her bottom one. She smiles.

Watch us.

My eyes are locked onto the woman and Eli less than two feet away as she tips her head to the side and draws closer to Eli. His eyes, those cerulean blue and sometimes stormy orbs that I fell in love with, pierce me now, and for a split second, I see hesitation. A flash of anger in his eyes. Then he stiffens, and those eyes now stay focused on my gaze as he lowers his head and moves his mouth over the woman's. His hand threads through her hair, pulling her head backward just a bit, and his other hand skims her throat and grasps her jaw. His tongue sweeps hers, the light glistening off its moisture, and their passion is as palpable as my own pulse. Not once does his gaze leave mine as he kisses her. The lights flash, the music thumps, and I can't do anything except stand there and watch them. As if I'm rooted to the wooden floor beneath me, paralyzed in place to stand and watch my fiancé engage in a sensual, sexually charged kiss with another woman.

I try to turn my head, but I can't. Literally, physically can't. Inside, I'm screaming. I'm dying. I'm having a mental Jerry Springer moment where I've kicked off my boots, yanking that bitch off the chair by her hair and whipping her ass for kissing my man. But it's all mental. I can't do a single thing except watch.

The woman drops her hand from Eli's chest and lets it drag slowly down his abdomen. He pulls her closer, and her hand moves over his crotch. Eli's mouth leaves hers and he kisses her throat, and his eyes are hazed and locked on to mine as his mouth tips up in a grin. All the while, Rhine's music jams the club, and everyone around us is rocking and singing, having a swell time. It's as if no one else notices that Eli and this woman are nearly having sex, right out in the open. Like no one else sees them but me. Like no one sees me, either. Where the hell is Noah?

What the hell's wrong with *me*?

I concentrate. Focus. I stare hard at her, then at Eli. *Stop, Eli. Let her the fuck go.*

For a split second, something flashes in Eli's eyes. It's so fast, and so short-lived I almost question if it really happened. He wraps his arms around her waist and pulls her onto his lap. He's now sitting on a barstool, and he drops his mouth to her temple. The woman smiles.

Then the smile vanishes. I see nothing but hard, ice-cold hatred in her eyes.

In a blurring motion, she waves one hand in a gesture over the crowd. Her lips move, but I don't understand the low murmur coming from them.

I feel the movement before I see it. It's a low-frequency hum that nestles beneath the music, gains tempo, and then just like the sonic boom in the forest, explodes. The windows of Hush 51 blow completely out, sending shards of glass pummeling into the streets. Screams begin penetrating the trance I'm in; lights are flashing and then extinguish. Shadows and the scent of human terror wash over me, and I'm dazed, standing there, paralyzed on the floor. One second, I see the blaze of Eli's eyes in the dark. The pale white skin of the woman he's holding.

Her face, completely morphed into full-blown vampire. Incisors twice as long as the rest of her jagged white teeth drop from her gums, and her face extends forward, bones accommodating the change. Her eyes flash bloodred. Dark veins snake across her alabaster skin.

In the next second, amid the crowd's panic, they're gone. She, Eli. Vanished.

Slowly, after a few seconds, my paralysis lifts. I shake my head. Even my vision has gone blurry. I shake my head again, and then my shoulders are grabbed and I'm yanked around. I'm shocked to see Rhine standing there, looking down at me. I didn't realize the kid was that tall.

"You okay, lass?" he says. "You'd best get out of here!"

"I've got her," Noah says, suddenly by my side.

Chaos is all around me. People are running,

knocking into me now, and my stupor is slowly vanishing. I glance at Rhine. "Thanks," I say. "Let's get these people out of here."

Patrons are running around, frightened and screaming, and everyone is trying to fit through the narrow, double oak doors of the club. Rhine and his band members have dispersed, trying to calm people, get them to calmly exit the club. It's not working.

My mind is jumbled. Eli, the woman. She's a vampire. I know that now. The Hush 51 patrons. Priority seizes my brain, and I push vampires out of my thoughts.

I focus on the human crowd.

Stop!

As if I'd pushed the PAUSE button on a DVD remote, everyone stops in their tracks. I waste no time in hurrying to the front doors. I kick open the props so they both stand wide. After a brief scan of the sidewalk and street, I notice people there have stopped, too. Amazing what a panicky human with tendencies can accomplish.

I run back inside, weaving through the stone-still patrons. Noah's standing there, right where I left him. Not moving.

Oops.

I grasp his hand, and catch his gaze. *Let's go.* I say that only to Noah.

His eyes immediately brighten, and then he scowls. "Yes, ma'am." He leads the way out of Hush 51, and once we're back outside, I glance at the patrons behind me, standing in a building that might not be so stable.

Everyone, fall into two single files and walk calmly out through the front doors.

As if a bunch of zombies being commanded by a voodoo priestess, the patrons all fall into two lines inside the club. Slowly, they start moving outside. I see now that they're not running one another over, stampede-style, so I grasp Noah's hand and pull.

"Let's go," I say.

Now he's in front of me, pulling *me* by the hand. "Pretty impressive, Poe," he says as we run side by side up the street, toward the river walk. "Not even sure I can pull something like that off." He grins and faces the street. "Human shenanigans never cease to amaze me."

We're running down High Street now, and it's a no-traffic, pedestrian-only road. Most of the businesses are closed for the night, but the streetlights illuminate the paved sidewalks, and the occasional open storefront beams its light's hue, causing shadows to stretch from sidewalk to sidewalk. The road itself is cobbled, not as old as Edinburgh, I imagine, but still pretty damn old. I'm barely paying any attention to Noah's comment as we hurry along. I've now got only one thing on my mind. Well, two.

Eli and that female vampire.

Who the hell was she? And why does it matter so much to her to see me suffer?

No words are spoken between me and Noah, yet we both know each other so well we're simultaneously searching the streets, the shadows, for Eli and the female. I home in on movements, too. Shifts in the air. Off-key sound waves that belong to neither a rat, nor a human, nor a hedgehog. I sense nothing.

Not at first.

My mind is working so hard, trying to sense and make sense of what's just happened, that I now realize we're at the curving walkway of the river Ness. I stop and stare into the water, its black depths glimmering with shards of light casting down from the streetlamps holding my gaze as I try to ignore the images of Eli embracing, kissing the female. Pain sears my insides. I feel as if someone a lot larger and stronger than me has sucker-punched me in the gut. I physically hurt. It almost doubles me over. I can't hear anything right now except the cries of my own self–pity party.

"Hey," Noah says, and he drapes his arm over my shoulders and pulls me against him. His body is hard, not so warm, but not so cold, either. Kinda like Eli's. It's weird, getting used to that lukewarm skin. I can feel it through Noah's clothes, even. Yet I take full comfort in it right now. I slip my arms around his waist and lay my head against his rock of a chest. "Don't beat yourself up, Poe. Even I was overpowered." He squeezes me. "That's one strong bitch. Must be old as dirt."

I lean back and look at him. "Do you think she's controlling Eli?"

Noah's jaw tightens. His eyes are murky in the shadows of the river. "I'm not convinced of that, darlin'. I wish I was." He sighs and crosses his arms over his chest. "She rendered me powerless back there, along with you. When you stopped, I stopped." He sighs. "But I could still see. Still hear. Still understand. And what I saw?" I look at him, and he looks down at me and shakes his head. "Damn, Riley. The grin on Dupré's face, that look in his eye? Even gave me the fucking chills. She's sick powerful if she can control you, me, and Eli, all at once."

A wind gusts by, and it strikes my face and makes me squint. It's chilly, maybe midthirties. I'm not uncomfortable, but I do notice the temperature. Sometimes I miss it, that very humanlike sensation of being frigidly cold and needing to bundle up and stamp my feet for warmth. Miss the absolute hell out of it.

"Something's wrong, though," Noah says out of the blue. "I can't put a finger on it. But I feel like there's something we're not seeing."

"With Eli?" I ask.

He glances at me. "With all of it." He grabs me gently by my jaw, forcing me to hold his gaze. "I've not been dead so long that I don't remember what it feels like to have your heart trudged on. Even if Dupré is being controlled by that bitch, it still pisses me off. And I'm sorry you have to suffer it. You've not been yourself since Edinburgh. Since it happened." He pulls my face closer, lowers his almost until our noses touch. "I miss the old, sarcastic, mean-ass, smart-ass Riley Poe."

I miss her, too. It's something that I just can't seem to help, though. Everything is darker now, since Edinburgh. Ugly dark. Coming from me, that's bad, because I've seen the shittiest, ugliest dark there is. This tops it. But maybe I've let it get to me. In a way I shouldn't have, I mean. Maybe that's part of what's blocking my abilities. I'm so blinded by grief and fury that I'm not using the extent of my tendencies. It's why that female was able to control me so thoroughly.

Maybe Noah Miles is onto something.

He grins, still obscenely close to my face.

"How come you've not even once pulled that satchel off your neck and tried to seduce me?" I ask jokingly. I narrow my gaze and wait for Noah's wiseass answer.

Instead, he widens his smile, turns my face loose, and fishes out his iPhone. After a few taps, he flips it around and lowers it. My eyes scan the picture fastened there.

Me. Noah. My mouth latched on to his, sucking his face off.

Then it hits me. I remember. The forest, after I'd dragged Eli and Vic out of the realm. Noah had used his oversensual vampire pheromones to lure me back to reality.

He'd saved my life by doing it.

Still. I glare at him, and punch him in the stomach. "Asshole. You had to take a pic of that?" I punch him again. Harder. "You literally took the time to take a pic? I was out of my mind."

"Ow," Noah says, ridiculously clutching his stomach. As if that had hurt him. "You don't sincerely think I'd pass up a photo op like that, do you?"

"Give me that," I say, and reach for it. He snatches it back. Lifts it out of my reach.

"Oh, hell no, Ms. Poe. Not on your life." He grins and stuffs his iPhone deep into his pocket. "Technology is a wonderful thing. And I've saved it to my hard drive, so stop fretting about deleting it off my cell—"

A sound distracts me, and I hold up my hand to silence Noah. He's listening now, too, and through the chilled night air, we both strain. I concentrate, breathe deeply, opening my senses. Closing my eyes, I zone out everything and envision my ear canal as a megaphone, siphoning all abstract noises and sharpening them. At once, I snap my gaze beyond the city lights. Up the river and higher. I strain so hard it almost hurts. Then I hear it. The slightest of sounds. It's a groggy, faint groan. Female.

Human.

And it's not a groan of pleasure.

I sniff the air, but it's too far away to tell. I can barely detect where the sound is coming from, and all I can do is start moving in that direction.

"Come on," I say, and start off at a jog.

Noah's right beside me.

At once, I stop, turn around, and take off toward the river. Within seconds, I'm at a full run. The moment my boot hits the walkway hugging the river, I leap, over the water, and land in a crouch on the opposite bank. I glance behind me, just in time to see Noah land beside me. I pause and listen for a half second. We're on the same side of the river as St. Andrew's, but north of the cathedral. I turn in the direction of St. Andrew's, and slipping through the shadows, we run. It's close to two a.m. now, and patrons have thinned and humans are scarce. So the whimpering I'm homing in on, growing louder by the second, worries me. We race up Duncraig Street and turn onto Kenneth, following the human's groans. I glance at Noah as we run, and I know he hears it now. There's a cemetery up ahead, the scent of aged decay penetrating my senses and drawing me closer and closer. Fearing to be noticed by anyone simply taking out the trash, I hasten down a dark alley, find my foothold, and leap up to the rooftop. When I glance to my side, Noah's there. We head across the rooftops, bounding over chimneys and slipping on tiles, until the sound of the human's heartbeat quickens. The cemetery is there, just ahead, and I pick up speed, leaping down from the roof and landing in a full run. We're still within the city limits, but the populated areas have thinned. Tomnahurich

Cemetery sits on a hillside, and as we hit the single graveled lane within, it starts to wind up the hill from the bottom. I can smell old death, bones, and rotted earth. My eyes search the area in front of me, and although it's dark out, the pale gray of the headstones stands stark against the blackness of night. Graves reach all the way up to the summit, but the human's quickened heartbeat pulls me off the path and into the wood. Through the pines and brush we race, and suddenly, I pull up short. On the far side of the hill, I hear it. Gurgling. Choking.

Panicking, I take off, and Noah's keeping up step for step. I jump up and into the tree limbs overhead, and leap tree to tree to save time. Then, below and ahead, I see them. I see Eli.

And the scene stops my heart.

The female from Hush 51 stands in the clearing. Eli is a few feet away, stone-still.

In the female's arms is a young woman, the other woman's mouth latched on to her throat. The girl's arms dangle, limp and lifeless at her sides. Her body jerks, convulses. Not all the way dead yet.

In the tree, my hand is pressing hard against the rough bark. Noah's arm goes around my waist and I know he's doing that to keep me from lunging down. In my heart I know we're too late.

The woman's head lifts. Blood trails down her chin. Jesus Christ, it's a lot of blood. She's looking dead at me when she smiles. Eli continues to stand, unmoving. Frozen in place.

When my gaze moves back to the female, she throws the human down.

Like trash.

Part Four

DARK WHISPERS

Make sure when your shift is over you go home alive. Here endeth the lesson.

—Jim Malone, **The Untouchables**, *1987*

Can you imagine what it would feel like to have your heart ripped out of your chest? Like, dig their fingers into your skin, break rib bones until those fingers thread through the vessels, find and squeeze your heart, and then rip it out of your body? I can. I feel like it just happened. I don't feel human anymore. Not alive. Not dead. I don't know if I feel anything at all, other than fury. And disgust. It sounds dramatic just to think it, much less truly feel it. Right now I don't give a damn. I want to hurt. Cause pain. Maybe even kill. Now that I think about it, maybe that's what she wants.

—Riley Poe

They are baiting you, Riley. You must leave. Do it now.

My body jolts as though I've been hit. I'm so taken off guard by the voice in my head that I nearly fall from the twenty-foot tree branch I'm sharing with Noah.

Go now. If they capture you, Riley, they won't kill you. They'll torture you. And there's nothing more you can do. The human is dead. Leave.

I stare through the pine branches and shadows at Eli and the female. My eyes drift to the lifeless body of the innocent human lying on the ground. I am so damn confused and hurt and angry, I feel as though I'm going to self-combust.

My breath quickens, and my energy gathers, but before my feet leave the tree branch, Noah's grip tightens around my arm. I know he won't let go. If I jump, I'll land with one less limb.

But if I jump, I'll still have one good arm left to fight with.

Then I hear it. I hold my breath and cock my head, zoning out everything else around me: the wind, the night sounds. I focus on heartbeats, separating the human ones from the animal ones. There. Back toward the river. And it's more than one, accompanied by breathlessness.

With a final glance at the female vampire, who wipes her mouth with her sleeve and grins at me, I look at Noah, and he knows. We take off through the trees, and I'm racing now toward the human heart that is beating faster and faster, matching the footsteps as it runs. The moment we clear the cemetery, we're at top speed, Noah's a few steps behind me, and . . . I was wrong. Not at the river. One street over. Down an alley. The crying and begging is loud now—loud enough for another human to hear. Noah and I round the corner at the same time.

It's a dead-end alley—a crossway between two buildings, with a small courtyard at the very end. A young couple stands huddled together, the guy shielding the girl. She's clinging to his back, her fingers digging into his shoulder so fiercely I can see her knuckles whitening from where I stand.

Two have them cornered—both males. Both

young. Well, young looking. They both turn and face me and Noah as we close in. I lunge toward the couple, and the girl screams. I glance at her. *Be quiet. Both of you run. Leave. Go straight home. Do it now!*

The guy stares at me for a blink, then grabs his girlfriend by the hand and starts to run, and I shuffle them to the side of the building, my back to them, my eyes on the males. Noah's in front of me now, and he's already morphed. One of the males leaps and tries to get past me to go after the humans, but I grab his leg and snatch him down. He lands on his back, and I'm on top of him. He surprises me, though. He's stronger than I imagine. He grabs me by the throat and flings me against the building. My head hits, and I know it's gonna hurt like hell in the morning. Out of the corner of my eye, I see Noah. He's got the other one. This one flies at me, and I yank my silver out of my waist sheath and jab the tip into his skin. His eyes grow large as he stares at me.

"Is she controlling you?" I ask. When he doesn't answer, I shove the blade in a little more. He grunts. "Who is she?" I growl. *What's her fucking name?*

The vampire stares at me with bloodred eyes. "Carrine," he says, and his voice is gurgly sounding. A smile tips his mouth upward. "She will kill you."

"I don't think so." I shove the blade into his heart. He falls against me. He's already convulsing when I shove him off, and the moment I'm clear of him I see Noah tear the other one's head clean off. Not pretty. He throws it down onto the quivering body and looks at me. In a blurring instant, his face shifts back. Flawless and perfect.

"You know," Noah says. He glances at the piles on the ground. "This is getting pretty god-damn old." He cracks his neck, as if there's a kink left over from his monster shifting. "What'd he tell you?"

I go over, kick the blade away from the messy pile of vampire leftovers, and clean it off on the pavement. Then my pants. So freaking sick, but I don't want to leave my blades behind. "Her name is Carrine. And apparently, according to him"—I incline my head—"she wants me dead."

"Yeah, that's nothing new," Noah says. He glances skyward; it's the first time I notice that dawn is near. "You hear anything else?" he asks.

I listen for a moment, then shake my head. "No, but I'll feel better if we run the rooftops, slip through a few streets before dawn breaks." I shove the blade back in its sheath and walk to Noah. "I don't know who Carrine is, but some-thing else is going on here."

"Like?"

I shrug. "Well, if I knew that answer we wouldn't be standing here."

Noah's face is shadowy, but I see him grin. "Let's go."

We head out. Run rooftops. Leap from build-ing to building. We even cross the river, scale St.

Andrew's Cathedral, and make a few laps along the river Ness. It stays silent the rest of the night. Well, all except for the fire department and clean-up crew still gathered outside Hush 51. What a mess. We keep our distance, though, and the closer it is to daylight, people are beginning their day and we're forced to slow to their pace. Nothing else occurs. No random vampires. No appearance of Eli and Carrine.

Just thinking his name with another female, vampire or not, hurts.

With Noah and me covering opposite sides of the street, we sweep the city center once more. Gulls scream and light on the rooftops, and as I inhale, the salty scent of the firth sweeps over me. Reminds me of home. God, I miss that stinky, pukey-smelling marsh.

The next couple of days are surprisingly un-eventful. No killings, not even a hint or scent of Eli and Carrine. We comb every club, seek out every rooftop, every darkened alleyway, and all along the river Ness. Nothing. The weekend is over now, and locals are returning to their weekly routine. Me and Noah are just turning onto Montague Row when the November sun peaks over the city's crest. I stop and turn, staring. Ever since I've been in Scotland, I think I've seen the sun maybe three times. I want so badly for all this bullshit to go away: the killing of innocents, the mystery of Eli. And how will I ever get the images of him kissing that female out of my head? Jesus, I hate jealousy, but I'm human, even if just partly, after all. I can't help some emotions. And watching the two of them kiss, touch?

I close my eyes for a brief second, and the sun rises and gleams through the clouds, shining on my face. My skin heats, just a little, and I inhale. For a moment, I'm lost. The sounds of the city, horns blasting, the low hum of conversation that hardly ever leaves me now. The wind is chilled and brisk this morning, and with it rides the sounds of seals barking from the firth.

I snap my eyes open, suddenly aware that I'm standing on the drive of our guesthouse, with my eyes closed. Looking like an idiot. Feeling way more vulnerable than I should ever, ever allow myself.

Noah's silver eyes are studying me with such intensity, such depth. No pity there. Only compassion. His eyes soften. "You're far from looking like an idiot," he informs me, once more delving into my thoughts. "Far. And don't go digging around in my head, either." He grins. "You might not like what you find."

It's tempting, I'll admit. To dig, I mean. Ever since all of the vampiric venom latched on to my DNA, I've been able to see past events in others' lives. All by a simple touch. I don't have any control over where I go once inside that soul's memory, but it's almost as if I'm actually there, in person, standing and watching whatever event is occurring unfold. The guys who schooled us all in the use of a broadsword back in Edinburgh?

Tristan de Barre in particular? Yeah, that was definitely something else to behold. He'd been a thirteenth-century knight who was murdered in his own dungeon, along with his men, the infamous Dragonhawk and his knights. In the vision I'd stood in a dank cell and watched, helpless to do anything about it. Then again, had I been able to, there'd be no Tristan de Barre today. And weirdly, although he was dead for centuries, there is a Tristan. Dead, wandering his lands with his men as spirits, then whack! His now wife, a forensic archaeologist, helped him break an aged curse, and he and his men were given another life. Another chance at mortality. Tristan and Gawan Conwyk, friends in life and in death, came together to instruct the WUP team in Edinburgh on the use of a broadsword. Sick teachers, both of them.

"Now, there's something I don't see nearly enough of lately," Noah says as he unlocks the guesthouse door. He turns. "You, smiling."

I walk past him. "Yeah, well, you know me, don't ya?" I move into the kitchen, open the fridge, and grab the half-filled soda bottle Noah had bought for me the other day. When I crack the lid, it barely hisses; it's flatter than what I like, but I guzzle it down anyway.

"All too well."

I look at Noah, and for a split second I think to tell him about the voice I'd heard, warning me to leave instead of attack Carrine. The voice telling me that she and Eli would not kill, but would torture me. I open my mouth, but something else comes out instead. "I don't get this, Noah. What do Carrine and Eli have to do with the rogue and newblood killings? I don't see the connection at all."

"I don't know, either," he offers. "But that's what we're here to find out, right? And to stop it."

"Yeah, we are," I answer. Then I throw the empty plastic soda bottle at the trash can. I throw it harder than I mean to, and I completely miss the can and hit the wall instead. It bounces and flings across the kitchen. I sigh and rub my eyes.

Noah grabs me by the shoulders and steadies me. Calms me. "Look at me," he says.

With another sigh, I open my eyes. "I don't get it, Noah. How can Eli look right at me and not know me?" I feel energy surging up inside me from the thought of Eli and the female together. Like a soda that has been shaken, and the lid is cracked and all the liquid fizzes out. That's me, right now, despite having seen the hesitation in Eli's eyes. Almost there . . .

"Riley, you have to get a grip, darlin'," Noah says, and ducks his head to make me look at him. Liquid silver glimmers. "Because, when we have human bloodlust, that's all there is. It consumes us. No matter what's occurred, that becomes the focus. To somehow, no matter the means, get that human's blood inside our bodies."

I look away, because it hurts to think about this. He grasps my chin and pulls my gaze back to his. "All reason, morality, humanity—it all goes away. Memories? Gone. Our vision sees nothing but blood. We taste it in our mouth by just the scent of it beneath the surface of a human's skin." He smiles. "You know this. You experienced it, Riley. I've got the memory of a sore neck to prove it. Remember? You ripped into it when you were blood-lusting."

Again, the need for comfort overwhelms me, and I slide my arms around Noah's waist and lay my head against his chest. I'm not very fond of this neediness I have lately. It sucks. Makes me feel so useless.

His arms go around me, and his hand cups the back of my head. "I'm not going to lie and say I got all the answers," he says gently. "But I will fight to the end to save Eli."

It's at that exact moment, it happens.

It's weird that it hasn't happened before now.

One moment, my cheek is pressed against Noah's chest; in the next second, *I'm standing in a mist-shrouded forest, the white vapor slipping through tall trees and underbrush. I look around me; nothing looks familiar. Ravens startle and fly away in a rush overhead. I glance around. At first, I see no one. Then I hear footfalls. Running. Breaking through brush.*

Then I see Noah. He's on foot, running through the trees. He's wearing brown pants, boots, a cream-colored long-sleeved shirt, and a brown vest. His hair is different—long, gathered at the nape of his neck, no dreads. He wears a tricorn hat, and is hauling ass. In one hand, a hatchet. The other, a rifle. Three men in red coats are chasing him.

Revolutionary War. Noah is a militiaman.

A shot rings out through the wood, and when I look at the redcoats, one of their rifles is smoking. The other two fire at Noah. One misses. One hits him in the shoulder, knocking him sideways and down. I fight not to run to him; it will do no good. I'm a bystander, watching a memory that's already happened.

Just as fast as he fell, Noah rolls and gets back up. He's now rounded and running directly toward the redcoats. All three are on their knees reloading their guns. Noah throws down his gun and with a wide arc, swings and sinks his hatchet right into the British soldier's chest. With his foot, he shoves the soldier off the blade and runs right at the other two. Blood is oozing from Noah's shoulder, but he ignores it and takes a lethal swing at the first soldier's throat. His head nearly comes clean off.

One redcoat left, and he's waiting for Noah and uses his gun to reflect Noah's powerful swing. The two fight, struggle. It's only now that I realize Noah's not a vampire. He's mortal. Impressive fighter. I can feel his rising adrenaline as the pair struggle to gain control.

Out of nowhere, another redcoat appears, and with a sword drawn, he runs it straight through Noah's back. Noah's scream pierces my ears, and every ounce of pain and anger coursing through him, I feel inside me. He sinks to his knees, his hand still tightly gripping his hatchet.

From the canopy above, a figure falls from the mist. The moment he drops and lands on his feet, I see it's Eli. He's dressed like Noah. His hair is longer, pulled back at the nape of his neck. His cerulean blue eyes almost glow through the mist.

In a blur, Eli moves, and he is suddenly at both men. He grabs one redcoat by the throat. The other, by the front of his shirt, and pulls him close. As I watch, Eli's jaw extends, his teeth drop long and jagged from his gums, and he rips into the soldier's throat. He throws him down and does the same to the second red-coat. The bloodlust that rushes through Eli also rushes through me; I can feel it, the scent, the craving, al-most as if I were experiencing it instead of him. Mo-tionless, I stand there and watch as Eli drops to the forest floor to Noah. Eli's no longer morphed as a vampire. He's Eli. And I can see pain etched into his features as he stares at Noah.

"I won't make it," Noah says. His accent is still tinged with Southern drawl, but it's older. "Find Elana. Take—" Noah starts coughing, choking. He grabs Eli's arm. "Take care of her, brother. I promised her I would care for her always. I . . . have to break this promise." He coughs some more, and it's more of a crying cough than anything else. It's filled with pain. Not physical pain, but emotional. I feel it inside me, too. "Do this for me," he begs Eli. "Please."

All of Noah's emotions run through me. He loves this girl, Elana. Was it his wife? His fiancée? Either way, the sorrow he's experiencing is mind-numbing. It's a different Noah than I know. I watch as Eli low-ers his head closer to Noah's.

"I can fix this," Eli says. "I can fix you. You can take care of Elana yourself."

Noah's breathing quickens, and he chokes.

"You must hurry and decide," Eli urges. "Now."

"I'll be like you?" Noah asks.

"Yes."

Noah closes his eyes for a moment, and his lips are moving. He's praying. Suddenly, his eyes open again and he's staring at Eli. "Do it."

Eli doesn't ask if he's sure; nor does he hesitate, not even for a second. He moves so fast I don't see Eli's face change. Don't see his teeth elongate. I only see his mouth move over Noah's throat and stay there for several seconds. When his head lifts, and he wipes his mouth across his sleeve, his face is Eli's. Not vampire. Noah is deathly still. I see no breath rising in his chest. His mercury-colored eyes stare blankly skyward.

Suddenly, Noah jerks, his body begins to quiver, convulse. Eli grasps his shoulders, holds him down. "Be strong," Eli growls, and his French accent is heavier now.

Noah's painful scream rips through the misty forest. Then his eyes flicker open.

Voices, footfalls in the forest. Eli's gaze snaps up, his hands still holding a now-ferocious and fighting Noah down. It's like . . . he's crazed, and those emotions soar within me, too. I can barely stand still.

I look in the direction Eli's staring, and I see what he sees. More redcoats. A lot of them. Like a rag doll, he throws Noah over his shoulder and starts to run. I try to move, to follow, but I can't. Moments later, the British soldiers rush by me. They're so close I can see the whiskers on their faces. They're chasing Eli and Noah, and before long, the mist swallows them all up.

Gunshots ring through the air. Screams. Terrified screams—

Suddenly, my eyes snap open, and Noah's shaking the holy hell out of my shoulders. So hard I feel like my teeth are clanking against one another. I focus on his face, his eyes. "Stop shaking me," I say.

Noah's jaw clenches. "I could've used my special method of pulling you from your mind explorations," he answers. His eyes lighten. "The one I reserve only for you."

He leads me to a chair and I sit. He squats down in front of me, and I look at him. "You never told me Eli is the one who turned you."

A smile tips his mouth. "You never asked. So what else did you see?"

I inhale, exhale, and look at him. "I saw you fighting British soldiers. But you were dying. Pleading with Eli to take care of Elana."

For a moment, Noah's mind goes elsewhere, and I know this because the look in his eyes softens and deepens and he stares away at some other point in the room. He finally looks back at me. "We were engaged to be married. She was . . . the sweetest woman I've ever met."

"What happened?" I ask. "After Eli changed you."

Noah rubs his jaw, and I can tell it's painful to recall the memories. I regret asking. "You know how it is when you're first changed. You're . . . out of your mind with bloodlust." A smile touches his mouth. "I don't remember everything, but

Eli later told me I gave him a helluva ride. He took me all the way south, to Preacher's kin. He left me there for them to cleanse me. The same way you were. Hasn't changed a bit."

I hesitate to ask more, but I might as well. Noah's my partner. My friend. Eli's best friend. I want to know. "What happened to Elana?"

Noah looks down at the floor between his knees. "By the time Eli made it back to watch over her until I was ready, she and her whole family had been killed." He looks up at me now, and his liquid silver eyes are watery. "Elana, her parents, and six brothers and sisters. All dead. Their house had been burned to the ground." He rises and walks to the window and looks out. "I . . . went nuts for a while. A controlled rampage, you might say." He turns and looks at me. "It started out that way, anyhow. Revenge, I assure you, can quickly turn into bloodlust. Eli had to come after me. I had to go through vampire detox once more." His eyes aren't sad now, but he's not smiling. "I avenged Elana and her family. But it was almost at too high a price. If Eli hadn't stopped me . . ." He shakes his head. "I don't know, Riley. I'm pretty sure you and I wouldn't be sharing the same guesthouse if it hadn't been for Dupré's determination to save me from myself."

I punch Noah in the arm. "Damn glad he did, then. There's no one else, except Eli, that I'd want watching my back."

We stand there in that little Inverness guesthouse kitchen, and we're silent for only a handful of seconds. But we know each other. We understand. And I understand a little more about the predicament Eli is in right now.

Noah's fingers lightly grasp my chin and pull my gaze to his. His eyes search mine for a few moments. "I know Eli better than anyone, Riley. He's a strong-willed soul. He'll come out of this. I swear I feel it."

Noah's encouraging words wash over me, and I'm soothed. I smile at him. "I needed that."

His perfect lips pull back into a wide smile. "I know." He kisses my nose. "All right, enough mind-diving for now," Noah says. "We got work to do."

"Hey, I told you I had no control over where the memories take me," I remind him. "I guess I'll just have to wait and see what it is you're hiding from me later."

Something stirs in Noah's eye, but I ignore it. No need to goad him.

"Smart girl," he says.

We get busy.

As we study the city map, I circle all of the most likely places a rogue or newblood would hunt. But as I stare at my markings, it starts to all seem useless. The red permanent marker I'm using starts to take up a lot of space. I shake my head, snap the pen lid back on, and throw it down. "Their attacks are too random, Noah. We're chasing too many directions. Too many damn what-ifs." I look up at him, and his eyes are glued to the map. "I feel like the only thing we're doing is running on my supersonic senses. So far, it hasn't been a hundred percent on the mark, either. Carrine has been able to control my mind, and she's killed an innocent before I had a chance to pick up on it."

He looks up at me now. "She controlled your mind, and mine, because she's strong as shit, Riley. Plus, you're distracted by Eli. We're not seeing it, but somehow it's all tied in together. Carrine, Eli, and the random kills." He shakes his head. "We need to find out more about her." He pushes away from the table and grabs his cell off the counter.

"Who ya calling?" I ask.

"Gabriel," he answers. "He's been in Scotland a long time. Maybe he's heard of her."

Gabriel not only has no last name to mention, but he's an immortal druid from centuries ago. He's WUP's Scotland contact. We stayed at his place, the Crescent, back in Edinburgh when we fought the Black Fallen. It'd be nice to have him here.

As Noah talks to Gabriel, I get up, nod toward my bedroom, and head to the shower. My body aches, and the beginning of a headache is nagging at the base of my skull. In my room I dig through my meager belongings—just the bare necessities, I guess. I grab clean panties and a cotton camisole and head to the shower. Once in the bathroom, though, I stare at the large porcelain claw-foot bathtub just a little too long. I decide to soak. Think.

Forget.

Turning the water on full-blast hot, I undress and wait for the tub to fill. I wrap my hair into a ball at the nape of my neck and bind it with a ponytail holder. Staring into the mirror at my reflection, I have to wonder where all of this is going. What's going to become of Eli? Of me? Of us?

No sooner do I slip into the water and lay my head back than the voice returns.

You make it very difficult to speak to you, Riley. You're so beautiful.

My eyes flash open and I glance around. Although I lost most of my modesty years ago, I drape my arm over my breasts. This time, I answer the voice.

Where are you, Athios? I ask in my head.

Prison. Hell. Call it what you will.

Athios was wrongfully nailed with the sin of a Black Fallen—a fallen angel engulfed in the darkest of magic. We defeated the others. He saved my life, all of our lives, by submitting his own. *What are you doing slipping around my bathroom while I bathe?* I ask.

It's hard to get you alone these days. Forgive me for indulging in your beauty. 'Tis all I have left.

Who is the female? Carrine? I ask.

She's apparently someone who wants your fiancé just as badly as you do.

That angers me. *Damn it, Athios. Are you going to help me or not?*

He laughs softly, almost a whisper. *You ask much of me, Riley Poe.*

Yeah, I know. I'm sorry, Athios. I wish there was a way you could escape . . . wherever you are.

Athios sighs. *What would the difference be? I'm in here without you, or out there, without you? Same prison to me.*

I love Eli, and that's never going to change. I have to help him.

I know. Which is why I even bother putting myself through this torture. To see you like you are, in my head, and know you're unobtainable. I'd rather be sliced in half.

Athios.

Another laugh. *I'll see what I can find out. Mind combing is a tedious endeavor, you know. And it's all I have at the moment. I'm bound here, in this place, Riley. And I don't know Carrine, except, of course, what she is. And that she's very, very powerful.*

I know. With a wave of her hand she caused some sort of a sonic boom in the club we were in. Blew out all of the glass. I had no power against her

Well, keep in mind that powers of the mind must be practiced, just as one practices swordplay. Practice on your partner. You've not even scratched the surface of your capabilities, Riley. Remember. Besides your own unique blood, you have all that vampiric venom floating about in you. I've seen your powers. They're only half developed.

I smile. *Is this a pep talk, Athios? Something to lift my spirits?*

You aren't hearing me, are you? Whilst you may have pushed aside our time together, I most certainly have not. It's all I have, those memories.

Guilt washes over me. Yes. I admit there was something between Athios and me. Something strong and powerful that I could not fight. We made love, after I thought Eli had been killed. It's something I've had to come to terms with. It's something I don't regret. And if I ever get Eli back to Eli, I will have to tell him. Hell, he may even already know.

It soothes my soul to know you at least don't regret our time together. But my point is, Riley, that you have a little Black Fallen in you, too. Along with all of the vampiric abilities. You've simply ignored it. And unfortunately, I cannot help you. Only you can bring them to light.

I close my eyes, and let my head drop against the hard porcelain tub. I purposely knock it a few times. And I groan. *I feel like I'm talking to Yoda. In riddles. What are you talking about, Athios?*

Who is Yoda?

I almost laugh. *No one. Just tell me what you mean instead of talking in circles.*

You have a few of my abilities inside you, Riley. When we made love, we became one, even for a brief bit of time. I left inside you a piece of me. My skills of the mind. Core energy that you can command. And perhaps a few powers that can help you manipulate the elements. Forces of nature. You can use them to fight Carrine, or anyone else who poses a threat. Hone them. Use them. I must go. If I'm caught, I may lose this. And I can't survive without at least speaking to you every now and then. I'll see what I can find out about Carrine. Watch your back. Stay close to Miles.

I will.

Just that fast, I know Athios is gone, out of my head. I can sense his presence is no longer there. I can't explain it, but I'm left with a sense of loss. Not the same loss that I feel with Eli, though.

That's becoming more and more unbearable.

Reaching up, I turn the hot water back on and let it heat the lukewarm water I'm sitting in. I rest my head back and close my eyes. Just a few more minutes.

My thoughts drift to Athios's words. I have Black Fallen traits now, too? That he left them inside me is . . . freakishly weird. Stronger mind control and power over the elements? Core energy? I'm like one of the fucking X-Men. What the hell?

Technically, Athios isn't a Black Fallen. He's not evil. And he sacrificed his soul to save mankind. But he's one powerful angel. I can't even begin to imagine grazing that kind of power. I don't want such intense mind power. What if it takes over me and I become some power-hungry half human hell-bent on revenge, throwing hurricanes and tornadoes at people? There're enough of those in the world. I'm not going to become one of them.

Hell no.

The hot water envelopes me, and I feel myself drifting. I don't really want to—we've got work to do. But drowsiness overcomes me, and I slip into a quiet peace that I haven't had in some time.

At first, I'm conscious of lying in the tub, hot water soothing my aching muscles and bare skin. Then it grows dark behind my eyelids, and I see nothing, I feel nothing. I lose the sensation of being submerged in hot water, and it's replaced by cold, blackness. My arms are weightless, probing into the murky surroundings like a mindless, rambling zombie with its arms held out before it.

Then, as if my thoughts have lit some sort of inner fire, adrenaline surges through me, and I feel energy gathering from my core. At first, it swirls there, like a satellite hurricane photo. Then it fires, explodes, sending lethal doses of that energy through my limbs. I jerk awake, almost leaping from my confinement. I land on my feet, crouching. Slowly, I stand. I'm no longer naked. But not dressed. Not like I normally am. It's almost like a bolt of the softest, gauziest material is clinging to my body, hovering close but unrestrained by straps or zippers or buttons. None of this do I see. I only feel it.

The power that soars through me doesn't escape; it's here, inside me, like a low-humming frequency. If a bug flew at me and hit my body it would zap and fry, bursting into flames, just like a bug lamp. Darkness still surrounds me. I'm totally lost, and I don't feel anyone else's presence here but mine. Like I'm in some weird time warp, floating around. Like Dr. Who. Except he's way more cool.

I lift my hand to push my hair from my face, and that same surge of power burns in the pit of my stomach, then shoots in a rush through my arm. I feel it clear to my fingertips. What the freak?

I lift my arms up simultaneously; the power surge that rips from both of my hands nearly knocks me off my feet.

Is this what Athios was talking about?

I feel like Patrick Swayze in the movie *Ghost*, trying to move the penny after he's dead. Pulling the energy from my core and rocking it out of my body.

Do I really have that in me? Or am I just dreaming?

It's then I feel the atmosphere around me shift, and I'm weightless once more. Darkness still surrounds me, and yet something incredibly familiar overcomes me; I can't tell if it's a sensation, or a memory, or what. But it's something I know very, very well. I'm actually starting to get pissed off. Am I in the goddamn bathtub or a dream? Loss of control now replaces that surge of power I felt moments before. I have control over nothing. I feel as though I'm crammed in a recessed hole in the wall: cold, dank, spaceless. I can't turn my head; I can't move my limbs. I don't think I have any clothes on now, no gauze, nothing.

The brush of a caress grazes my waist, my hips, and the familiarity of the touch knocks the breath out of me. I crave it now, and although I can't see it, I want it.

Invisible hands move over me, and heat trails the caresses, almost uncomfortably. I can't move, although I want to; I can only stand here and receive. A grip moves through my hair, pulls it back enough to tilt my head. The touch is erotic, exciting, and my heart pounds, slowly but hard. Lips brush over mine, moist, full, seductive all at once. The sensation moves to my throat, across my collarbone, while hands cover my breasts. Arousal soars through every nerve ending in my body, and a silent moan is swallowed by the deepening of this strange, weightless kiss. Hands leave my breasts and move over my ribs, and strong fingers dig into my flesh as the kiss consumes me. I know it, this mouth. I can't place it. I only know I have to have it.

Those strong fingers ease from my hips and move down, over my thighs, and then, without warning, slide between my legs. I'm caressed there, *right there*, a seductive touch by an invisible hand, directed by someone who knows me, knows my needs and exactly how much pressure it takes to bring me to my knees. It makes my head spin, that sexual touch, and I gasp for air as the first wave of orgasm ripples through me. Then a heated breath replaces gentle, strong fingers, and that surge of power, that orgasm, crashes over me in tumultuous waves, and I feel myself slipping.

At once, I'm knocked backward, almost painfully, and my eyes jerk open. The water in the bathtub is cold; my body temperature has lowered. I'm in the guesthouse. Inverness.

My gaze lifts, and from the corner, a figure emerges from the walls. He stares back at me.

Eli.

For a moment, our gazes are locked. Wordless.

His pupils dilate, fixing on mine. He knows me. I can sense it.

"Do it, Eli. Do it now," a female voice commands. Carrine.

He hesitates; then his features harden. His face shakes, blurs, morphs.

And he lunges for me.

I scream, not a girly, terrified scream, but one of anger, of hurt. Of self-preservation. He's above me, though, so fast I don't even see him move until he's right at me. His hands go around my throat and he squeezes, thrusts my head under the water. I hold my breath and my eyes are open as I struggle. I see his face, all morphed and horrible, hovering just above the surface. My arms and legs flail. Jesus, he's going to drown me. Where's Carrine?

Then something grips me. Inside. Athios's words. I focus, forcing all of my anger and desperation to one location in my body, at the very core. It bursts free, and I surge out of the water at him. He's back against the wall now, and he lunges at me. I've never seen him so . . . horrifying. Just as we meet, he's gone. I hit the wall. He has totally vanished.

"Riley!"

Noah's here now, and he's grabbed a towel and draped it over me. I'm lying on the floor, crumpled. "What happened?" he asks. He lifts me, towel mostly wrapped around my naked body, and carries me to my bed. Laying me down, he follows me, his head bent over close enough that his dreads drop against my chest. "What are you doing?" Noah's voice is angry, raspy, and his eyes flash fear.

I shake my head. "It was Eli," I say. A lump forms in my throat, and I swallow past it. "He was there. Then . . . Carrine commanded him to kill me. He hesitated, Noah. He knew me. I could see it in his eyes." At least, I think he did. And I think he was there.

Was he? Really?

"Riley, Eli's not a ghost," Noah says. He grabs my chin and looks me over, brushing a fingertip over my cheek. "You're scraped," he says. "I walked in just as you leaped from the tub. No one else was in here but me." His eyebrows pull together. "What else happened?"

I stare at the ceiling and exhale. "I had . . . an experience."

Noah waits.

So, I semi-explain, leaving out the mind-numbing orgasm part.

I tell him everything else. Including my convo with Athios.

Noah's eyes harden. "So you're dreaming of Eli killing you? And you have fallen angel traits cooking inside you, along with all the other venom that's making you crazy?" He shakes his head. "This is fucked-up."

"I'm not so sure that was a dream, Noah," I say, and clutching the blanket to my chest, I sit up. "I was wide awake when I came out of that . . . bizarre state of existence. I looked around, knew I was in a bath of cold water, knew I was here, in this guesthouse, in Inverness." I grab his hand, and it's clenched into a fist. "It's like . . . Eli was part of the wall, part of the wainscoting. He"—I shake my head, dredging up the picture of it—"emerged from the wood. Almost like, I don't know. He was camouflaged or something."

Noah's disturbing eyes study me with severe intensity. "Was your sex dream with him?" he asks.

I really have to think about it, and I hate that. "I thought it was him," I answer. "I couldn't see a thing. Total pitch-black darkness. But in my heart, I felt it was him." I glance toward the en suite bathroom, and I envision the corner from which Eli emerged. "Now I'm not so sure."

"Why?"

I climb from the bed, my arms holding the towel against my body, and I walk to the window and pull the drapes back. Something has propelled me to do this, and I have no clue what.

But I do it. It's midday, but the sun has disappeared, leaving the sandstone buildings and gray stone in a murky, dreamlike frame. Pedestrians are walking along the sidewalk in front of the guesthouse. My eyes drift across the street, where a single figure stands out and catches my eye. Female. Wearing a hooded jacket. Dressed in all black. I can't see her face.

I don't need to.

The building she's leaning against blurs, and the figure blends into it. Or disappears. One second, there. The next, gone.

Whatever.

Noah's now at my side, looking out of the window, too. But I know he doesn't see what I just saw.

"What did you see?" Noah asks.

Tell him what you see, Riley.

I close my eyes, and the motion makes my chest rise, fall, and it hurts. I feel pain inside my chest.

Go on. Tell him. He wants an answer. Give it.

The words are cold, and I can't help shivering. I continue to stare out the window.

And just in case you're completely blind, he wants to fuck you, too. Always has. He thinks about it constantly. I'm surprised at his control.

I shake off his words and just breathe. "Carrine is stalking me."

Noah grabs me by the shoulders and turns me around. His face is hard as he stares down at me. "What do you mean?"

I stare up at him, unable to answer at first. Inside, my stomach is flipping around like I'm on a fast-as-hell roller coaster, unable to stop.

You didn't think that fucking angel was the only soul who could get inside your head, did you, Riley? You think because you fucked him, you have his powers, too? I'm here now. We'll see just how strong you really are. Imagine someone cutting open your skull and stuffing a live beetle inside, then sewing you back up. Imagine those tiny little feet scratching back and forth, back and forth, over your brain and bones until you begin clawing at your scalp, ripping open those stitches just to pull that beetle out. To make the insanity go away. It's going nowhere. That sensation is me, Riley. And I can't wait to show you a few things.

Only the violent shaking of my shoulders brings my vision into focus, and I stare blankly into Noah's eyes.

"What the hell is going on, Riley?" he yells. His fingers are digging into my biceps now. Painfully so.

It's been a long time since I've felt fear. I feel it now.

"Riley!" Noah yells again.

She's laughing inside my head now, and she won't stop. I drop my hands from my towel and clutch the sides of my head. I push—hard. My eyes squeeze tightly shut.

"It's Carrine," I say without looking at Noah. "She's inside my head now. She won't . . . get out. Laughing, egging me on. I can't take it, Noah—"

Then, at once, she's gone. Just like that. My

vision, my mind, is completely clear now. Free of the torture. Free of the bugs.

Noah's hand lifts, and I only now notice he's grabbed my towel off the floor and is lifting it back to cover me up. With one hand he holds the towel in place, and with his free hand he uses his thumb to wipe at my cheeks. Only then do I notice the tears that have started streaming from my eyes.

He sighs and pulls me against him, and I let him. His lips press against my temple. "What's she doing to you, girl?" he says against my skin. "What the hell is she doing to you?"

I'm thinking clearly now. I hate it, but I am. Part of me wishes I could just stay suspended in some kind of weird dreamlike state—a fantasy world where everything was right, going my way, and I was the winner.

That's not my reality anymore.

I look at Noah, and the care in his eyes almost pains me.

Almost as much what I have to say out loud. Just thinking the words rips into my heart.

"I'm going to have to kill them, Noah," I say.

Noah just stares at me. Speechless.

My voice almost doesn't sound like it belongs to me. Sounds like someone else speaking. It quivers, breaks. More tears spill. "I'm going to have to kill Carrine and Eli."

Part Five

❊─❊

THE NESS BOYS

But there's many a slip twixt the cup and the lip.

—William H. Bonney, *Young Guns*, 1988

I'm not one who usually exhibits much control, but I've sincerely tried to respect Riley and stay out of her head. I have now failed. It's been nearly impossible. So I have brushed off my failure and entered. What I see there scares me. The odds have changed drastically now. With Riley's heart and her brain colliding, the outcome cannot possibly be a good one. There has to be an intervention. No matter the cost. Her life is at stake, as well as what little humanity is left in her. Even I can see that. And I'll do whatever it takes to make it right. Even if it means starting a vampiric war of epic proportions. Nothing and no one matters to me except Riley. Nothing.

—Victorian Arcos

Noah stands with his back to me while I dress. Surprising, I know, because twice today he's seen me buck-ass naked. I guess the decency in the core of his soul rose above the perverted, sexually charged vampire in him.

"Not my fault you can't keep your naked parts covered, Riley," he offers. "Doesn't make me a pervert. Not really."

Trying to make light of the situation, no doubt. I try really hard to put Carrine's words about Noah aside, but it's hard. I can read minds, too. And yeah, I'm not an idiot. Noah isn't only just a powerful vampire with the trait of severe seduction. At his core, he's a man. I'm a woman. He's attracted to me. And I'd be a liar if I didn't say he's not sexually enticing. But my love for Eli has always doused that in me. There's no one I want more than Eli. I want him back the way he was when I first met him. Not this monster he's become. Even if Carrine is controlling him. How much of Eli is left? Anyway, not once have I ever felt threatened by Noah Miles. Just the opposite. He's placed nobility and a vow to keep me safe over any sexual tension he may feel. That takes strength of crazy proportion. Especially for a vampire.

Thoughts are crashing over me like violent waves, even as I pull on my clothes. Confusion rocks me, and I can promise you, I don't like feeling out of control. Oh, hell no. Too many years spent like that. Now I like total control. Of myself. My thoughts.

But now someone else has been pulling the strings to my brain. Carrine and Eli. The other half of me.

The half I have to kill in order to survive.

I just can't believe it's come to this. I'd rather Eli had stayed . . . Jesus Christ, I can't even think it. Would I have rather he stayed in that alternative realm? How can all this be happening?

After yanking a black ribbed tank over my head, I pull on a pair of low-rider army green cargos and button the fly. My hair is still wet and hanging in dripping hunks, trailing water down my back, when a knock sounds at the door. Noah and I share a look, and he moves so fast his form is nothing but a blur. Seconds later, the front door creaks as he opens it. Voices. Slightly familiar. I hurry down the hall and round the foyer.

Just as I step into view, my eyes collide with Rhine's. The young lead singer and bass player from the street, from Hush 51. All of the band members are now trailing in behind Rhine, and stand in a half circle in the living room.

"How'd you guys find out where we're staying?" I ask.

Rhine's gaze latches on to my arm with the dragon inked into it. A slight smile touches his lips before he looks at me. "We've come tae help."

I glance at Noah, who is leaning against the doorjamb, arms crossed over his chest. He looks at me and gives a slight shrug. I step closer to Rhine, give the others a brief once-over, then look back into the young guy's gaze. "What do you mean, help us? What is it you think we need help with?"

"Och, gel," Rhine answers with a grin. A glint of mischief lights his green eyes. "You'd be surprised at wha' we could help ya wi'. Sort of how ya helped us all quit smokin'. How ya saved all those people at Hush 51."

"Aye. An' how ya can run like the devil," Pete says. A grin slashes across white teeth. One eyebrow lifts.

I narrow my gaze.

"Do ya ken where ya are, lass?" Rhine says

with a very appealing grin. "You're in the bloody Highlands. 'Tis no surprise tae any o' us that your mate here is a bloodsucker, although it took us a while tae figure it out. Not like us tae take so long." Rhine cocks his head and studies me. "You're . . . somethin' altogether different, though."

I'm staring at Rhine, and I gotta admit, he's . . . impressive. Young, but pretty stable. Solid and cut, like he works out. No skully today, and his close-cut dark hair and flawless complexion make those green eyes and dark lashes definite eye-catchers. His smile widens, as if he can read my thoughts.

Impossible.

I focus. Just to be sure.

Nope. Total, one hundred percent mortal.

Noah chuckles.

"What happened back at the club? I watched. Saw the whole bloody exchange between you and that bloodsucker bitch," Rhine said. "Froze me solid, she did, but I could still see." He laughs, and it's a deep, scratchy, sexy sound. "She ain't the first one we've seen, either."

"Aye, we know that's who's behind the murders here," Gerry says. He's the shyest of the bunch, I'd have to say. Wide brown eyes and dark close-clipped hair, his face baby-soft flawless, his voice soft. But when he speaks, it's listen-worthy. "We've seen plenty." He grins slightly.

"We've killed plenty, too," Tate adds. Not the shy one, I notice, and a little husky. Maybe even the class clown. His wavy auburn hair flips over his ears and his eyes are the color of dark honey. And from the size of him I believe he can kick some serious ass.

"Aye, and it's been quiet for a while. Until you showed up," Rhine says. "Fancy that."

There's silence as Rhine and I hold a staredown. His gaze is locked on to mine. "You think we're killers?" I ask.

Rhine doesn't hesitate. "You'd be dead as dust if we did."

There's a little tension in the room. More from me than anyone else, I imagine. I don't like a threat. I don't like a pack of young human hunters sniffing us out, either. I guess I'd been so consumed with Eli and the female, and the other killings, that I'd totally misjudged Rhine and his friends. Even more so than simply thinking they were thugs.

They're goddamn hunters.

I'm staring at Rhine, still trying to wrap my brain around it all, when Noah speaks.

"We don't have time to babysit," he says.

Just that fast, Rhine whips out a silver blade and is holding it against Noah's throat. The others all have similar blades in the hands.

What the hell?

I'll give Noah Miles some cred. He doesn't morph. He remains totally calm. But I can see inside his head. *Ri, this little prick has a fucking silver blade at my neck. Wanna get him off?*

Yeah, I'll get him off, Miles. Gotta hand it to him, though. He's pretty quick. Might use him and the guys after all. And he's not so little.

Get him off now, Poe. I don't want to have to kill him.

I focus on Rhine, then the guys. *Drop your silver, boys.*

The clap of blades hitting the hardwood floor resounds in the room. Noah moves to stand beside me. It all happens so fast the guys' puzzled faces are almost comical.

Rhine gives me a nod. "Aye, like I said. You're somethin' altogether different, lass." He shrugs at Noah. "No hard feelin's? Was just provin' my worth, ya ken?"

Noah returns the nod in silence beside me. I cock my head, studying the guys. "What I don't ken is what makes you think we aren't the bad guys."

Rhine smiles. It's a lazy, sexy expression that I'm sure brings many a young girl to her knees. "Because you"—he casts a glance at Noah— "and he don't add up. No' tae mention what happened at the club. You both saved a score of humans, whilst those other two bloodsuckers escaped. And I can sense it." He inhales, exhales. "So do ya want our help? Or are we wastin' our time here?"

I glance up at Noah, and he gives a slight nod. I move across the room and stand directly in front of Rhine. His eyes flash interest, and strangely enough, I detect no fear. Not one ounce. I don't know if that's good or bad. I've got to know more. We can't have their young mortal lives balancing in our hands, especially when I don't know what the hell is going on with my own psyche. I'm as unstable as Eli. With my gaze fastened on his, I grasp his hand and hold it between both of mine. His pupils dilate, just a fraction. Then I close my eyes.

I stand in a dank brick courtyard amid tall oaks and overgrown shrubs. A stone apartment complex rises before me. A window on the second floor is open, and a ripped curtain hangs in the gaping hole. No lights are on. I can't tell what time of day it is; no sun, no shadows. Just murky gray. A light rain falls. Shouting falls from the open window, and a thick, heavy accent trails out.

"Ya fookin' loser!" The sound of fist connecting to bone rings out, and a slight whimpered growl follows it. "I told ya tae give me all o' it! Dunnae ya hide the quid from me, boy!" Another punch. Another growl. "What do ya have tae say for your pathetic self? Pathetic, aye, just like your fookin' useless mother!" A slap this time, and another. Another. A scream this time. A woman's scream. Laughter. "Och, boy, you dinnae like your whore mum tae be slapped, aye? Too fookin' bad, then." Slap.

I can move, and I race toward the doorway leading into the apartment. Inside, the stairwell is cold and smelly, and I creep up the steps to the next floor. I open the door and move into a hallway lit by a single bare bulb at the end of a corridor. Beneath my feet, ratty red-and-blue-plaid carpeting. Three doors to my left, I stop and listen. The door is cracked, and I step inside.

The moment I'm inside, I see Rhine. He's kneeling beside a woman, lying on the floor. Rhine looks a little younger than he is now. Maybe fifteen. His hair is longer, and it curls at his ears, the nape of his neck. He has a huge red welt across his porcelain cheek, and one eye is swollen and blackened, and his nose is bleeding. His lip is split and bleeding. He looks a goddamn mess.

All from the hands of his father. I know it's his father. Rhine looks exactly like him, only his father is older, bigger, meaner. And drunk as hell. Holy shit.

Rhine is comforting his mother, who's whimpering, sobbing. He's shielding her from the hands of his abusive dad. God, I hate abuse. In any form.

Rhine's father grabs him by the back of his hair and hauls him off his mother. I stare at Rhine's face, and it's awash with so many emotions; I feel each one. Fear. Hatred. Love. Loathing. Pain. His father yanks his head back and turns him, slamming the young Rhine against the wall. The older man holds him there by his throat.

"You dinna fook wi' me, lad," he says. "I'll kill you and that whore on the floor."

Rage illuminates Rhine's green eyes. Just as a burst of energy surges out of him, and he uses all of his young might to throw his father off him, a figure moving so fast I almost don't notice it hovers over the woman on the floor. He stands there, looking down, and I can only see the back of him. Tall. Broad shoulders. Dark blond hair, long, tied back.

And pulseless.

I blink. A vampire?

"What the fook are ya doin' in my house?" Rhine's dad yells. He shoves Rhine down and faces the newcomer. Rhine scrambles to his mom, grabs her by the shoulders, and helps her up. Rhine's father is a big guy—easily six feet five—and the vampire is eye to eye with him. Then the drunken man glances at Rhine and his mom, then back to the vampire. He throws back his head and laughs. "Och, you fookin' that whore? You fancy that, aye?" He laughs again, and the vampire remains silent. "You best check your cock, make sure it hasna rotted off—"

The drunk man's words die in his throat as the vampire lunges, morphs, and piranha-like fangs drop jagged from his gums. Without a single sound, he clamps down on the man's jugular, shakes his head a time or two, and Rhine's father's head comes clean off. The vampire spits it out and it rolls across the floor and stops an inch from my feet. Widened eyes filled with frozen disbelief stare up at me. Blood oozes from the torn ligaments and flesh. I fight the urge to throw up. The rest of the body on the floor begins to quake, convulse.

Rhine's mother screams; Rhine throws his arms around her and pulls her face to his chest, guarding and shielding her, and she sobs against her son. Those haunting green eyes of his stare at the vampire, who's now completely changed back. I can feel the pounding of Rhine's heart as he battles his fears, and as adrenaline charges through his veins, it also rushes through mine. The vampire crosses the room and stops a foot *in front of Rhine. For the first time, he speaks. I can see his face now. Chiseled jaw. Straight nose. Long lashes. Gray eyes.*

"I'm sorry I had to do that," the vampire says. "I had no choice."

His accent is . . . not Scottish. It's something else. Not English. Not Irish. Something I can't place.

"Lela, 'tis me." The vampire reaches a hand out to Rhine's mother. Rhine slaps his hand away, and the vampire smiles. But his mother turns her head, and she gasps.

"How did you know?" she asks the vampire. She looks up at Rhine and caresses his cheek with her hand. "It's okay, son. He willna hurt you."

Rhine's heart is beating hard; his breath is fast. He holds his mother tightly. He says nothing, but his eyes drift to the form of his headless father, lying crumpled and dead on the floor in a pool of blood.

"Rhine, I've loved your mum for as long as I can recall," the vampire says. "And it's pained me to see you both endure this hell. 'Tis over now. This . . . is no more."

Rhine slowly lifts his gaze to meet the vampire's.

The vampire reaches into the pocket of his long black trench and pulls from within a sheathed knife. Flipping the snap that keeps the blade secured, he takes it out. He shows it to Rhine. " 'Tis pure silver, boy, and 'tis the only thing that will kill others like me. They're no' all good. Most are killers. Your father was one. Did you know that?"

Rhine, wordlessly, nods.

I'm slightly in shock. Rhine's father was a vampire? An abusive, drunken wife- and child-beating vampire? What the hell? How is that possible? Didn't see that one coming.

The vampire turns the blade, hilt first, and offers it to Rhine. He takes it.

"Keep it with you, boy," the vampire says. "Straight into the heart is the fastest kill. Be sure before you use it. We're not all killers." The vampire casts a long, loving glance at Rhine's mother. "You're a fine son. Keep a watchful eye over your mum here. She loves you verra much." He again reaches into his trench; this time, he withdraws an envelope. He hands this to Rhine as well. "Take this and go. Gather what little means something to you, and leave this hellhole. There's enough here to buy a house, new clothes, a car, and whatever else you might need. For years." He glances at Rhine's dead father's remains: a pile of ashes. "Just leave that here."

Before Rhine can respond, the vampire moves. He's gone. Out of the apartment. I glance around. He's nowhere.

I blink, and I'm back, standing in the guesthouse, directly in front of a grown-up Rhine. My hands still hold his, and his green eyes, aged beyond his years, stare down at me. He doesn't say anything; he's waiting on me.

"Do you know what just happened?" I ask.

A grin tips his mouth. "Aye. My theory's accurate. You're a bloody voyeur."

His friends laugh.

I glower at him, and he gives me a nod. "Aye. You saw a rather nasty chunk o' my life." He sighs. "And now ya know my horrors."

I drop his hands. "But you're human."

One side of his mouth lifts into a smirk. "You're no' the only one wi' a few tricks, girly."

"So you have traits, like me," I say. "Like what?"

Rhine shrugs. "No' much, mind ya. I canna run, or jump like you. I canna go at will into others' memories." He sighs. "But I can sniff out a bloodsucker. My hearing's pretty sick." He shrugs. "I'm fairly strong."

His band members chuckle. "Och, that's the verra least, eh, Rhiney boy?" Pete says.

Rhine shrugs again. "I'm no' much of a braggart."

"Let me get this straight," Noah says from behind us. He walks up and stands next to me. He looks at Rhine. "You have tendencies? Care to clue me in?"

"His father was a vampire," I offer, keeping my eyes on Rhine's. He stays silent and lets me do the talking. "He carries traits, like a human with tendencies."

"Father was?" Noah asks.

"My da had a unique disorder," Rhine says, and we're still watching each other. "Liquor fooked him up." His eyes soften a little. Saddened, maybe. "He wasna always like that, though. I can remember him as a wee lad. He . . . treated me and my mum well." He sighs. "But once the liquor got in him, it dulled his vampirism. Eventually, it overcame him. He became a typical, fooked-up drunken vampire. Similar to drunk humans in that they eat very little whilst they drink ou' of their gourd. He still fed on human blood occasionally. But his body became absorbed with alcohol. It changed him. Still a vampire, aye, but only a shadow o' one. Sloppy. His brother came one day and, what would you call it?" He smiles at me. "Intervened?"

The pain in Rhine's eyes makes me sad for him, and I know he can tell it. "Anyway, my mum died no' too long after that. Cancer. My uncle came back after that, made sure I finished school and didna become a street punk." He grins at his friends. "Taught me things. Valuable things." His green eyes turn stormy. "Then a couple o' years ago we had a surge in rogue vampires here. My uncle was killed. And it's been me and my mates ever since."

Noah glances at me, then the rest of the band. "And what sort of tricks can you little humans perform?"

"Och, they're just the fiercest fightin' fookers you'll ever meet, lad," Rhine tells him. "They've helped me keep Inverness fairly cleaned up ever since. No one faster with a blade o' silver." He glances at me. "Except mayhap the dragon girl here."

Noah rubs his eyes, and sighs. A big, exaggerated, airless vampire's sigh.

"We need the help," I offer to Noah.

He glares at me. "You're not helping." Then his silvery gaze turns to Rhine. "What you saw in the club? Even we aren't certain what we're dealing with. The male?" He inclines his head toward me. "That's her fiancé. He hasn't always been a prick."

"Nice," I say.

Noah goes on. No holds barred. Holding nothing at all back. "He's possessed or something. And you saw the female. She controls him and has a power even I've never seen before."

A smile lifts Rhine's mouth. It's a characteristic of his that's pretty damn appealing. Poor, poor young human girls.

"I have."

Me and Noah both look at Rhine. The others chuckle.

Rhine rubs his jaw. "As I said before, you're in the Highlands, my friends. 'Tis a place unlike any other. Like a kaleidoscope, 'tis nothing ever the way you think it is."

"Stop with the rhymes and tell us what you mean," Noah says. "My patience is growing thinner by the second."

Rhine laughs. "Aye, well, that female? She's old. An' before she was a vampire, she was a fookin' witch."

It's almost . . . funny, the way the Scots swear. It's not as menacing, or as vulgar, as the American version. Like, it's okay to swear. It's almost distracting. Every time Rhine says *fookin'*, I want to laugh. "So, how do you know all of this?"

Rhine shrugs. "I've seen one like her. When

my uncle was killed. Fookin' witchpire cast a bloody spell that controlled his mind long enough for her tae take his bloody head. I'll ne'er forget it."

"But you've never seen Carrine before?" I ask.

"Never. That night at the club was the first time. She's a slippery one, though. We've no' been able tae track her. Fookin' witchpire."

"So, she's a witchpire. Great," Noah says. "So you boys are experts on all things paranormal, or just vampires?"

Rhine shares a look with his bandmates, then turns to meet Noah's gaze. "Aye, we're pretty much experts on everythin'. Ghosties, vampires, werewolves—you name it. We keep Inverness safe. My uncle taught me everything he knew before he died."

Noah glances at me. "How ya holdin' up?"

I nod. "Okay so far." I know he means my mind, and whether or not Carrine is prying into it again. I look at Rhine. "Have you heard of St. Bueno's?"

Rhine gives a single nod. "Aye. O' course."

"My fiancé and another were cast into another realm. A Hell-like realm. I went after them. Got them both out. Only my fiancé changed." I hold his gaze, filled with questions, curiosity. "I think he's being commanded to kill me now. And he and the female may be behind the random killings here."

"That's shit luck, lass," Pete says. "Damn sorry for it."

With a slight nod, I acknowledge Pete's words.

"I've heard of those realms," Rhine admits. "Ne'er been in one myself, though." His eyes search mine. "You'll have tae tell me about it, lass."

"So just you five keep Inverness safe?" Noah asks.

"There're more of us," Rhine claims.

Noah and I share a quick glance. "What do you mean?" he asks.

"After my mum died, it left just me," Rhine begins. "And my band here, o' course. We've grown up together. But I knew it was up tae me, tae us, to keep this city right. There was nowhere else for us tae go, so we set out tae make sure the bloodsuckers stayed clear. We went tae the streets, gathered forces." He gives me a lazy smile.

"How many?" I ask.

Rhine shrugs. "Fifty or so."

Impressive. "All human?"

Rhine nods. "There're a few English in the bunch. Do they count?"

The other Ness boys chuckle.

Rhine holds my gaze. "Many make the mistake you both did. Thinkin' we're street thugs. It keeps us covered well enough."

"How do you know where to look?" I ask.

There's a flash in Rhine's green eyes that makes me like him. "We just make ourselves seen," he admits. "And we always run in packs."

I grin back. "Like some vampire-hunting *Lord of the Flies* ring, huh?"

"Och, girly," Tate says. "We hardly limit ourselves tae vampires only."

"Aye, that would be bloody boring," Gerry claims.

I turn, looking at Noah. *We can use their help. We're running in circles right now, and Jake and the other WUP members are tied up in a wolfy war.*

They're humans, Riley. No offense, but any one of them could be killed, at any given time.

Noah. We're outnumbered and alone. Rhine and these guys? They run in packs. You take a lion. Fierce. Lethal. Deadly. But you surround it with a pack of angry men with spears and guns? Lion doesn't have a chance. We need them.

We stare at each other, me convincing, Noah deciding.

"Och, you two are bloody talkin' tae each other, aren't ya?" Tate asks.

I slide a look his way and lift an eyebrow.

"Magic," he says in a low voice. I soon realize Tate is the Ness Boy with no filter.

All right, Riley. I guess we've got no choice.

We don't. And I trust them. Whatever happens, I trust Rhine. He went through some major shit as a kid. It's made him stronger. Like me.

Noah gives me one last, long stare, then turns to Rhine. "There're a few things you need to know." He inclines his head to me. "About her."

Rhine meets my gaze and nods. "Then it's best if the whole lot o' us knows at once." He smiles. "I dinnae know 'bout you, but I hate repeatin' myself. You can stay at our place." He looks at Pete and the others. "Meet the boys o' the 'Ness."

Noah gives me a quick glance, and I nod. Pretty cute bunch of guys. Yeah, they look like punks, but if you look deep and hard enough, you'd think you were staring at a hooded lot of Abercrombie models. Yet they fight vampires. Who would've thought?

"Let's pack up," I say.

So we do. As Rhine and the others wait, Noah and I gather what little belongings we have, throw our weapons into our gear bags, and clean out the fridge. An unexpected turn of events, to be sure. I mean, who in the hell would ever have guessed a gang of human boys was running the show in Inverness? Rhine being the only one with a tinge of tendencies. It blows my mind. They all must be some tough little bastards.

Being good tenants, we place the trash in the can outside, and the key in the drop box. Rhine walks up to me at the curb. "Your chariot awaits."

I glance over his shoulder at the two Rovers, parked with engines running.

"Need a hand wi' those?" he says, inclining his head to my two duffels.

I shrug out of the one holding my clothes and hand it to him. "Thanks."

Rhine takes it and walks to one of the Rovers. He opens the hatch and throws it in. Noah's at the other Rover, and he glances at me. "See ya there," he says, and climbs in.

"Guess you're ridin' wi' me then," Rhine says

with a mischievous grin. "Let's go." He quickly introduces me to the driver, Chess, and we head out.

The Scots, I notice again, have a wicked accent. I never tire of hearing it. We climb into the backseat, and both Rovers pull out onto Montague Row.

"Where're we headed?" I ask Rhine.

"My da's brother left me a fair bank account when he died," he says. "I used it wisely, as he had advised me. Invested some, saved some, and bought the Rovers, a motorbike, and an old hotel on the other side of the river." He stares at me. "So tell me about this fiancé o' yours." He mock-frowns, his dark eyebrows stark against his alabaster skin. "You sure you want tae marry a bloodsucker? Or is there a chance you might fancy a younger human wi' no' so many tendencies?"

I shake my head. "Obviously excessive flirting is one of them." I glance out the window as we cross the river. "I'd die trying to save Eli from whatever fucked-up hell he's in," I say, then turn back to Rhine. "But I'm not sure that's going to happen."

Rhine's eyes soften. "I dinnae mean tae be disrespectful," he apologizes. "Although I'd be lying if I said I wouldna give it a go if he weren't a factor."

I grin. "I can read minds, junior. You could lie, but I'd catch you."

His eyes flash, then move to my inked wing at

the corner of my eye. "You took a glance into my past," he says. "Tell me about yours." He nods to my ink. "I see you fancy body art. I gotta admit, I fancy it on ya."

I can't help laughing. Rhine is kinda like a junior version of Noah. "Before . . . all of this, I spent my days and a lot of nights at my ink shop. I'm a tattoo artist by trade."

"Interesting. And that dragon's tail winding round your arm there," he says, inclining his head. "Where does that lead?"

I smile. "My back. I'm slightly famous for my work in the States."

Rhine nods appreciatively. "Well, then, we'll just have tae exchange ink shows once we're settled."

Pete turns around from the front passenger seat and looks at me. "Master ink artist, aye? Have you more than just your dragon and wings, then?"

I grin. Pete's cute, with expressive blue eyes, wiry, and a scar on his chin in the place so many kids get them after slipping off the monkey bars on the playground. "A few more."

Pete returns the smile. "Then a fine exchange we shall have."

"Pete here's chicken tae get inked," Rhine says. "Scared o' needles."

"Shut the fook up," Pete argues.

"Scared o' needles but doesna mind pokin' a bloodsucker in the heart with a blade," Chess adds. A little older, maybe twenty-one, Chess has a matter-of-fact mannerism that belies the mischievous glint in his hazel eyes. He grins at me through the mirror, and I grin back.

I stare at the three Ness boys with interest. They've all taken me by surprise.

It doesn't take us long to reach Rhine's hotel-turned-slayer's shack—and it's far, far from a shack at all. After we cross the river, the Rover turns down several streets until we've just reached the edge of the city limits. Chess turns down a long tree-lined drive that leads to an ivy-covered stone building, four stories high. It's flanked by enormous trees with wide spread branches.

"Welcome to the Crachan," Rhine announces, and he puts on a proper British accent, so different from his sharp guttural Scot's brogue. "I do hope you enjoy your stay immensely."

Laughter erupts from Chess and Pete. We pull in, winding around a large half-circle drive. It sort of reminds me of Gabriel's Crescent . . . just not as creepy. There are a few vehicles parked along the front, and several motorcycles. The Rover stops, and we get out. The other one arrives, and Noah joins me. We stare up at the Crachan, pronounced *Cracken*. It's a pretty big place.

"Welcome to the Hotel California?" I sing to Noah.

Noah eyes me. "Should I worry about the kid?"

I move my gaze to Rhine, who's now on his

cell phone a few feet away. His back is to us, but I hear the muffled snort. "He heard you," I say, and smile. "He's a lot like you, Miles."

"That's why I asked if I should worry."

I shift my duffel on my shoulder, the weight of the blades and scatha almost a comfort. Rhine stuffs his cell in his back pocket, shoulders my other duffel, and joins us. He nods at Noah. "This way." He turns and we follow, making our way up the graveled walkway. I notice it's not too shabbily kept for a bunch of guys. Impressed again.

We walk through a pair of tall, intricately carved and thick wooden doors and into a cavernous open hall. Like many old manors, I notice, it has a massive fireplace occupying one wall. A huge flat-screen takes up another wall, and a few sofas, several chairs, and a long wooden coffee table sit before it. A few guys occupy the chairs and sofa. They glance our way.

"I'll show ya tae your rooms," Rhine says. "Most of the others aren't home yet." He leads us to a sweeping staircase at the end of the foyer. "One of the top requirements to reside here." He glances at me as we start up the steps. "Gotta be employed."

"Good idea," Noah says. "What's another requirement?"

Rhine stops at the second floor and steps onto the landing. He grins. "Can't be a fookin' scaredy-cat."

"Good requirement," I say. Rhine inclines his head, and we follow.

"I'll put you two across the hall from each other," Rhine says, and looks at me as he stops. The room number is 208. The door is wide open. "I'll get your keys whilst you both settle in," he says, and walks into the room, sets my duffel on the floor in front of the bed, and comes back out. When he passes Noah, he grins. "Aye. You've plenty tae worry about." Then he hurries up the hallway at a jog and disappears down the steps.

Noah looks at me from the hallway. "He's a little more intense than I first thought."

"I told you he heard you. Besides, he's got a lot on his young shoulders," I return. "He's all right in my book."

Noah smiles. "I know that." He shrugs on his bag. "I'm going to call Andorra and give him an update. And check back with Gabriel about Carrine."

"I'll be over here," I say, and turn and walk into my room. The hotel itself is old, as in a hundred years maybe, and although large, it's modest with a blue-and-black-plaid theme, sparsely furnished, but clean. A double bed stands against one wall, a tall chest of drawers, a straight-back wooden chair and desk. Walking to the bed, I drop my weapons duffel on top of it. I unzip the bag and pull out my scatha.

"That's a wicked piece of armor," Rhine says at my side. I'd heard his footfalls as he climbed the steps, so it didn't surprise me for him to be speaking in my ear. "What is it? A crossbow?"

I like the way his *r*'s roll and his *o*'s sound like ooh. "It's an ancient device, newly built." I hand it to him, and he palms it gently. "It's a scatha. Medieval design."

He turns it over, inspecting it thoroughly. "How does it work?"

Digging into a side pouch of the duffel, I retrieve one of the empty cartridges Gawan Conwyk had left me. "You take a prefilled cartridge of mystic St. Bueno's Well holy water." I reach over and drop the loading lever. "Load, lock, and pull back the release." I look at him, and his eyes glint with interest. "Then you blast to hell all sorts of demons and whatever else is lurking in the shadows of the underworld."

Rhine's large hands move deftly over the scatha, and as if he'd been doing it all his life, he quickly unloads the cartridge and hands it back to me. "And you plan on going back into this demon-filled underworld, aye?"

I shrug, and he hands me the scatha. I run my fingers over the cool metal, then look at him. "I will if I have to."

Understanding gleams in his eyes, and he gives a slight nod. "I hope one day your fiancé knows what he's got."

"I've always said he was a lucky fuck," Noah says, striding into the room.

"I'll have to agree wi' ya there," Rhine adds. "Ready tae meet the Crachan boys?"

"Just one thing, Rhine," Noah says. "Something you need to know about Riley here." He looks at me. "Besides having the DNA of four vampires, along with newly acquired traits of a fallen angel, she can move faster than any vampire I've encountered—myself included. She can scale a three-story building in under ten seconds. Her fighting skills are unmatched. Lethal. And she can read minds at will." He glances at me. "Her fiancé is being controlled by the witchpire, Carrine, who has decided to crawl into her brain and try and drive her crazier than what she already is. She's up to her eyeballs in deep, emotional shit. Just so you know."

Rhine nods. "I'll keep that in mind." He inclines his head. "Let's go."

We follow Rhine down the corridor, and I take notice of his demeanor, his movements, and I realize that we've really never been completely introduced.

"You got a last name, Rhine?" I ask.

He looks down at me as we walk, and smiles. "MacLeod."

I nod. "Poe." I incline my head to Noah. "Miles."

"Now we're all like bloody family," Rhine says. We hit the landing and I'm slightly overwhelmed by the small crowd that's gathered in the great hall. My eyes scan the group, and including the other three I already know, plus Chess, there's at least, I don't know, thirty guys from what appear to be between the ages of fifteen and twenty-five. They're parked in sofas, on chairs, and on the floor. No lie, it's a gruff-looking bunch, and if I ran into any of them on the street, I'd almost bet my life they were thugs.

I have a feeling I'm about to get schooled. Again.

Rhine jogs ahead of us and moves over to the hearth. He beckons to us, and we stand next to him and face the crowd.

"Right, then, I know some o' you've already heard about these two," Rhine says. His voice carries over the hall, a raspy sound that belies the crooning tone he creates when he sings. "Noah Miles, Riley Poe. Both from America. They'll be stayin' for a bit, and they need our help."

Total silence. Not a single solitary word comes from the guys. Their eyeballs are all focused on us, interested and curious, but no one speaks. So I decide to break the silence. I glance at Rhine, just to make sure he's cool with it, and as if he knows what I'm up to, he nods once. I face the crowd of slayers.

"You know there're vampires in Inverness," I begin. "Miles and I belong to an organization—Worldwide Unexplained Phenomena—and we're assigned to take care of it." I meet the questioning eyes of the guys. "Unfortunately, one of the vampires is my fiancé."

A few jaws drop. A few brows furrow.

"I'm a human with tendencies. Venom from four vampires, plus a little something from a fallen angel that I haven't quite nailed yet—no pun intended—clinging to my DNA." I nod at Noah. "He's been a vampire since the American Revolution." I smile at the wide-eyed crowd. "We won that, by the way."

"Fookin' English," one guy says. They all chuckle.

Scotland, I've noticed, is still fiercely proud and fiercely independent from Mother England.

I also notice a few of the guys getting restless, glaring at Noah. I focus, scan a few brains, search through a couple of thoughts. I point at a guy now sitting on the edge of the sofa, scowling. Young, twenty maybe, edgy. Solid as a pile of bricks. "You throw the blade you've got jammed into your boot there and I'll be on you in a bad way, before you draw your next breath."

"Fookin' whatever—"

I fly, straddle him, and yank the blade from his boot. I hold it to his jugular. Icy blue eyes widen as they stare at me.

"Fookin' sick," one says beside me.

I glance at him, the blade still pressed to the throat of the one I'm straddling. "You ever hear of a Strigoi?"

His brown eyes fix on mine. "Aye."

"I have three gens in me," I add. "Don't *fook* with me."

The guy swallows hard enough it almost echoes.

Just that fast, I'm off the lap and handing the guy his blade, hilt first. He takes it and nods. "Sorry, then," he says.

I look out at every single face there. "You don't know me, and I don't know any of you," I say. "But we're here to stop the killing of innocents, just like you are."

Several nods make it clear to me that I have their attention now, and I return to stand between Noah and Rhine. Next, I give in detail Noah's and my history regarding the Gullah, Savannah, and Charleston, and how Noah isn't salivating by all the strong young pulses gathered in the room. More than a few look at poor Noah with notable discomfort, but I put them all at ease by letting them know his eating habits. His role in Charleston as Guardian finally puts them at ease.

Then Noah steps up and clears his throat. "One thing more you need to know about Riley," he says, his Southern drawl commanding, raspy. "Because she has the most fucked-up DNA in existence, she doesn't typically sleep every day, like you. She unexpectedly falls into a narcoleptic coma every few days or so." He looks at me. "And she's due one at any time." He looks back at the guys. "She does exhibit a few signs you might want to look out for. Disoriented. Stumbles. Weakness. Difficulty expressing words. Eyes start rolling in her head. If you notice, she has no trouble at all with any of these. And when her body has had enough, she'll start to slow down. Then fall out, sometimes for two days. So if you notice her acting bizarre, catch her before she hits the ground."

I pass an uninterested glance at the TV, but something catches my eye. It's the local news. "Can you turn that up?" I ask the one who is closest to the remote. He nods, and ups the volume. A young woman is broadcasting. Her smooth skin belies the fear I can see in her eyes as she reports.

"Two more bodies were discovered this morning, both in close proximity to the Eastgate Shopping Centre," she says. Behind her is the entrance to the center, the large Eastgate letters standing out from the Celtic design behind it.

"Shoppers are encouraged not to linger after dark," the reporter says. "This may be the handiwork of a serial killer. Take full precaution as the victims are neither all men nor all women. So, everyone, be careful. Rachel Canns, Inverness Live."

I look at Noah. I don't say anything. I can't. Two more victims, right out from under our noses. Was it Eli? Has he become nothing more than a blood-seeking monster? Carrine is controlling him. She can make him do whatever she desires. Maybe she's making him do the killing now? The thought totally sickens me.

Noah barely shakes his head, reading my thoughts. He turns to Rhine. "We need to hit the streets. What's your method?"

All humor has disappeared from Rhine's face. His mouth is pulled tight, eyebrows drawn. "We break into lots o' no less than six. Scour the city. Run the streets." He glances to the guys and inclines his head. "Jep there, we've known each other since we were wee lads. He knows every nook an' cranny in the city."

"Aye," Jep answers. He's tall, lanky, maybe twenty. His hair is longer, pulled into a ponytail. A scar slashes across his forehead, through one eyebrow, and disappears. He looks like he can kick some serious ass. "We got six groups now. More will join as they get off o' work and such."

"There're a few still in school," Rhine says. "They never miss a day."

I nod. "Pretty little organized freaky society you got here," I say. "I'm impressed."

"We do all right, yeah," Rhine agrees. "Ready?"

I nod. Several others voice their *ayes* and *yeahs*. Most stand up, shuffle their feet, and glance around, waiting on instruction, I suspect.

"I guess we should split up," Noah says to me. In his eyes I can see doubt; he *so* doesn't want to split up. We have no choice, though. To have me and Noah together wouldn't make sense.

I nod. "Yeah, we should. Spread the powers around a little."

"Noah, you can run wi' Jep and his crew," Rhine says. He grins at me. "O' course, it's only right if you run wi' me, lass. In case you drop into one o' your comas."

I narrow my gaze. "Of course."

We break up into six groups. The adrenaline gaining speed and rushing through the Ness boys is palpable. I can almost see it floating in the room. It all but quakes with their readiness, their hunger. Like a live thing. It's absolutely incredible.

My group forms, and besides me and Rhine, there's four others I'm introduced to. I'm terrible with groups of names at once, so I push that worry to the recesses of my brain; the last thing I need to concentrate on is trying to keep straight thirty names.

From now on, they're the Ness boys to me. All of them, except Rhine.

"We'll take city center," Rhine announces to the others. "Everyone else spread out and take our regular routes. After hours, we'll slip into Eastgate, see what's on."

Many voices agree with varying degrees of accent, and the groups disperse. Outside, the sky has fallen in dark shades of gray and purple. Duel lampposts at the end of the Crachan's drive are lit, illuminating the street beyond. I inhale, and a sensation of pure evil washes over me. Different from Edinburgh, but still evil. It's met with a sense of urgency, too. Something else that I can't put my finger on. I'm sure it has to do with the fact that it all revolves around Carrine and Eli being the cause of it.

And that straight up makes me ill.

I close my eyes, inhale again, and let it out slowly. I gotta do this. I have to make things right. Whoever is calling the shots for the killings, they have to be stopped. If Eli's involved, and can't be saved . . .

My body shivers at the thought. Panic wells up inside me for a moment. Eli's face flashes behind my closed eyelids, and he's the old Eligius. My Eli. Sexy. Loving. Noble.

Then, in a blur, that face of his changes and he's the Eli in Hush 51, the same one with the hateful glint to those cerulean eyes I love so much.

"Hey," Rhine says. He's standing by my side, a good six inches taller, and seeming far older than his nineteen or twenty years. Those knowing green eyes study me for a second. Study me like he's known me longer than a few days. "You gonna be okay?"

I glance around me, up toward the darkening skies, and watch as the Ness boys separate and start their routes. If a pack of humans are hell-bent on keeping their streets and innocents safe, then I can do no less than every single thing I'm capable of.

I decide to put my own desires aside.

The old Eli wouldn't expect anything less.

My gaze returns to Rhine's, and I give him an assuring nod. "I will be. When all this is over, and the killings are stopped, and this city is safe again, then yeah, I'll be okay."

His mouth lifts at one corner and the smile lingers in his eyes. "Magic. Let's get goin', then, aye?" He inclines his head toward the street.

I push my heavy heart aside and fill the void

with sheer determination. We start off down the drive, four other Ness boys behind us.

We're on a vampire hunt.

I have a feeling there'll be bloodshed from both sides.

Part Six

——◆◆◆——

SEDUCTIVE FOE

If my calculations are correct, when this baby hits eighty-eight miles per hour . . . you're going to see some serious shit.

—Dr. Emmett Brown, Back to the Future, 1985

Yeah, Riley. I don't know her all that well, but what I do know, she doesna take much shite off no one. That includes me, Miles, and more than likely, her bloodsucker boyfriend. As a human wi' tendencies myself, I can sense a power wi'in her that is unlike anything I've yet seen before. Miles said she had fooked-up DNA. I can goddamn well believe it. Yeah, what I wouldna give to keep her.

—Rhine MacLeod

We walk up and down the streets of Inverness until well after ten p.m. Rhine has gotten a few calls on his cell, but nothing panned out. We're making our way up High Street for the umpteenth time, and I glance at the city center. Newer buildings mixed in and side by side with the older ones; some with coned turrets, others with tall spires. All flat fronts with colorful store signs above the doors. And the ever-present double arches of McDonald's gleaming golden yellow in the shadows.

"This time o' year we mostly have just the locals runnin' the streets," Rhine says beside me as we walk. There're three of us on one side of the street, three on the other. I nod and glance at the patrons. Foot traffic has definitely slowed down for the night, and most of the businesses are closed. "Mostly university students," Rhine says, and shoves his hands into the pockets of his brown leather jacket. He's wearing a dark blue skully, and it stands stark against his pale skin. "Anything?"

I tune my hearing, keying it to a lower frequency, and I pick up only small bits of animal pulses, baby hiccups, and so many heartbeats it creates a low hum in my ears. I shake my head and look at him. "Nothing out of the ordinary."

We're on the streets for another two hours before I see him.

At the far end of the sidewalk, standing against the building. The shadows swallow him, but I can see. I can smell.

It's Eli.

Beside him, Carrine.

The moment she sees me, she smiles. My eyes drift to Eli, and his gaze collides with mine. He stares at me, and that expression of recognition flashes in his eyes. Carrine moves in front of Eli, presses her body seductively against him, and I notice the muscles flexing at his jaw, and his brow furrowing. He looks angry. Then all expression fades, his gaze clouds, and he widens his stance to accommodate her. His arms go around her waist as they start making out, and his hands grope her buttocks and pull her hard against his crotch. His soft moan rides the breeze and hits me in the gut. We're walking toward them, and my pace quickens. Rhine's hand closes over mine, holding me back.

"Don't," he warns. "Wait."

No sooner does he say it than Eli lifts his head and looks directly at me. We're about fifteen yards away when a young woman rounds the corner close to them. So fast I'm unsure it happens, Carrine grabs the girl by the arm, pressing her between her own body and Eli's, and when I blink, they're gone.

The young woman's heartbeat is racing. That much I can hear.

"Fookin' A," Rhine says under his breath, and starts to jog. I fight not to pass him. "So that's your bloody boyfriend?" he asks.

"Yes," I answer. "And the female. Carrine."

As we run, and round the corner, we find it empty except the long shadows stretching across from the buildings. Rhine grabs his cell and makes a call. "At the Eastgate shopping mall. Round the back entrance." He ends the call and stuffs his cell into his pocket. At the same time, he withdraws a silver blade. The other Ness boys from across the street have joined us.

"Ready?" he asks me, and I nod. "Good. We'll take the male alive if possible, aye?" he clarifies to the others. "But dinnae endanger yourselves, lads. Us first. Then him."

Rhine grabs my hand and tugs me toward the alley. "This way."

Squeezing between two buildings through a narrow cobbled close, we slip through the back of Eastgate and Rhine climbs the first-story fire escape. He glances back at me, still on the ground. I leap up to him. Admiration glints off the streetlight shining in his eyes. "Now?" he asks.

I listen closely; the human's racing heart is coming from within the mall. "Still alive. In there."

Rhine leads me up to the roof. I could have climbed and leaped a lot faster, but I would've had to just pace waiting on him. We breach the top and he leads us to a single door. It opens under his hand, and we hit the stairwell leading back down and into the mall. I don't even ask questions as to how he just opened a rooftop door to a public shopping center. I figure he's got connections.

Inside the building, the human's heart races wildly. We exit onto the ground floor, and we're in some old-fashioned-looking market section. High wooden-arched beams peak like a cathedral above our heads. Several shops, their doors closed and locked down, line the walk.

"The Victorian Market," Rhine offers. "Department stores and food court that way." He points. "Which way?"

I listen. Footfalls. Faster. Louder.

Just then the young woman comes running from around the corner up ahead. Her heart is floored, and the fright on her face, the sheer terror, drops my own heart to my stomach.

Out of nowhere, a figure flies down and tackles her.

I leap. No thought. No process. Only action.

Vaguely, I notice Rhine and the others hauling ass behind me. And others, around, swarming in. I focus on the woman and just as the male—not Eli, just a rogue—drops his teeth, I lunge and knock him on his back. With my hands around his throat, I spare a quick glare at the woman. "Run. Toward those boys. They'll help you."

She simply stares at me, wide-eyed.

"Go!" I yell.

Something flashes in her eyes, and she scrambles up, whimpering, and the last thing I hear are the rubber soles from her hikers squeaking on the tile.

Hoping Rhine and the others deal with her, I turn my attention to the rogue. He's strong as shit, young. Newblood. His eyes are red, flecked with yellow. His face is fully morphed, and as I hold his mouth away from me, his jaws are snapping like a goddamn rabid dog's. We struggle, fall backward, and he throws me against the wall. The moment my back hits I lunge back at him as he's darting away, heading for the running woman. I grab his ankle, yank him down. He's on top of me again, holding my hands pinned above my head. Drool falls from his jagged teeth and onto my chest.

I focus, stare at his face until it becomes a pinpoint; then I suck in a long breath, and just as his head hurls toward my chest, I explode power. He flies off me and lands against the far wall. He's up and lunging at me, but now I've yanked my silver from my waistband. I thrust it into his heart as he falls against me.

The rogue drops to the floor, quivering.

Done.

"Riley!" Rhine's voice yells from above me. I glance up. There are Ness boys everywhere. As there are vampires everywhere.

It's hard at first glance to tell them apart.

At first.

Then they're all perfectly crystal-clear.

Males. Females. I spot them now, scattered over the mall, hanging from the upper floor, pacing the food court. All young. Void of heartbeats. Void of emotion or compassion. Vampires.

Just like Savannah, when my little brother, Seth, was bitten by Strigoi Valerian Arcos.

Goddamn, I hate that they're so young. My eyes scan the upper floor of the mall. No sign of Eli or Carrine.

One vampire, a female, lunges directly at me.

Everything happens in slow mo after that.

Somewhere, from a music store, I suspect, Kansas cranks out "Dust in the Wind" over the mall intercom as I take down the female. She's out of her mind crazy with bloodlust, and I waste no time in ending her swiftly. She falls into a quaking heap at my feet, and I withdraw my blade and wipe it on her coat. Her teeth are still snapping as she begins to disintegrate.

My eyes are everywhere now, and for a brief second or two, I catch Rhine and some of the other Ness boys in action. Rhine fights up close, and he sincerely reminds me of a younger version of Noah. Fights like a mad dog.

The other Ness boys throw, and within ten seconds I notice three vamps are taken out on an air-lifted silver blade. The moment it does the job, the Ness boys retrieve their blades. I catch sight of Pete, who's joined us. He's fast.

Just then I see Eli. He catches my eye and disappears around an upstairs turn. I free-run up to the food court, determined to confront him. Or kill Carrine. Preferably that.

My heart, although megaslow from all the vampire venom coursing within me, still feels like it's slamming against my ribs as I see Eli disappear. Thoughts race through my head as I spare a glance down at Rhine and the others. There are still a few rogues left. After watching what I'd just seen, I don't think I'll question Rhine and the Ness boys. Ever. Badasses, every one of them.

Not bad for humans.

The moment I round the corner, I draw up short. So fast I almost lose my breath. Eli's standing directly in front of me. It's like swallowing a sword, standing there looking at him, looking at me, with bloodred eyes laced with hatred. Then they focus, lock on to mine, and lighten. Recognition passes over his face. I can see it, plain as day, even through the shadowy closed mall. He stares hard at me, cocks his head to one side, studying me. For a moment, those blood-lusted red eyes return to cerulean blue.

I push aside my aching heart and concentrate. I focus on his face, then beyond, deeper, to his memory. *Eligius. It's me. Riley. Please, can't you see me?*

Again, Eli cocks his head to the side, his eyes focusing on me.

Eli? Please . . .

Kill him, Riley. He's no longer your love. You must do it.

The voice startles me. It's not Eli's. I'm . . . not sure who it is. Can't worry about it now. Focusing again on Eli, I take a step back as he advances slowly. His eyes are unchanged. He is focused solely on me.

"Eli," I say out loud. If I had something to hit him with, I would. Right in the head. Maybe that would knock him out of his bloodsucking trance.

Then Eli stops. He's still staring directly at me, but in silence. I can't tell what he's doing. I focus on him once more, hard. Trying to worm into his thoughts. There's something there—I can't see. Can't get through.

It's no use, Riley. He's no longer the same as before. There is no conscious thought left in his memory. Not of you. Not of his family. Only bloodlust. You know this. Don't you?

"Who the fuck are you?" I yell at the voice. My eyes, though, remain locked on Eli's. I can sense a buildup of power, of strength. Like a lion stalking its prey, like a cat in the yard with its ass in the air, stalking a butterfly. The buildup is so intense it sends waves of electricity toward me.

Eli's eyes fade, then turn red. Any second. He's going to lunge, rip my throat out . . .

My hand slides to the back of my waistband, grips the silver blade there, lowers. My fingers tighten around it. I'm ready. I don't want to be, but I am.

Kansas is still playing over the intercom. "Carry On Wayward Son."

How freaking ironic.

Do it. Go on.

I hear it before I see it. I react.

And it all happens at once.

Behind me, a whirring noise. I know it's a blade. I leap. Grasp it. Catch it by the blade. It tears through my skin, and it's sharp as hell. Warm blood trickles down my outreached hand, down my arm, beneath my leather jacket.

Eli leaps toward me.

We clash in midair.

The weight of his body takes us both down to the tiled floor, and he lands on me. With one powerful swipe, he's knocked the blade from my hand. His gaze slides over to the blood oozing from my palm. His head shakes, so fast it blurs, and jerks to a sudden stop. No longer Eli now. Our eyes meet, just for a split second.

"Eli, please," I whisper. "It's me."

Before I can gauge his reaction, a body flies out of nowhere and slams into Eli. He's knocked to the floor.

Noah.

And he's fully morphed, too.

"Noah, don't!" I yell.

Then everyone freezes. No one moves. No one even slides a glance. But I can see her. Hear her.

Carrine moves from the shadows of a store-front, and into my view. She's wearing tight leather pants, black heeled boots, and a black leather vest over a billowy white shirt. Her hair hangs long. Her face, flawless, white as snow. Lips red. Beautiful.

"You're not as powerful as you think, Ms. Poe," she says. She steps over Eli and Noah, frozen in a locked position on the floor. I can do nothing more than stare at her. A lazy smile stretches plump red lips over her teeth. She walks toward me and stops a foot away. Her eyes travel over me, down to my boots, then back up. "Do you know what I was before all this? Before sucking the blood from human vessels became my only means of survival? No? Well," she says, moving in a circle around me. "I was a master of the dark arts, from a long family of proud Highland witches. You see, I have Pict blood running through me, Ms. Poe." She laughs. "Well, I used to. And 'twas verra old blood. Filled with magic and spells and potion recipes that I'd honed over the years." She stops again and faces me. With a long, elegant fin-ger, she pushes a hank of my hair from my eyes. "Then I was changed. My life, stolen. But," she says, moving again. "I . . . adapted. Yes, that's the perfect word for it. Adapted."

I'm frozen to the floor. My joints and limbs

paralyzed. What the hell! I stare into her insane blue depths. She is not going to kill me. I'm not going to die. Not like this.

Leaning forward, she presses her lips to mine, lingers, and pulls back. "You will," she says.

In that brief moment, I think she's right.

Then she grins. "But not now. Unfortunately, it's not time. You see, I am under intense orders myself. My savior freed me from my prison. 'Tis the verra reason I'm even walking the Earth again. I have no choice but to wait." She smiles at me. "But when it's time, you'll know it." She turns, walks back toward Eli and Noah, clutched in a frozen frantic fighting stance on the floor. Carrine stares down at them. "Och, damn," she breathes. "He's a fine one, too." She shakes her head. "I can smell his erotica." She looks at me. "However do you stand it? I want to fuck him right now, just standing here."

I can do nothing more than stare hatred at her.

She sighs. "Such a pity."

Fear, fury, and the need to make sure nothing else happens to someone I love gathers in one place, deep inside me. Everything else around me blurs but Carrine. She is up and at the forefront. Although slowly at first, I draw in a long, deep breath.

When I exhale, it's a maelstrom of fury.

The sonic boom that comes forth from me isn't as colossal as the one Carrine had delivered back at Hush 51. But it's big enough. Forceful enough.

It blows Carrine off her heeled and booted feet.

Then my joints release; I can move. It hurts at first, but I break free.

At the same time, Carrine, who's landed several feet away, leaps to her feet. She yells in an unfamiliar language to Eli. Beckons him. He shakes free of Noah and, without sparing me a glance, runs to her. They disappear into the shadowed recesses of the storefronts. Just as I leap to take off after them, my ankle is grabbed and I hit the floor.

Noah has a grip and he isn't letting go.

On my stomach, I turn and look at Noah Miles. He's on his stomach, his arm outstretched, his strong fingers gripping my ankle. We stare like that for a moment. I know now I can't go after Eli and Carrine. Another time, maybe. Not now.

Only when I notice Rhine moving toward us do I try again to get up. This time, Noah lets me go. We both stand, and in seconds we're surrounded by Rhine and no fewer than fifteen Ness boys.

"Well, then," Rhine says, and he yanks off his skully and rubs his hand over his short-clipped hair. "That was . . . interesting."

The low drone of the others talking in hushed voices buzzes in my ear. I look at him. "That's putting it mildly. She could have walked up and killed every single one of you."

"Witchpire," Rhine says. "Looks like I may have underestimated her a wee bit."

I stare. "A wee? That's more than a fucking wee, Rhine."

Several of the others chuckle.

"Oy, lass," he says, and chucks me under the chin. "No need tae worry about us Ness boys." He glances out across his brethren. "We just have a bit more studyin' tae do. That bloodsuckin' bitch willna get the better o' us again."

Several *ayes* from the Ness boys affirm his words.

"It coulda been the end o' you, fool," I return in my best Scottish accent.

That brings out a deep laugh from Rhine.

Even Noah chuckles.

"Right, then," Pete says from the crowd. "At least we killed us quite a lot o' bloodsuckers this night."

"Aye, and saved that wee girl, too," another said. "That's, eh . . ." He starts counting on his fingers. "Eight bloodsuckers down, one fine lassie saved."

"We're fookin' heroes!"

I glance at the watch on Rhine's wrist, and I pull it closer. It's almost five in the morning.

Where did all the time go?

Everythong's looking hazy. Did I just say everythong? I mean everything.

I'm staring at Rhine, and his face is blurring, too. I squint, stare harder, trying to focus.

"I think we should go," I say, and start to move. "I'm hungry as holy fucking hell on goddamn wheels."

I take one step, swagger, then two more steps, and I'm walking straight toward Rhine. A large, cocky grin spreads across his face, and straight white teeth glare at me. "What the hell's so funny?" I say. I shake my head, trying to clear the fog. "I gotta get something to eat. Sugar's low."

"That ain't it, darlin'," Noah says. "Rhine?"

Just as the words leave Noah's mouth, I start to fall. The Kansas track playing over the mall's intercom has been set on repeat, apparently. We're back to "Dust in the Wind." I fall into Rhine's arms, and his face is inches from mine. "I love that song," I say. "But I wish they'd play 'M-M-M-My Sharona.' The Knack. I love that one, too."

His cocky grin is the last thing I see. "Yeah, I know."

Blackness washes over me, and I feel weightless; voices around me soften, mumble, and weave together until I can't understand anything anyone is saying. It's a low hum, vibrating around me. Sleep washes over me, and I float until I feel . . . only peace.

My eyes flutter open, and a thick white mist floats all around me. The ground is slightly squishy beneath my feet, but still solid. The scent of clover and something else unique and twangy fills the air, my nostrils, and I inhale. I see nothing but the sallow vapor around me. I'm outside. On a slight incline. I'm climbing.

After a while, I stop and squint, trying to peer

through the mist. What am I doing here? Where am I? I continue looking around, searching . . . for something. Or someone. I don't know right now.

Then, ahead, I see a figure. The mist thins enough for me to make out a little. Tall. Wearing all black. Dark hair. Wide stance. Arms hanging at his side. Then he lifts one of those arms and beckons me with his outstretched hand.

Is it Eli? I think it is. My pace quickens, and I hurry, stumbling up the hill, using my hands now to grab on to clumps of dead heather to pull myself along. Not sure why I don't just hurl myself upward. I try . . . try to jump, move as fast as my tendencies will allow. They don't work here. I'm breathless from the climb. I'm just a regular ole human.

Go figure.

I'm closer now, and the figure—it's Eli, I can tell—stands at the top. The wind picks up, catching the tails of his trench and billowing it open, like a black cape, or the outstretched wings of a giant raven. He awaits me. I sense no threat. No hatred. No violence. Only . . . desire.

I reach the top, and a space of about six feet separates us. The wind tears through the vapor, scattering and swirling it into a mass of white soup around his body, obscuring his face. I step closer. "Is it really you?" I ask. "Eli?"

"Don't speak," he says. "Come here."

An uncertainty claws at me, but I'm helpless to stop my feet from advancing toward him. His arms open, like raven wings, and unable to do anything else, I walk into them. His arms close around me, pulling me against his lukewarm body. His hand splays against the back of my head, holding me securely to him. Lips caress my temple. His other hand lowers, caressing my lower back, and then lower still, over my buttocks. When he pulls me against him, his hardened state of arousal is evident as it pushes at my groin. Something worries me; I can't figure it out. So overcome by finally having his arms around me, I ignore the worry. I only want him. Eli.

In the next instant, he leans, catching me under my knees, and scoops me up. I still can't see his face; so much mist. He begins to walk with me, and I rest my head against his chest. It's hard, muscular, as are the arms that hold me.

He leaps, and we're weightless for a few moments, and then he lands solid on the ground, his arms tightening around me. He's walking now, and I can't see anything. We stop. A door opens. Creaks as it closes behind us. His footfalls sound against a hard floor, echoing in my ears. It almost sounds as though we're in a tunnel.

I try to open my eyes. I want to see. We're inside now, so the mist can't obscure. I try to speak, but my throat tightens. I can't talk. I can't move. Panic seizes me, and I feel my heart pound. Adrenaline surges within me as my alarm rises. I'm paralyzed.

"Shh, shh," he soothes. He presses his lips to my temple, and it calms me.

He continues to walk with me, and now we're moving up. Stairs. We're climbing now, and finally, we level once more and he moves with me down a corridor. I inhale, and all I can smell is his spicy scent. It's . . . somewhat familiar. A door opens. Closes.

He lowers me, my back sinking into a soft, downy bed. I can see now, but the room is cast in shadows. No candles. No lamps. Only a sliver of moonlight through the small crack in the drapes across the room. I can see his silhouette. He pulls his arms out of his trench, drops it to the floor. His fingers begin to unbutton his shirt, and soon he drops it, too. I see only his outline. He's bare from the waist up.

When he moves over me, his body settles over mine. A heavy, muscular thigh wedges between my legs, pushing them apart. Bracing his weight on his elbows, his hands on either side of my head, he slants his mouth over mine and kisses me.

"Touch me," he commands in a whisper against my lips.

Unable to stop myself, I do as he says. My hands encircle his back and trail up his spine, and the muscles bunch beneath my fingertips. He deepens the kiss, tasting my lips with his tongue, then moving his mouth to my throat. His groin grinds against me, his erection hard against my thigh, and his hand moves from my head to my breast, lowering over my stomach until his hand finds my skin beneath my tank. Over my ribs, he pulls my bra aside to find more skin, and caresses me. His mouth finds mine once more, and he kisses me hard, frenzied, and panic seizes me once more.

Something is terribly, terribly wrong.

He lifts his head then, leaving my lips. His hand covers my breast. His heavy cock pushes against me.

The moonlight catches enough of his profile for me to see.

Shock.

Fury.

Panic.

With all of my might, I shove him off, and I leap up. Free at last.

He leaps, too. He's off the bed. Standing, backing away from me, wordless.

Anger surges inside me, and I lunge—

"Fook me!" a voice grunts beneath me as we hit the floor. My vision is foggy at first, but soon starts to clear. I stare at the figure below me. I blink several times. It's getting clearer now.

"Shit!" I mutter, and scramble off Rhine, who I've got pinned beneath me on the floor of my room at the Crachan. I extend a hand. "Rhine, I'm sorry! Did I hurt you?"

Rhine grabs my hand and I yank him up. The fool is grinning at me.

Grinning.

"Aye, ya did," he says, still smiling. "But I was warned." He rubs his jaw, his eyes locked on to mine. "'Twas worth it, I'd say."

I'm still somewhat dazed; I glance around the room, at the window. Light gray spills from behind the drapes. It's daylight. Late afternoon.

"You've been out for forty-six hours," Rhine explains. "That's some bloody dream you were havin' there."

I walk to the window and pull the drapes aside. Cars and pedestrians are moving along the street at the end of the Crachan's entrance. I turn my head and look at Rhine.

"What are you talking about?" I say.

Rhine rubs his chin and walks to me. He ducks his head. "You dinnae remember what you just did?"

"I'm scared to ask."

Rhine chuckles, a throaty, guy sound. "Miles warned me no' tae wake you, but you yelled. I came in, and you were breathin' hard, like you were angry, and trapped maybe." He shrugs. "I shook you, called your name." He grins now. "Next thing I know, you've got me on the floor. Like I said . . ." His smile widens. " 'Twas worth it."

My mind searches, scrambles to make sense.

All at once, it hits me. My dream.

I pray it was a dream.

Panic seizes me. Panic and a deep, cellular fury.

It wasn't Eli.

I fly to the door and yank it open.

"Eh, Riley?"

I turn and look over my shoulder at Rhine, still standing at the window. His eyes lower, down my body, then back up. "No' that I'm no' appreciatin' the beauty o' it, but I'm feelin' a bit stingy and unsharing." He inclines his head toward me. "Dinnae ya want tae get some clothes on?"

Only now, when I glance down at myself, do I realize I'm standing in my Crachan room, with Rhine at the window, staring like a hungry wolf, in only my sports bra and boy shorts panties.

Jesus H. Christ.

I rush over to my duffel and start yanking out clothes. My mind wonders briefly who exactly pulled the other ones off me, and I quickly push the thought aside.

I've got new worries now. Newer and bigger.

"That is . . . simply amazin'," Rhine says.

I look at him. He's staring at my back. I turn to my duffel, pull out a pair of soft, old, faded jeans, complete with raggedy holes, and pull them on. "Thanks," I answer. I've got other things on my mind, though, and Rhine's appreciation of my inked dragon is not top priority. Finding a white long-sleeved tee, I yank it over my head and stuff my arms into the sleeves. Turning, I sit on the bed and start pulling on clean socks. "Where's Noah?" I ask. Spying my boots, I grab them, yank them on, and pull the zipper on each.

"Och, he just went out," Rhine says. "As in fell asleep. What's wrong?" he asks.

My dream washes over me as I stand, and it almost makes me dizzy.

No way is this happening.

"Riley?" Rhine says. He's moved closer. Concern lights his green eyes.

I shake my head and go to my weapons duffel. I pull on my leather holster and start loading my sheaths with blades. I shove one in its place at my ribs, and I look at Rhine. "That dream? It included an unwanted and unexpected intruder." I shove the last blade in and find my jacket draped over the end of the bed. I pull it on. "I gotta fix it."

"Whoa, lass," Rhine says, and moves to block me at the door. "Noah made me swear that I'd watch o'er ya whilst he sleeps." He shakes his head. "You ain't goin' nowhere wi'out me."

I see the determination in Rhine's eyes. I also know that I can render him paralyzed if I want to. But maybe it's not a bad idea to have a backup? Might prevent me from what I'm not too sure I can't restrain myself from doing.

Killing the fucker from my dream.

Just thinking it makes me boil inside with fury.

"How long's Noah been out?" I ask. I'm standing in front of Rhine now.

"About an hour and a half," he answers.

His eyes search mine curiously. I know he's trying to figure me out. Wondering if I'm going to throw some crazy hoodoo whammy on him. It's damn tempting, but I don't. Instead, I give him a nod. "Come on. I can use the backup. Just you and me, though. No Ness boys this time."

Rhine studies me hard for a second or two, then opens the door. "Aye, the two o' us, then." He heads out into the hallway. My eyes drift across, to Noah's closed door. My hand is reaching for the knob now, and I open and step into his room.

Noah's crashed on the bed, under the covers like some regular ole human, bare from the waist up. One arm is resting across his abdomen. His chest doesn't rise and fall with breath; I still can't grasp that sometimes. I stare at his face, so peace-

ful and still. Long lashes brush his flawless skin.
Sun-bleached dreads hang loose around his
shoulders.

He's not waking anytime soon. Unlike what
most humans believe, vampires don't hunt all
night and sleep all day. The ones I know only
have a few hours of rest every few days or so.
Sometimes daily, depending. Noah hasn't rested
in . . . I can't remember when. A long time. He
may sleep for hours now.

And what I have to do can't wait.

He'll be so pissed.

He'll get over it.

I back out of Noah's room and quietly close
the door. In the hallway, Rhine waits. Wordlessly,
we start up the corridor and hit the steps at the
same time. Downstairs, the flat-screen is on.
Three Ness boys sit on the sofa and chair. I pause
when I see the movie they're watching. *E.T., the
Extra-Terrestrial.* Memories from my youth, before I turned into a wild child, crash over me. My
mom sitting on the sofa in our little apartment,
watching it with me.

"Great picture," Rhine says beside me. "One
o' my favorites."

I look at him and grin. "Cintus Suprimus."

"Zero Charisma." He gives me a crooked
smile.

I'm impressed that Rhine, who is at least eight
years younger than me, can quote one of my favorite random quotes from a favorite movie.
"Let's go."

When we get outside, the sky is still light, with fading lavender and gray hues. I start toward the drive.

"I got a better idea," Rhine says, and inclines his head toward the row of motorcycles parked on the side of the Crachan. "Since it's just the two o' us."

"All right," I agree, and start toward the bikes.

What is it about me and guys and bikes?

Rhine swaggers up to a black Harley, straddles the seat, and turns the key. He starts the engine and it rumbles to life. With his legs, he pushes it backward and stops where I'm standing. "Get on," he instructs. He pulls on a helmet and pushes a pair of shades on and hands me a helmet off one of the other bikes.

I strap it on, straddle the seat behind him, find the foot pegs, and slide my arms around his waist.

He turns his head. "Where to?"

"City center," I say without hesitation. "We'll park and walk from there."

"You got it," Rhine says, and clicks the gears. He takes off down the drive and turns the bike toward Inverness's city center.

My mind races as Rhine weaves through traffic. The sun, previously hidden by the looming Scottish winter skies, cracks through now, just a golden orange thread between shades of purple and gray. The wind hits my face, and it's brisk and biting, and I inhale deeply. Rhine's body is hard and warm. I can hear the thumping of his young, healthy heart. Humanity. Something I sorely miss. I squeeze tighter, and his head tilts slightly toward me in response. I hope I'm not sending the wrong signals to him. I just feel a sense of vulnerability overcome me that I want squashed out. I don't want to feel it. I want to do what I have to do, fix what needs fixing, and be the hell done with all of this. I want to sit back and watch *E.T.*, eat some pizza, and not worry about the safety of others. I want Eli beside me. I want him out of whatever hell he's in.

Jesus, I *miss* him.

My heart aches, like someone is physically squeezing the life out of it.

Rhine pulls his bike along the curb and stops it. I dismount and take off my helmet. He stays straddled and tugs his helmet off and hooks it on the handlebars.

"You okay?" he asks. He takes his shades off. The late afternoon is fast turning into an early Scottish winter's eve. Dark at four thirty. That's such bullshit. "Aye?"

I glance around, taking in my surroundings. We're on a side street, close to High Street. There are pedestrians moving about. Mostly locals. I've learned to tell them apart now. Tourists are more, I don't know . . . colorful. And the expression of the locals is different. Friendly, but unimpressed. If that makes any sense. "I will be." Looking at him now, I sigh. "Believe it or not, I'm actually glad you came with me. Sometimes I really need a warm-blooded, human hug."

That sounds stupid as hell. But I had to say it.

Rhine grins. "Oy, what do ya know? I'm warm-blooded and human." He winks. "Hug me anytime ya get the urge, lass."

I shake my head and fight a grin. I feel like I've got two Noahs now. I give in and smile, then glance up the street. Then I study Rhine. He has to know what's going on. It wouldn't be fair to keep it from him. I sigh. "What we're walking into here is a nightmare, Rhine. This vampire? I've dealt with him before. He was the first one to poison me with his Strigoi venom, back in Savannah. He didn't want me dead, though. He wanted to keep me. Make me become his mate. And I'm pretty damn sure now he's behind everything here. Carrine, Eli—it's him. Valerian Arcos. He's powerful as all holy hell. Just so you know."

Rhine's eyes shine with understanding. "Aye, I'll keep all that in mind. But I willna leave ya, lass."

With a nod and a deep breath, I focus. Everything around me goes silent, and blurry. I hear and see no one. I'm singling out one in specific. Like flipping through the channels on satellite, my mind spins and spins.

Then I've got him.

The hairs on my neck stiffen, and I stare down High Street. Past the double arches of McDonald's, a sidewalk café. The shade of the building falls over the sidewalk tables, but he's there. I sense him.

And he senses me, too.

He knows I've come.

I'm sure he knew it all along. He's controlling everything. Every goddamn thing.

"This way," I say to Rhine, and I start up the street. Past several storefronts, past McDonald's, past the tartan shop, I walk steadily toward the outdoor café. The only sound I hear is my boots making contact with the sidewalk. I vaguely see Rhine, slightly behind and beside me. I know he's not going anywhere. It would've been useless to try and get him to stay behind. Knowing him, he would've chanced waking a sleeping vampire, just to make sure I wasn't stepping into danger.

I may still be.

But I don't think so.

At the café, our eyes meet. I know he's watched me, from the moment I turned into view. Seeing him here, now, is slightly shocking. Infuriating. Disgusting. My hands clench at my sides into fists. Fury boils inside me.

I walk directly to the table, and before I realize it, Rhine is pulling the seat out for me. I sit down. He stands behind me, his hand on my shoulder. A few other tables are occupied by humans. All of them sipping tea and coffee, having a bite to eat, chatting. Wrapping up their day. None of them have any suspicion that a coldhearted murderer is in their midst.

I'm looking at the one sitting at the table, facing me.

A smile touches his mouth. His chocolate brown eyes soften as they stare directly into mine. His dark hair is pulled back into a perfect ponytail. His features are flawless.

He's a monster inside all of that beauty.

"Riley," he says seductively. He draws a deep, exaggerated breath, as if air could move through those lifeless lungs. He spares Rhine a brief glance before lowering his gaze back to me. "I didn't expect you to bring along a chaperone."

Rhine's grip tightens on my shoulder. It comforts me.

I steady my gaze directly into that of Valerian Arcos. "Does your father know you're here?" I ask. "Or your brother?"

An easy smile falls on Valerian's full lips. "Of course not. Why would I tell them such?" His gaze drops to my breasts, then back up. "And have them ruin our time together?"

Fury seethes within me, and I briefly focus on one mind. *Vic, your brother is here in Inverness. I can't talk right now, but you need to know. And warn your father. I may very well kill the fucker.* "We'll have no time together," I say calmly. "What do you want here, Valerian? You're breaking serious codes, you know."

"Codes my father and ridiculous little brother vowed to uphold," he acknowledged. "Not me. Besides," he says, his voice lowering, "I've come for a much different reason than you think."

I cock my head and study him. "I'm not a helpless human you can push around," I remind him. "So you'd better tell me what it is you want—"

"I could have fucked you in your sleep, love," Valerian corrects, interrupts. His voice is low, almost crooning. And it's all matter-of-fact. "You enjoyed every touch, every swipe of my tongue. You liked it. And you were powerless to fight me." He smiles. "But you know that, don't you?"

The tension building in Rhine's body surges through him to his fingertips, where his grip tightens.

"I've always known that about you, Valerian," I say. "I know something else, too."

He smiles and strokes his chin. "And what's that?"

I lean forward, my gaze locked with his, and run my fingertip over his knuckles. "That you're such a pussy, the only way you can get inside girls' panties is in a dream."

Valerian's face hardens, for the briefest of seconds. Then he smiles. "That's what I adore most about you, Riley Poe. Crass American that you are, you've got that special, oh, I don't know . . ." He in turn grasps my hand with his. "Fuck appeal. It's terribly irresistible."

I yank my hand away.

Rhine moves forward, and I reach up and grasp his hand with mine. It stops him. His heart is pounding a mile a minute. Fury rolls off him in waves. I know Valerian notices it. And of course, he doesn't even acknowledge it. Arrogant bastard.

"But as I insisted before, that's not why I'm here," he says, and leans back in his chair. He's dressed in head-to-toe black. His skin clashes seductively. "You see, I'm so enamored of you that I cannot sit back and watch you be killed mercilessly. 'Twould be . . . quite a loss."

I narrow my gaze. "What are you talking about?"

His smile is cold. "Your fiancé, Riley. You do realize there's no saving him now, hmm?" He leans forward again. "He's partaken of too much human blood, love. He's awash with it. He can no more control it than you can control me. His vampiric brain is crazed. He doesn't know you anymore. Or his family. He knows only the female. And his next meal. And I can promise you, my love. No root doctor potion can fix him now." His brown eyes soften as he looks at me. "You've got to put him out of his misery."

Valerian's words hit me hard. I fight not to gasp. "Where are you getting your meals from?" I ask. "And since when do you care enough about Eli's misery to want it ended? And what do you know of the female?" Carrine's words ring in my ear. *"You see, I'm under intense orders myself. My savior freed me from my prison. 'Tis the verra reason I'm even walking the Earth again. I have no choice but to wait."*

Valerian gives a slight shrug. "I'm merely en route to my destination and thought to stop by and encourage you," he says. "Like I mentioned before, I hate to see such fine fucking material as yourself wasted. And if you wait too long, trying to"—he waves his hand in the air—"save Dupré's soul, you will get killed yourself." His eyes turn molten. "And I truly do hate that thought." He smiles. "And I've only fed once since my arrival. I'm not greedy, you know, but I must survive."

I pin Arcos with a glare. "You freed Carrine, didn't you? And you've given her orders to control Eli." I cock my head, staring. "Why? Why go through all that? If you simply wanted me, why not just take me? And how did Victorian end up in Romania? How did he simply vanish from the forest?" I draw closer to him. "What are you, some fucking magical fairy bloodsucker?"

Valerian's expression doesn't change. His chocolate eyes lock on to mine and he stares. "That female he's with? She's a witch, no?" He shrugs. "Maybe she used her magic to send my brother back home. Perhaps you should ask her all of your questions. I don't have the answers."

Anger rages through me, and I grab his arm. His eyes light up with interest. "Leave here, Arcos," I warn. "And don't touch another human." I rise and lean over the table. "I will kill you myself."

Valerian's brown gaze flashes at the challenge; then he chuckles softly. "Oh, Riley. How easily you forget." He looks at me. *Turn your lovely self around and kiss that paltry human boy you've brought along with you. Go on. Do it.*

I turn where I stand, slip my hand around Rhine's neck, and pull his mouth to mine. I kiss him, deeply.

Do you see the power I still possess? You may stop now. The sight sickens me. I simply wanted to prove myself to you. Now you must kill Dupré. He'll only hurt you in the end. Kill you. Dead. Do what you wish to his lover.

I pull away from Rhine's mouth. His eyes are glued to mine, green flashing curiosity. I turn and look at Valerian.

"I'm not an idiot, Arcos," I say, and I move away. "I've known what has to be done since I arrived here. Now leave Inverness," I warn. "Before I call the House of Arcos and tell Daddy what you're up to." I won't tell him I've already sent word home to Vic. Better if they surprise him.

Valerian casts an unworried smile. "As I said, I'm just passing through. Heading to Ireland for a jaunt."

"That's too close," I advise. "Go farther. And stay out of my head."

Valerian chuckles. "Or what, pray tell?"

I edge closer to Valerian's chair and straddle his lap. In my peripheral I notice several bypassers and other cafégoers turn their glances toward me.

I don't care.

Valerian's eyes widen as my hand pushes open his black woolen coat. His stomach is hard, lined with lean muscle. Not bulky strong. Just . . . well, aristocratic strong, if that makes sense. I let my hand move over his ribs, distracting him.

My other hand grasps the silver blade tucked into my boot and I lift it.

One hand on his crotch.

His eyes turn darker.

My other hand goes to his heart with the blade.

Just that fast, Valerian's eyes flash the tiniest bit of fear. Just before they ice over.

I smile. "So you see," I say, and press the blade just a little harder, beneath his coat. I grab his crotch harder, too. "I'm not the pushover you think I am." I lean my mouth to his ear. "I could end you right now, Arcos. It'd be so easy." I move my face in front of his, our eyes inches apart. "And all I did was use a little bit of pure, unadulterated human female skill."

He stares at me. "That, my love, would be a mistake," he advises. "One day, you may just seek my help."

I slip my blade back into my boot and get up. "I highly doubt that. Now go. Tonight. Or I'll make the call. Not just to your father. But to Eli's."

Again, a tinge of fear replaces the cocky spark of fire in Valerian's brown eyes. He gives a slight nod. "Very well. You'll see what I mean soon enough," he warns. He spares Rhine a glance. "Perhaps your little human friends can keep you safe enough." He smiles. "For a while." He rises from the table and buttons his woolen coat up to the throat. He stands in front of me now, looks down at me, and I briefly wonder why vampires are so goddamn beautiful. What a waste.

His smile bares straight white teeth. "Very well, my dear Riley. I'm on my way. But if you need me at all, please . . ." He lifts my hand and brushes his lukewarm lips over my skin. "Call me. I will hasten to be by your side."

With one last lingering stare, he gives a slight bow, turns, and heads down High Street. I stare at him until the shadows swallow him up.

Then he's gone.

And I mean gone. Just that fast, he's out of Inverness. On foot, I sense his presence getting farther and farther away. I can't believe he even dared approach me. Or maybe he really is stupid enough to pull all that shit and not think I would eventually recognize him?

"Riley?"

I turn and meet Rhine's gaze. A sheepish expression crosses his face, and he smiles. "Do . . . you remember wha' you just did?"

I smile and punch his arm. It's funny to me that Rhine's brogue is void of the letter *t*. "You mean that kiss? Yeah, I knew I was doing it." I incline my head in the direction of Valerian. "But it's better if we let him think he made me do it. I may never have gotten rid of him otherwise."

His green eyes flash. "I'm no' sure if I like the idea of you doing it unawares, or on purpose."

I smile and we start back toward the bike. "I

can't let everyone know all of my secrets," I say. "Had Valerian realized he wasn't overpowering me, I may not have been able to slip inside his head like I did." I knock shoulders with him. "I didn't mean to use you, Rhine. For what it's worth, you are a fab kisser."

Rhine cuts his eyes at me and shrugs. "I've been told that a time or two," he admits. "Never by an older lass, though."

"Watch how you say that word *older*," I warn. "I'm fast creepin' toward thirty and not liking it much."

When we get to Rhine's bike, he throws his leg over it and sits for a moment, staring at me. The sun has dropped now, and a streetlight casts his face in half shadow. He watches me, studying me closely. I'm sorely tempted to slip back inside his brain, just to see what he's thinking.

But I don't.

Finally, he shakes his head. "Get on."

We pull our helmets on, and I crawl onto the back of the bike and wrap my arms around Rhine's middle. "We've got a vampire to awaken," I say. "And trust me when I say shit's about to hit the fan."

"I believe it," he says, and pulls into traffic.

Oh yeah. Shit is definitely about to hit the fan.

What Arcos doesn't know certainly won't hurt him.

And I've got a wealth of information, just from our little café chat.

And I love that he doesn't even know the secrets he gave to me.

That's what he gets for fucking with a human with vampiric tendencies.

And a little fallen angel dust, thrown in to boot.

Part Seven

+—◆—+—◆—+

SOULLESS

This one, this one right here. This was my dream, my wish. And it didn't come true. So I'm taking it back. I'm taking them all back.

—Mouth, The Goonies, 1985

Oh, dat girl of mine. She crazy in da head and gonna git herself kilt if she don't look out. I'm worried about dat Eli, too. I think he might be too far gone for even me to help him, that's right. He done slipped way into dat mess of bloodlust. My baby girl might have to make a choice she ain't gonna like too much. If she does, well, den, we will have to go and get her. No tellin' what she'll do.

—Preacher

The second we walk into the Crachan, I can tell Noah is still asleep.

I don't know what it is, or how I can sense it. It's just one of those qualities I've acquired that have no rhyme or reason in my human brain. Which is really a joke, considering. As if anything in my world makes sense.

"I'm going to wake him," I tell Rhine. "Be right down."

"Aye," Rhine answers, and disappears through the hall.

I hit the stairs and take them two at a time. One plus for long legs, I guess. I take the corridor at a jog and ease into Noah's room.

I'm not prepared for what—or who—I see sitting in the chair against the wall, opposite Noah's bed.

My little baby brother.

"Seth!" I choke out. I hurry to him, and at the same time he rises and launches at me, full weight. I catch him, and we embrace.

I'm shocked we're no longer eye to eye. Rather, I have to look up at him. And I'm wearing spike-heeled boots.

"Ri!" he says into my neck. "I've missed you!"

For a moment, I forget all the craziness that's become my world, forget vampires, blood, silver blades, and saving humans. I just inhale the familiar scent and feel of my little brother. I squeeze him tightly, and it takes me back to . . . before. That in-between time when I ran Inksomnia with my best friend, Nyx, and I tattooed for a living, and ordered Chinese food and had low-country boils with my Gullah family. I let it engulf me, for just a minute.

Then I pull back and scowl up at my brother.

My eyes widen. "Holy crap, Seth." I finger his chin. "You've got freaking whiskers!"

Seth Poe grins, and the fact that he's now almost seventeen blows me away. His dark hair is close-cut, like Eli's brother Phin. Nicely arched dark eyebrows frame green eyes, just like mine, with long lashes most girls envy. But there's a hardness about him now that wasn't there before. In a way, I'm glad. He's strong, and he's grown.

And in another way, it saddens me. Innocence gone.

"I've been growing whiskers for a year now," Seth says.

"Four single whiskers do not count, bro," I remind him, and he grins. "What are you doing here anyway?" I stare at my brother, amazed at his physique. Although his are not nearly as severe as mine, he, too has tendencies. Strigoi tendencies. It's what started all of this hell. Seth, on a dare by his pain-in-the-ass buddies, accidentally set free the entombed and deadly Arcos brothers. Seth was then drawn into Valerian's Lost Boys' cult in Savannah, and . . . Jesus Christ, I almost lost him.

Thanks to Eli and his family, he was saved.

And we realized Victorian Arcos wasn't nearly as lethal as his brother, Valerian.

It's been quite a hellish ride ever since.

"Your inspection of me, Ri, is kinda creepin' me out," Seth says with a grin. "Anyway . . ." He takes both my shoulders in his hands. "I kept having this bad feeling about you here," he admits. "Preacher did, too. So he and Eli's dad sent me."

Eli. God Almighty, just hearing his name hurts. And saying what I have to say will hurt even more. "I have to tell you something."

"Whoa, why are there so many Poes in my room?" Noah says, awakened. He's sitting up now, still in bed. Dreads all over the place. He leaps from beneath the covers and, thank God, he's wearing a pair of black workout pants. He's barefoot, and in two steps he and Seth meet in the middle of the room. Noah pulls my brother into a fierce bear hug.

"What in Sam Hill are you doing here, boy?" Noah asks Seth. Noah's Charleston drawl is appealing, and a little sensual. Especially when he's serious. It gets, I don't know . . . stronger. Almost like the old Noah, prevampirism, Revolutionary War Noah, is there, in his voice. Appealing.

Seth shrugs. "I got a bad feeling." He looks at me. "About her."

"She tends to stir that feeling in almost everyone she meets," Noah says. He's looking at me hard now, and I can tell he knows something's up.

"How did you know to come here?" I finally ask.

Seth looks at me. "Jake Andorra told me you were in Inverness. Once I got here . . ." He shrugs. "I first went to the guesthouse you were supposed to be staying in. When you weren't there, I just walked around until I . . . sensed you. I guess we look enough alike that the guys who were here let me in." His eyes are questioning now. "What is it you have to tell me?"

"It's Eli," I say, and my throat constricts. I'm keeping focused, not dwelling on the fact that the very soul I love with all my might is the same one who's turned dark, killing innocents, and doing so has made it almost seem surreal. To explain it? Say it out loud?

Pain. Deep, throbbing pain that starts in my gut and twists up my spine, to my throat and grabs on so fiercely I find it hard to even breathe normally.

But I do.

"What about Eli?" Seth asks.

"He's turned, Seth," Noah answers for me. "For the very worst."

I look at Noah first, and I know he sees the appreciation in my eyes. Seth sits down in the chair he'd been in when I first walked in, and I finish telling him everything about Inverness. About how I'd gone into the alternative realm, dragged both Victorian and Eli out, and saved them. How Victorian had ended up back in Romania. And how Eli had grown fond of human blood, and Carrine. The killings. The Ness boys, and Rhine. Everything. My little brother sits in stunned silence the whole time I speak.

Then I have to tell both Noah and Seth the latest.

About Valerian Arcos.

Now I have two pair of stormy eyes staring at me. One green. The other pure liquid silver.

Both mad as hell.

Noah speaks first. "What the hell, Riley?" he says. "You knew it was him and you went anyway?"

I shoot a glance at Seth. He's waiting on an answer, too.

"I took Rhine with me," I answer.

"No, Rhine insisted on going because I made

him swear he would watch out for you while I slept," Noah corrected.

"Nah, that's no' exactly right, either," Rhine says from the doorway. "I'd have gone, no matter what." He eyes Seth for a moment.

"Rhine MacLeod, my little brother, Seth Poe," I introduce. Rhine walks over and shakes Seth's hand.

The two look each other over, and Seth nods. "You've got tendencies."

Rhine nods in return. "Some." He glances at Noah. "She kissed me."

Noah's brow lifts. "Is that so?"

I shake my head, glare at Rhine, and sigh. "Clarification. I had to make Valerian think he had one over on me so he would leave. He instructed me to do it." I slide a sideways glance at Rhine. "So I did."

"And what did he want?" Seth asks. "Does his father know he's here?"

I nod. "I slipped Victorian the message, but Valerian doesn't know that. Anyway, when I threatened to tell his dad, he didn't seem overly concerned. He basically told me that Eli was far gone—too far for help. And that I needed to kill him before he killed me."

"Did he mention the female?" Noah asks.

Again, I nod. "Said she's just some female latched on to Eli. But I think he knows a lot more than what he's letting on. Carrine told me at Eastgate that her savior had freed her of her prison. That she was basically under his command. Could be Valerian."

"But we know she's a witchpire," Rhine adds. He looks at Seth. "Witch. Vampire. Old as bloody hell."

"I think Valerian wanted his presence known," I say. "He claims he's killed only one innocent here in Inverness." I look at Seth. "So far there've been five. And that's not including the new-bloods."

"So what are you doing?" Seth asks. "To keep the city safe?"

I glance at Rhine and Noah, then at my brother. "Same thing we were doing in Savannah. Run the streets."

"Only the lot of us, we're human," Rhine says. "I'm the only one wi' any tendencies, and they're mild compared to your sister's abilities."

Noah's pacing now, and pulling on a white T-shirt over his head. "I don't like it." He ties his dreads back with a leather band. "There's more to Arcos's appearance than to simply tell you how much he doesn't want you to die. He's full of shit. He knows something."

"Och, that's no' all he said," Rhine offers. "He fancies Riley here." He looks at me. "A lot."

Noah makes a sound, almost a swear, in his throat. "I can only imagine. Still," he says, "there's something else going on."

"He left," I tell him. "I can sense his absence. He's gone from Inverness."

"Well, unfortunately, Eli is still here," Noah says. "And Carrine. And they have to be stopped."

"Why don't we just capture Eli and bind him?" Seth asks. "Take him back to Savannah so Preacher can take him to Da Island for detox." He looks at me. "Like we did with Ri?"

"What if it's not Eli?" I offer. I walk to the window and pull the drapes. The city is ablaze with streetlights. The castle is illuminated on the hill. "What if the killings continue, even without Eli as a factor?"

"We'll kill Carrine, too," Noah offers. "I'll make a call to Andorra."

"Meanwhile," says Rhine, "we'll be hittin' the streets tonight." He looks at Seth. "You hungry?"

"Starved," Seth admits.

"Well, let's go get some grub." Rhine inclines his head to the door. "Riley?"

"I'll be down in a sec," I say, and look at my brother.

He reads my mind because he comes straight to me, pulls me into another embrace.

"It'll be okay, sis," he says into my hair. "Whatever it takes, we'll get Eli home and Preacher will make all of this right."

"I hope so, bro," I say. I squeeze him around his middle, locking my hands together. "God, I hope so." I pull back. "Go. Eat. I'll be down in just a bit."

"Okay," Seth says, and leaves with Rhine.

"I have to admit, Riley," Noah says. He's

kicked off his black workout pants and is pulling on a pair of dark jeans. "Something doesn't sit right with me about Arcos." He buttons his fly, his stare remaining on mine. "There's just more to it than him slipping into your dreams, then telling you to kill Eli. That's just . . . too simple."

"I don't know," I answer. "What motive would he have? Why doesn't he just kill Eli himself? Why go through all this?"

Noah's standing in front of me now, and he taps me on the nose with a forefinger. "Because, darlin'," he says. His mercury eyes all but are illuminated. "That would be a big fucking no-no, now, wouldn't it?" A smile lifts his mouth. "He can't touch Eli Dupré. The Gullah, not to mention Eli's entire family, would storm Romania and the House of Arcos would become a bloody vampire battleground. Senior Arcos knows it. And so does Valerian."

I laugh. It's almost too stupid to say out loud. "So Valerian seriously thinks he can simply put the Arcos whammy on me and make me kill my own fiancé?"

Noah shrugs and pulls on his boots. "Maybe."

Maybe, indeed.

"Well," I say, grabbing Noah's leather jacket off the foot of the bed. I watch as he sheathes a few silver blades in the holster he's now strapping on over his shoulders. "Whether Carrine is commanding the rogues, Eli, or Valerian . . ." I shake my head. "Either way, they have to be stopped. Maybe Eli doesn't have to die.

"Why the rogues? What's the—I don't know—rationale? If Valerian in fact set free, resurrected, whatever—Carrine, why?" I ask.

Noah strokes his chin. "Maybe Valerian doesn't have as much control as he thinks. Or," he says, meeting my gaze, "maybe he does, and he's just a sick bastard who gets off on the chase. The killing of innocents. And it's no secret he loathes Eli."

"Maybe he set Carrine free in order to use her for her witch powers?" I muse. "Valerian mentioned that could be how Vic disappeared and made it back to Romania."

"Could be," Noah answers.

I move to stand directly in front of Noah. I look up. "If there's even a slight chance of capturing Eli and getting him back to Da Island, we gotta make it happen."

"It's going to take more than just us to subdue him," Noah says. "He's . . . full-on rabid, Riley. You were bad enough as a human with tendencies." Noah takes the jacket from my hands and eases into it. His eyes never leave mine. "When we took you to Romania? God Almighty Damn, girl." He chuckles. "You nearly tore the plane's wiring out of the walls. You were some kind of out of control. Can you imagine what a full-blooded, blood-lusted two-hundred-plus-year-old vampire would be like?"

"I can imagine."

"He's strong, Riley. Damn strong," he says.

I head to the door and stop, and Noah's right behind me. I look up. "You scared?"

He smiles. "Hell yeah, I'm scared." He shoves his hands into his jacket pocket and spreads it out like a cape, exposing the leather holster, sheaths, and blade hilts. "Just as I'm scared as hell that I'm gonna poke myself with one of these goddamn silver blades and turn to dust."

"You're not going to turn to dust, Noah," I answer, and we both step out of the room. He closes the door and locks it, and we start up the corridor. Suddenly, I stop.

"Hey, I'll meet you downstairs," I say, and turn back to my room. "I need to change."

"Why?" Noah asks, and starts up the hall. He throws a grin over his shoulder. "Can't you run in them things?"

I take a look at the high-leather heeled boots I'm wearing, and shrug. "I can. For a while."

Noah waves and hits the staircase. I turn and hurry into my room. I shut the door behind me and walk toward the bedside table. The moment my fingers graze the knob, I freeze. It's dark, with only a small haze of streetlight shining in through the cracked drapes. The window is open, and cold November Highland air rushes in.

I'm not alone.

A sensation washes over me, and slowly, I scan the shadows. I search the other side of the room, and I turn back.

I gasp.

Eli is standing in front of me. A foot—twelve inches—is all the space that's between us. His body is tense—so much I can feel the power rolling off him—and every muscle is rigid, hard. His eyes are red—not the beautiful cerulean I'm used to. But he's not morphed into his vampirism. Only his eyes are different.

My vocal cords are frozen. My body is paralyzed. I stare hard at him, wishing him to recognize me. Why is he here? How the hell did he *get* in here?

His head cocks to the side, and he's studying me so hard I feel adrenaline surge through me and realize it's fear. I want to scan the room. Is Carrine here? Commanding him to kill me? Or to torture me, as Athios had warned? I want to run. I want to call out to him, scream his name, make him see me.

I want to touch him. So badly it hurts. Maybe if I do, he'll remember me. He'll remember us.

I concentrate. Focus. Holding his bloodred gaze, I breathe in. Out. Slowly, I lift my arm, reach my hand out to him. I'm grabbing blindly, gently when I feel his hand beneath mine.

For a split second, confusion flashes over Eli's features. So quick I almost miss it. He could kill me so fast. I've seen how swift he turns. It's little more than a blur, and his jaw extends, jagged teeth drop sharp and white, and he'll go for my throat. He could snap my head right off like a dandelion. Right now he's hesitating. And he's alone. Is his resistance to Carrine's control strengthening? Is he remembering me?

I swallow, pushing past my fear. My heart

throbs inside my ribs, and I have to concentrate to keep my breathing under control. Staring, willing him to recognize me, I hold my hand against his.

"Eligius Dupré," I whisper. "Eli, please, come back to me."

Eli's nostrils flare. His head cocks farther to the side, and his eyebrows pull together into a frown. He's considering. Studying.

Or remembering?

"Riley, what's the holdup?"

Noah's voice startles me, and on instinct, I drop my hand and glance toward the door just as he enters. His face hardens, just that fast.

I turn my head back to Eli.

He has disappeared. My eyes move to the window, and the drapes are still fluttering. Hurrying over, I peer out into the night, my eyes searching the shadows, the street, the walk.

Eli's gone.

At the window, I sag against it.

Noah's beside me, his hand on my shoulder. "He could have killed you, Riley." He squeezes me, his fingers digging into my bones. "I wouldn't have been able to stop him, darlin'."

"Yeah," I agree. "I know that." I look up at him. "He hesitated, though. Looked as if he was trying to figure something out." I shrug. "Or figure me out. Do you think he remembered?"

"Hard to say." He grasps my jaw gently and turns my face up to his. "If anyone's capable of reaching a vampire through a bloodlust phase, it's you." He kisses me, a fast brush across the lips. "You're kinda unforgettable, you know. And I'd like to keep you around for as long as possible, so if Eli approaches you again, call me." He taps my temple. "In here." He drops his hand and shakes his head. "Swear to God, for a human with so much power, you don't utilize a third of it."

"I guess I wasn't thinking," I admit. "Except to try and make him see me."

Noah chucks me under the chin. "I know." He inclines his head. "Let's go."

I finish changing, Noah helps me gear up, even though I don't need the help, and we head out. Downstairs, Seth and Rhine stand together, talking.

Riley, please. I can barely stand this—being here, and not there. How are you holding up?

Vic, it's okay. We've got a little unexpected help from a group of hunters here in Inverness. They're apt. Kick-ass apt. We're doing fine. I promise.

I don't know what's happening, Riley. I don't like it. I have a horrible feeling about everything. I should come.

No. You stay put. At least until we get things figured out here. Eli is here, Vic. And he's not himself. He's being controlled by a witchpire, of all things.

Damn me. Haven't heard that term in quite some time. Please. Don't be overzealous with your abilities. Keep Miles with you at all times. I beg you.

I don't think I have a choice anymore. He's on me like glue.

*Good. And a warning: The moment I feel you've
upset the balance of safety there, I'm on the first plane
to Inverness. I swear it.*

I'll keep you posted, Vic.

You'd better.

I finish my mind convo with Victorian Arcos
and hit the living area. My eyes scan the room.
My brother. He's here. And I haven't seen him
in . . . weeks. Since before Edinburgh. I walk up
to him, and he drapes a lean arm around my
shoulders and pulls me close. I look up at him.
"We run together tonight, bro," I say.

"Lads, you know where tae go," Rhine says to
the twenty or so Ness boys gathered in the hall.
A few faces are ones I haven't seen yet. "Rob,
Tate, Jep—you'll run wi' us."

The Ness boys break down into groups and
start filing out of the door. Noah walks over to us
and places a hand on mine and Seth's shoulders.
He squeezes us both.

"You two Poes don't stir up any extra unwanted
trouble," he warns. "And don't approach Eli or
Carrine alone. If you cross paths, call me."

I nod. "We will."

"And if Arcos—either one—tries to get to you,
don't entertain that, either."

I throw Noah a grin. "Yes, Mother." Noah
probably never will trust Victorian Arcos, but I
do. He's on our side, and I don't think he ever
was as evil as everyone claims. I feel lighter now.
More hopeful. The possibility that Eli is trying to

resist Carrine lifts my spirits. I want to save him. So bad.

Noah waves and disappears out the door. We're right behind him.

Outside, the air is cold and the wind brisk; a fine mist falls, and I pull my hair into a ponytail. Scanning the front of the Crachan's lot, I notice Noah's already disappeared with his group. With Rhine in the lead, we head off.

We run the city for four hours before I notice anything. Seth and I have scaled a row of buildings, and we leap the rooftops as Rhine, Tate, Rob, and Jep jog the sidewalk below. It's just after ten p.m. I stop, listening.

Seth stops, too. The thigh-length leather coat he's wearing conceals as many silver blades as I have on me. A skully keeps his hair plastered down. "What is it?" he asks.

I lift my chin, smell the air, zone all city noises out. Streetlights illuminate side streets, and I cast a glance over the cityscape. Coned turrets and spires from the city center jab the air, and the castle sits light up on the hill, holding sentry over the city.

But something's not right.

"What is it?" Seth asks again. He, too, scans the skyline.

I shake my head, stare at the rooftop under my feet. I close my eyes.

Then I hear it. Not a faint word, but a voice, in my head.

Ah, ma chère. *There you are.* Bon. *I want you to remember something very important*, oui?

My eyes flutter open, then shut again; I'm desperate not to lose what was happening.

"Riley, what's going on?" Seth says at my side. He grabs my chin and forces me to look at him. I do, but I smile, press two fingers to his lips to silence him, and close my eyes.

Yes, ma chère, *there you go. I need your complete concentration to speak with you as such.*

"Mr. Dupré," I say in my head. "You could've just called me on my cell."

Eli's father chuckles. "*Now, what good is having such fine, combined inhuman tendencies if not to use them thusly? My dear girl, I won't keep you long, but I want you to know only this. My son loves you deeply—more than his own existence. Never has he given his heart away to another, since our human life. Only to you. And other than my love for my beloved wife, I've never seen another vampire love so completely. If anyone can dredge him from the hell he is in and save him, it is you, my darling. Remember the blood coursing through you is filled with more than simply Arcos's Strigoi. You have Dupré in you as well. You always will. Bring my son home*, ma chère."

"I will, Mr. Dupré. I swear it," I answer. "I . . . ache inside without him. All the time."

"*Ah, well, that's because he's the other half of your soul*, chère. *You, us, and what we are? It was meant to be. From the very start. Take care now, and stay close to that Miles boy. He'll keep you safe.*"

Strong hands are shaking my shoulders with violent force.

"Riley!" Rhine growls.

I ignore him for a moment more.

"Thanks, Mr. Dupré. Could you please send your other sons to help? Time we start wrapping things up here. I'm so ready to come home. With my fiancé."

"Ah, ma chère, how often must I remind you to call me Gilles? And Eligius's brothers are already on their way. They'll be in Inverness by morn."

"Thanks, Gilles. I promise, I will bring him back safely."

"I've never doubted that you will."

I open my eyes to find Rhine and Seth glaring at me. I smile. "I'm okay, fellas. Just having a little head convo with my future father-in-law." Jake Andorra must have spoken with Eli's father. I pray I can keep my word. I incline my head to the street, where Rhine has been staring holes at me for the last few minutes. "Let's go."

Seth follows me down to the street, finally leaping to the ground. Rhine stares hard at me. "What's up?" he asks.

"We've got a little help coming in the morning," I offer. "For now, take us to the darkest dregs of Inverness."

A knowing gleam shines in Rhine's eyes. "This way," he offers, and turns and heads into the shadows.

With a nod, Seth and I follow Rhine and the other Ness boys into the darkness.

I'm tired of all this bullshit.

I want my fiancé back.

I want that witchpire bitch to turn to dust.

And I want to get the fuck out of here.

Part Eight

※━━◆━━◆━━※

BLOODBATH

You must make your own life amongst the living and, whether you meet fair wind or foul, find your own way to harbor in the end.

— Captain Daniel Gregg,
  The Ghost and Mrs. Muir, 1947

It must be bad if Riley and Noah are sending for us. I don't like it. And Eli must be fucked-up in a serious way. That has to be driving Riley completely insane. There is no one else for Eli except Riley. They're meant to be together. Even in bloodlust, I can't believe he's not tried to get at her. And whatever or whoever is controlling my brother? Vampire, witch—doesn't matter. Dead fucking meat.

—Séraphin Dupré

There really aren't dark seedy dregs in Inverness. The city is pretty clean and kept up. But because Rhine knows the underground fight circuit, as well as which clubs operate from the back room, so to say, he knows a few places to hit. The kind of place that might be harboring a vampire or two. Maybe even Carrine.

I refuse to say Eli's name with hers now. It's totally clear to me that he's being controlled by her; she has some ancient witch power that makes him do what he does. But he proved to me the night before that something in his brain still remembers me. The way he looked at me, as if trying so hard to remember. Despite his bloodred eyes—totally opposite of how he typically is when he turns, which is white eyes with red pinpoint pupils. We'll fix this. Make it right. Once and for all.

One place Rhine knows in particular is tucked away near the outer city limits, in the upper floor of an older apartment building. I've been in places just like it back home. We encountered a place very similar in Charleston, and the vampire fight club.

Sometimes you just can't keep the rotten apples out of the barrel.

Even with the Ness boys around.

By now, I've called Noah and him and his group has joined us. I quickly tell him about my head convo with Gilles, and that Phin and Luc are on their way over now.

Noah nods. "Good. I told Andorra we needed to separate Eli from the female and get him back home to Preacher." He looks at me. "It's going to be one hell of a plane ride back."

"No doubt," I answer, then glance up at the darkened apartment complex. Chunks of sandstone and brick are missing; the window is cracked on the entrance doorway. "We gotta clean this mess up first."

Noah inclines his head. "Ladies first."

I give him a sidelong glance. "You know, I really miss the old Noah."

He quirks an eyebrow. "What old Noah?"

I grin. "You know. The one who used to egg me on in a fight? Remember how proud you were in Charleston when I killed my first newling?" I chuckle. "Remember that nasty fight club we went into there?" I mock-glare at him. "You were ringside, laughing. Cheering me on."

Noah grins. "Yeah. That was before the vow."

My eyes soften at him. "Yeah. I know."

Memories light his silvery eyes, though, and he punches my arm. "That was some crack shootin' in that ring, though, Poe."

I shake my head. "That's what you said then, too."

"I know."

"Ri, you're not fighting tonight, are you?" Seth asks.

I shake my head. "Not if I don't have to."

"These fights move round fair quick," Rhine offers. Seth is standing beside him. "Rough bunch of lads, ya ken? They're in it for the money. An' you dinnae fook wi' their quid."

"I ken," I answer. "Just a quick appearance. Just to see if we can flush her out."

Her meaning Carrine.

We slip into the complex and climb the stairs. Shouts, swearing, and the acrid scent of blood, sweat, and cigarette smoke fill the air in the corridor. The moment we clear the stairwell, I see a large, bald, inked guy standing outside one of the rooms.

I look at him. *Move over and let us in. Don't follow.*

By the time we near him, he glances away, steps aside, and we walk directly into a large room. Dimly lit, smoke filled, and after a quick glance it looks like several rooms gutted out. Fifty humans fill the area, and it's shoulder to shoulder as we all separate and scan the arena.

So far, nothing but humans. Mean, tough-as-shit, fighting humans. But still humans. Music thumps, hard, heavy, and mixes with yells carrying through the room. Two guys fight in the center of a human ring of onlookers. Bare from the waist up, and barefoot, both of their faces already bloodied. Both of equal size, I can barely tell them apart. Both have close-shaven heads. One has a chunk of chain mail inked into his shoulder. There. That's the only difference I can make out.

That same guy lands an elbow punch to the other guy's nose and blood starts spurting. He hits the floor, writhing in pain. He doesn't get up. Cheers fly from the patrons' mouths; money is exchanged.

Then the lights flicker. Several glance upward, to the bare bulbs swinging overhead. One by one, the bulbs crackle and break, until the very last one lighting the room pops out. The room is cast into darkness.

Noah, get my brother out of here.

Too late. The room is filling with newbloods. I can sense them now. Ravenous. Crazed.

I sense her. Carrine.

The screams begin.

Filled with shadows and terror, it's total chaos in the closed-in makeshift arena. I can't see. I can't move. I'm getting knocked from all sides, trapped in a sea of panicking human bodies. Had she followed us here? Followed me here? What's her drive? I'm lost, but one thing I know for sure. I can't let these people die. And my brother is in here. Rhine. Noah. The other Ness boys.

Souls I love and care about.

I brace myself, standing with my legs apart, stiff, and I inhale. I close my eyes, ignore the bodies slamming into me, and push all of my focus, my power, my concentration, to my center. My core. I feel it, burning as if I've swallowed gasoline, followed by a lit match. It scorches me until I throw my hands up and release it.

Before it leaves me, I stop it. Midair. Suspended.

Everyone is still. Frozen. I can't see faces, and I can't see who is who. But I can tell no one is moving.

I focus my words, choose them carefully. *All humans, leave. Now.*

Immediately, bodies start to hustle. Heartbeats have slowed down to normal, and they're all around me. Feet are shuffling out of the door.

After a few moments, I can see how many figures are left. I see Noah's dreads. Beside him, Seth and Rhine. I can plainly tell them from the other four left standing. All males.

And they're vampires.

We're trapped in a dark building with four other vampires.

I feel my control slipping.

"That's because you're weak," a female voice carries to me. "Pathetic and weak."

"What do you want?" I ask Carrine in the dark. She can read my mind. She thinks she can control me. She's got another goddamn think coming.

"Oh, I don't know," she says. "Eli? What do I want?"

My heart drops at his name on her lips.

Silence.

My eyes shift as I wait. Eli's resisting her again. He's getting stronger. My heart soars with hope.

"Eli!" Carrine screams. The sound vibrates within my chest. Makes the fine hairs on my neck stiffen. *Witchpire*. More like banshee in full-blown menopause.

"Her blood, sliding down your throat," my fiancé growls from the shadows. I hear the hesitation, the contempt in his voice. He's fighting her.

Carrine laughs. "Oh, my love, you know me oh so well."

Sickness pools in my stomach. None of this makes sense. My mind whirls as I struggle to hold the other vampires in the room in place. Yet my thoughts race around the fact that there's no good reason Carrine wants me, out of all the blood she can choose from. Why?

I hold my concentration, and I'm straining every internal muscle I have to do it. "Why me?" I ask her.

"Your unique blood could empower me beyond conception," Carrine admits. "I would never have to be under another's control again, like I have been for so many centuries. It's a private hell, a torture I'll no longer endure. Now bring her to me," she commands.

I see his figure weaving between the dead-still bodies of my loved ones, and the other four vampires. I know his swagger, no matter that it's bloodlust driven. Eli's fiery gaze lights on me, close. He pauses, those bloodred eyes fixated on mine.

A blinding light accompanies a sonic boom, and we're separated, all of us knocked backward. The light remains, and the bodies are stirring. Eli stands before me, confusion darkening his reddened eyes. I duck beneath him, pulling my blades, and by the time I reach Carrine I've left three of the rogue vampires convulsing on the floor.

Carrine's eyes flash the tiniest bit of fear; then she laughs, swipes her hand out, and another boom knocks me backward. I land on my backside and skid hard. The wall stops me, stuns me for a second.

The light is still blaring when I look up. There is no sign of Carrine and Eli.

Seth takes out the rogue who lunges at him, driving a silver blade deep into its heart.

And standing in the center of the room is someone I don't expect.

It's not my light, my boom that just chased away Carrine.

My eyes blink, and I walk toward Athios.

A once-fallen angel. Now condemned to . . . something. Somewhere. I'm not entirely sure what. He's nothing short of breathtaking. Tall. Elegant, yet very masculine. The white long-sleeved linen shirt pulls at his broad shoulders and grips his biceps. Thick, muscular thighs are encased by perfectly tailored dove gray slacks. Long silvery blond hair hangs straight past his shoulders, and he wears it pulled half back and secured with a silver clip. His eyes are nearly the same color as his hair, a shade darker maybe. Silvery. Not mercury, like Noah's. He's . . . beautiful.

"I've no' much time," Athios says, and grasps my shoulders. His eyes fall on my face, and he pulls me to him in a tight embrace. I allow it. He kisses my temple and pushes me gently back. "Forgive me for that. I cannot help myself. And it pleases me that you think me beautiful. Not that it does me any good in the long run."

"Believe it or not, I'm so glad to see you. What are you doing here?" I ask him. Noah, Seth, and Rhine have joined me.

"Your skills are no' honed enough," he says to me. "And I couldna allow her to kill you, Riley."

I give a short laugh. "Well, thank you for that," I say.

"You've got to lure them," Athios says quickly. "Back into the realm. There, you must kill Carrine. She is no' here naturally."

I look at him, his pure illumination making his face chiseled, beautiful in the shadows. "What do you mean?"

"Valerian Arcos," Noah answers for him. "Am I right?"

Athios spares Noah a glance. "You are." He looks back at me, and his eyes soften. "I couldna see it before, clearly. But I finally broke through Carrine's mind. She had a fiercely guarded charm protecting it, but I saw. Valerian has resurrected Carrine. But she's far more powerful than even Arcos suspected."

"She was a witch, aye? As well as a bloodsucker?" Rhine asks.

Athios faces Rhine. "Aye, a lethal combination."

Rhine slides a glance to me.

"Valerian Arcos encountered Carrine centuries ago. The dark evil she delved in as a witch rivals that of the Black Fallen. Combined with her beauty, she became an obsession for Valerian." He glances at everyone, then back to me. "Even back then, the magic controlled her. Nothing mattered more to her. She convinced Valerian to change her—that the combined powers of a witch and a vampire would leave them invincible. Like now, she grew too greedy. Valerian entombed her. But . . ." Athios strokes my chin with his knuckles. "You rise above all of that. Your blood, Riley. Your DNA. It's like a moth to light for Valerian Arcos. He felt she, of all souls, could be the one to defeat you. But Arcos didna count on Carrine's lust for power to overcome her. She's an ancient, with Pict blood and dark magic coursing through her. She hungers now for your unique and powerful blood, Riley," Athios continues. "She is overpowering Arcos. She's using her witchery to fight against him, even though he's been commanding her. She's breaking free."

"What about Eli?" I ask. I grasp his hands. "Please, Athios."

His profound stare sinks straight through me.

"It's because of my love for you that I cannot see you suffer," he claims. "Whilst Carrine is strong, Eli is, also, extremely powerful. He's resisted killing innocents. But Carrine has fed him. Her victims. She's shared, and their blood has inevitably turned him into full bloodlust." Athios's eyes soften. "Valerian is forbidden to kill Eli. Which is why he's engaged Carrine into trying to force you to do the deed. You were lured here by the killing of innocents. Carrine has beckoned the rogues, and has turned a few newbloods herself. You must lure them both—Carrine and Eli—into the realm, and be prepared for a fight. You have to kill her in there, and 'twill no' be an easy task tae accomplish. She will have all of her faculties about her, Riley. But you'll also have yours as well. You're as strong as she. And you must kill her." He looks hard at me. "And leave your love inside."

"Leave Eli inside the realm?" I ask.

"Until you kill Arcos." Athios glances up. "I must go. 'Tisna safe. For any of us." He kisses me again, briefly, and nods. "Until—" he says.

The light snuffs out, and we're alone once more.

"Why does everyone love you so much, Riley?" Rhine asks in the shadows. "Have you bewitched every male around you?"

"Nah," I answer, and I'm searching for the way out. "It's the ink."

Noah chuckles. "This way, Poe," he says.

We find our way out of the darkened complex

and run the streets until dawn. Now that I know Carrine, originally controlled by Valerian Arcos, has been pulling away from his control. Causing the disturbances in the city without his command.

And Eli is trapped in the middle.

All because of some insane obsession Valerian Arcos has with me? Rather, my blood. That's the trigger. Not me, Riley, the person. Arcos doesn't know me. He doesn't know that I love *The Goonies*, can quote most of *Young Guns*, and like to bake. He doesn't know me at all. It's all warped and twisted around my dumb-ass blood. He's always wanted it, even while entombed in Savannah, before he and Vic were set free. And now that my DNA has Strigoi and Black Fallen traits, he's insane with wanting it. He'll never get it.

Some of the other Ness boys had called it quits earlier. Jobs. Real life. I'm pretty impressed they're all juggling it so well. So organized, for such a young group of humans. Males at that. The rest of us, Rhine included, encountered a few stray rogues Carrine had set upon us earlier. Two more innocents had died while we fucked around in that complex. We ran until we flushed them out. One male, one female. Rhine shocks me with his speed and accuracy with the silver. The Inverness police were already busy at the scenes, and by the time they find the vampiric remains, they see it as nothing more than little piles of ash. It's all over the news, and even in the café we stop in to grab coffee, it's the talk of the shop. Serial killer running amok in Inverness.

People are scared. I can smell their fear.

"You look tired, Ri," my brother says as we walk up the sidewalk. He drapes an arm over my shoulder. The people of Inverness are hustling about, going to work, school, getting on with their lives.

"Yeah, I'm feeling it," I answer, and meet Seth's worried gaze. "How you holding up, bro?"

Seth ducks his head. "Holdin'. Riggs told me to tell you he misses you," he says with a grin. "Zetty, too. And of course Preacher and Estelle, and Nyx." He scratches his head. "And all of the Duprés, I guess." He chuckles. "Pretty much everyone."

With a sigh, I lay my head on my brother's shoulder. "I miss them all, too." Sliding an arm around his waist, I squeeze. "I've missed you most, though."

Seth kisses the top of my head. "I've missed you, too, sis. All this will be over soon. It'll be right again. I know it."

"Gosh, you two are just so darn sweet," Noah says from behind us.

Rhine chuckles.

Suddenly, the hair on the back of my neck bristles. My gaze lifts, away from the sidewalk I'm walking on, and it cuts across the street.

Nothing.

But everything inside me screams *Eli*. He's watching me, curious.

Back at the Crachan, I shower, change, and in thirty minutes meet the others downstairs. I'm starting to wind down, feel weary, but I want to go with Seth, Noah, and Rhine to pick up Eli's brothers at the airport. I've missed them. And, I confess, there's some comfort in having Luc and Phin close. Almost like having a piece of Eli with me.

We take two Rovers, and I ride with Rhine. Although the sun is hidden, the gray-white of daylight is bright. He wears a dark pair of shades as he weaves through the streets to Inverness's airport. Noah and Seth follow behind us in the other Rover.

"I can go wi' you, ya know," Rhine says. "Inside the realm." His gaze is straight ahead, on the road, but I can tell by the clenching of his jaw that he's worried.

"It's too dangerous," I tell him. "You're strong, and fast as hell with the silver." I cover his hand with mine. "But no way could you keep up in there. I'd constantly be worried about what you were doing instead of concentrating on what I had to do."

An amused grin lifts one side of his mouth. "You worry about me, Poe?"

I punch his arm. "Hell yeah, I worry."

I can't see his eyes behind the shades, but his mouth gives it all away. He full-out grins. "That makes me sor' o' feel like a baby. Havin' a lass worry o'er me so much."

Rhine's accent is heavy, and at times I have to

concentrate on what he's saying to get the meaning. "Get used to it," I say. "It's what I do. Ask
anyone who knows me."

Rhine hits the volume to the radio, and a tune
filters through the speakers of the Rover. His
gravelly, unique voice overtakes the artist's, and
he claims the song. I listen, amazed, and when
he pulls into a parking spot and shoves the Rover
into park, I smile at him. "I think I could listen to
you sing for hours," I admit. "You've got to send
me some music when I leave."

Rhine takes off his shades, and green eyes
study me. "I'm gonna hate tae see you go."

I shake my head. "You probably say that to all
your band groupies."

Opening the door, he steps out. "Only tae you."

Noah and Seth join us, and together the four
of us hurry into the small airport to await Phin
and Luc's flight. It's on time, thankfully, and just
hit the tarmac. I stand, staring out of the huge
Plexiglas overlooking the runway, and watch
other planes land and take off. Memories assault
me, and I can't help tracing time back to the day
I first met the Dupré family. The first time I un-
derstood that vampires existed. Luc and Phin
were both so eager to show off their skills. I remember how they leaped like frogs on crack
across Gilles's parlor. Scared the holy shit out of
me back then. Cracks me up to think about it
now. Seems like I've known them all for years.
Eli? Forever.

"Hey, come on outta there," Noah says by my

side. "Before you start bawling all over the airport." He drops his arm over my shoulders and gives me a shake. "Look at Luc and Phin. They're tripping over each other to get to you first."

My memory of Eli and our first official introduction simmers inside me as I focus on the present, and Eli's two younger brothers pushing past each other and the passengers filing out. Each has a duffel swung over his shoulder. Phin's dark blond buzz cut and black shades stand in contrast with his perfect pale skin. Luc, whose hair is longer, brushing the collar of his black leather jacket, has a wide white smile. Both are making a beeline straight to me. When they reach me, they drop their duffels in unison. Phin reaches me first, throws his arms around my waist, and picks me off the floor. I fall into his embrace and squeeze.

"Jesus Christ, Poe," he mutters against my neck. "I've missed the holy hell outta you!"

A wash of emotion hits me, and I breathe in his familiar scent. "I've missed you, too."

In the next instant, I'm pulled directly out of Phin's arms and am now enveloped into Luc's strong embrace. "Sis," he says against my hair. He's a little quieter than the rowdy Phin, and his French accent is a little stronger. Every feeling he has rushes through me, too. He pulls back and kisses me on the cheek. The trademark Dupré cerulean blue eyes stare down at me, so much like Eli's it almost hurts to see them. "It's not been the same without you guys around."

Phin laughs. "It's been flat-out boring as hell at home without you."

Luc kisses my cheek once more. "That is for Gilles and Elise. They miss you terribly."

I stare into his gaze. "We'll all be home soon."

Noah and Seth exchange manly bro shakes and side hugs with Eli's brothers, and then introductions are made between the Duprés and Rhine, and we make our way through the semi-crowd of people filing out of baggage claim.

As we leave the building, I'm sandwiched between Eli's brothers, each with an arm draped over my shoulders. We cross the parking lot, and at the Rovers, Phin doesn't let me go. He inclines his head to the backseat, and we climb in. Luc shoots him a glare and then jumps in the front with Rhine. We head back to the Crachan, and by the time we arrive, I've updated Luc and Phin on all the events to date in Inverness. They are not surprised when I tell them Valerian Arcos is behind it all, and that he resurrected Carrine to control Eli, making me believe my only choice was to kill him. Fury makes their eyes turn dark, and I know that if Valerian makes the mistake of showing back up, he won't survive.

And that, of course, will start an epic war between the vampire families.

They needed to stand in line, though. I've already had fanciful visions of shoving silver into Valerian's heart myself.

Luc and Phin are completely impressed with Rhine and the Ness boys' work in the city, and by the time Rhine pulls into the drive, they're pretty much up to speed.

Noah and Seth join us, and we all walk in. Pete is squatting down in front of the hearth, stoking a roaring fire. Two other Ness boys are plopped onto chairs, eating bowls of cereal. I'm pretty sure, by the furtive glances Pete and the others pass Luc and Phin when they're introduced, they're freaked out by their houseful of vampires.

We sit on the sofa, Luc and Phin on either side of me. Noah and Seth fall into chairs. Rhine throws himself down in front of the hearth, onto the floor.

We discuss our next move.

"If Carrine is everything you say she is," Phin says, rubbing his buzz-cut head, "she'll know when you try to get to St. Bueno's to fill those cartridges."

"That's why me and a few of the other lads should go alone," Rhine offers. "She'll focus on you, Riley." He inclines his head to Luc and Phin. "And on you."

"He's right," Noah agrees. He looks at Rhine. "You've got to do this now." He inclines his head to me. "The longer she waits, the stronger Carrine becomes."

"Why do you have to go in alone, Ri?" Seth asks. His green eyes are hazy with worry. "I don't get it."

"Well," I answer my baby brother, "our theory is, since Carrine was a powerful witch before she became a vampire, she can manipulate inside the realm. I saw a piece of it before." I smile at him wryly. "What if she, I don't know"—I incline my head to Luc—"manipulated him to act against me?" I shake my head, the thought making me sick inside. "I couldn't face having to fight one of you."

"Well, I for one am dying to see this scatha of yours," Phin says. He looks at Rhine. "When will you leave?"

"The sooner the better," Rhine says in his brogue. He glances at me. "An' from the looks o' it, lads, Riley here is about tae crash."

I focus on the handsome young Scotsman, and realize my vision has in fact gone blurry.

"Yeah, look at that goofy look on her face," Phin says, leaning back and staring at me. He lifts his hand in front of me. "How many fingers am I holding up?"

I stare. "One. And your mother would beat you if she saw that," I say.

I am feeling weary, though. "I'd feel better if Seth went with Rhine and the others," I mumble, and lay my head over onto Luc's shoulder. "Make sure at least . . . eight of you go, huh?" I try to focus on Rhine, but his face has become distorted. My eyelids grow heavier and heavier.

"Och, there she goes," Rhine says, his voice fainter now. His voice sounds like he's talking from a concrete tunnel.

"I'll take her up," Noah says, his voice even fainter. "You boys will find some V8 in the fridge."

I feel my body go weightless as Noah leans down and slides his arms under my knees and shoulders, lifting me into the air. The room is spinning as he's taking me upstairs, and I concentrate on his features to keep from becoming dizzy. "There's gotta be a way to fix this narcolepsy," I mumble. "Don't like it."

My head rests against Noah's chest, and his deep rumble vibrates against my ear as he chuckles. "None of us like it, Ri. It's dangerous." He stares down at me. "We'll get Preach to figure something out once we get home."

We're moving down the corridor now, and I feel like I'm floating, Noah's movements are so fluid and graceful.

"Why, thank you, ma'am," he says, grinning. His white teeth flash in the shadowy hallway as he makes his way to my room.

"Key's in my pocket," I mumble.

The slight pressure of his fingers slipping into my back pocket keeps me focused. He unlocks my door, and we ease inside. When he lowers me to my bed, he pulls off my boots, unfastens my leather holster, and pushes the straps over my shoulders and sets it aside. His hands search for blades, find them, and set them on the bedside table. Silver free, he pushes me back and pulls the woolen plaid blanket up to my chin. He tucks me in.

Through my fading consciousness, I grin and ease my hand out from beneath the wool. I graze his cheek. "Thanks, Noah. What would I do without you?"

The room is gray and shadowy, but I can still see his face. With his hands, he grasps both sides of my face, lowers his mouth to mine, and kisses me gently. I'm conscious enough to know it's not a sexual gesture—surprising, since it's coming from Noah. When he lifts his head, the mercury silver of his eyes soften. "You won't ever have to find out, darlin'."

I turn my head into my pillow and the weightiness of sleep lulls me in. "I'm going to tell Eli you kissed me like that," I manage to mutter. "He's gonna kick your ass."

Noah's soft chuckle is the last thing I hear. "He'll understand completely."

Then I'm swallowed up in shadows. In my sleep, unavoidable memories assault me as I lie here helpless. Memories of Eli. The first time he touched me. The first time I had him inside me . . . and the first time he told me he loved me.

"Tell me."

My eyes flutter open, and I'm no longer in my bedroom at the Crachan. I'm . . . nowhere. In darkness. Suspended in weightless pitch. But the voice I know. I should be fearful, but I'm not. It's Eli.

"I saw you through my storefront window, back home," I say.

"Where's that?" he asks.

"Savannah. You're one of the city's guardians, Eli. You and your brothers, Luc and Phin. Your little sister, Josie. And your parents. Gilles and Elise." I sigh, and it hurts my chest.

"Guardians for what?" he asks.

"*Against rogue vampires. You keep the humans safe, Eli.*"

At first, he's silent. Several moments pass. "*I want to know more about . . . you.*"

I blink back tears, but I'm in sheer darkness and can't even tell if they fall onto a surface. I'm suspended, like floating on a cloud. "*I'm your fiancée, Eli. We've . . . been through a lot together. You've saved my life more than once.*"

"*What about . . . us?*" Eli inquires. I can tell he's treading on treacherous ground. He's curious. Not trusting. Unsure of himself. Of me.

"*Can you touch me in here?*" I ask. "*In this place?*"

He pauses. "*Oui.*"

My insides are shaking like crazy. "*Come here, then.*"

I can't see him; don't see him move. But I feel a shift in atmosphere, and in the next instant, Eli's here, in front of me. "*Be still,*" I command. "*Don't move.*"

"*Not . . . safe,*" he mutters. I can tell he's losing control.

"*You won't hurt me,*" I say. I'm not completely sure of that, but I can't help trying this. I lift both my hands, and my palms grasp his firm, stubbled jaw. Energy radiates from him, and fear rolls off him in waves. I pull his head down, closer to mine. Gently, I press my lips to his.

The moment of contact feels like lightning. The current that surges through me, through Eli, is palpable. Energy pings through every nerve ending, shooting down my legs, out of my arms, and harboring in *my core. I gasp, and he does, too. I kiss him gently, and in that kiss, I show Eli every raw emotion I possess. All for him. At first, he holds dead still. He's so still I wonder if he's ready to sink his fangs into my flesh. To kill me. To lose his will to fight.*

Then, hesitantly, he kisses me back.

Although I can't see him, he's everywhere. His lips move almost shyly against mine, as though it's a teenage boy's first kiss. Endearing. Heartfelt. And I drink him in.

I press my body toward his, seeking comfort. The comfort of Eli.

"Get away from her, Eli," Carrine's voice interrupts.

Eli goes still, but his lips remain against mine.

A surge of power fills the weightless space we're suspended in, and her bansheelike scream fills my body.

"Move!"

Fear and instinct make me force the energy building from my core out of my limbs, and now I'm hurling through the darkness, so fast I'm dizzy. . . .

"Calme, l'un a peint enbas," a voice says gently. A hand grips my shoulder. "Riley, wake up."

My eyes flutter open. Phin is staring down at me, the lamplight spilling over his chiseled features as he studies me. I smile. "Painted One. I haven't heard that one in a while." He'd said *quiet down, Painted One.* Something Eli had said to me. It's what the Gullah and the Guardians all call me. Painted One. Because of my ink. That seems like such a long, long time ago.

"You were . . . dreaming," Phin says with a half-cocked grin. "I'm pretty sure it was of my brother—ow!" Phin rubs his forehead where I've just thumped him.

Although I'm joking at first, my humor fades and is quickly replaced by an almost . . . panic. Pain. Dread. "Phin, I miss him." My eyes sting from tears. "I have to get him back. Just then, he was trying to remember me. Us. Our life before all of this."

Phin traces the inked wing at the corner of my eye. "He will, sis." His mouth tilts in a grin. "My brother's will is stronger than you think. And his love for you is a powerful thing. I gotta say, though. He's one lucky bastard."

I roll my eyes and push the tears from my cheeks. "That's borderline perverted of you to pitch a tent in my dreams about your brother. My fiancé, don't forget."

Phin shudders. "I didn't stay long." He eyes me. "I just wanted to make sure you were okay. At first, you were calm. Then you started to freak out. So I woke you. You've not been sleeping that long. Less than fourteen hours." He pushes my hair back, picks up a fuchsia strand, rubs it between his fingers. "Think you can make it, *chère*?"

I push up on my elbows and stretch. "Yeah, I'm ready to get on with it. Did Rhine and Seth and the guys get the cartridges filled?"

Phin nods. "*Oui*." He reaches down and pulls up the scatha, and grins. "I couldn't wait. This thing is sick."

Luc pokes his head in the door. "You woke her?" he asks, eyeing his sibling.

"It's a good thing I did," Phin says, grinning at Luc's puzzled expression. I slap his arm. He holds the scatha up to his brother. "Check it out."

The bed sags as the other Dupré brother sits down. He grasps the weapon and turns it over, thoroughly inspecting it. I tell them of Edinburgh, and how two ancient knights—one a once-Earthbound angel to boot—taught the WUP team how to properly use a broadsword. Both were now completely mortal, but badass to the bone and a wealth of knowledge. "Gawan told us where to find the mystical sacred water to fill the cartridges." I reach over to the medieval-designed crossbow and show them where the cartridges load. They both watch on in interest. Phin's buzz cut and Luc's fashionably longer-haired heads both bent over the scatha. "And he instructed me to seek out the alternative realm there. I want this to be over. I . . . need Eli back."

Both of Eli's brothers look up, understanding and love making their eyes glassy. Luc grabs my shoulder and squeezes. "I know, sis. We'll get him."

I lean my head against Phin's shoulder. "It's so easy sometimes to just want to . . . walk away. Be normal." I incline my head toward the window. "Like them. Everyday people, going about their daily lives without a clue. Ignorant." I inhale Phin's unique scent. His vampiric scent. Reminds me of a cedar fire. "I want to be ignorant sometimes. But that's so damn selfish. I hate even thinking it."

Luc ducks his head. "We'll get him, *ma chère*," he says. "I vow it."

Then, at once, I stiffen. Luc and Phin feel it, too, because both of their backs go straight, and Luc stands and walks to the window.

"Something's not right," I say, and I kick out of the covers and stand. A draft catches the skin on my legs, and I glance down, not remembering Noah taking off my pants. I spy them at the foot of the bed, and I hastily shove my legs into them. Grabbing my boots, I sit on the bed and yank them on, too. I'm crossing the room now, and I find my silver holster and shrug into it, stuffing blades in all their proper places. When I'm finished, I leave the leather halter I'm wearing in place, forgo the jacket, and hurry to the window. Next to Luc I stand, peering out. Shadows shift, stretch.

Movement. Above us, below us.

A sinking feeling crashes over me. Familiar. Terrifying.

"This place is surrounded," Phin says, peering over my head. "Fucking bloodsuckers."

It barely registers in my head that my soon-to-be brother-in-law, who is a vampire, is calling other vampires bloodsuckers. The Gullah would be so proud.

"Luc, take the stairs. Tell Noah and the others what's going down," I say, pushing up the window as easy as I can. "Phin?" I stick my leg out, straddling the sill, and make eye contact with Luc. "Watch Rhine and my brother," I ask. "Please."

"You know I will," Luc says, and he disappears from my room. I give Phin a silent nod, and he's blurring with rage. Pulling my legs up, I grasp the ledge and push hard. My body flips upward and I land on the roof. Crouching, I search the darkness. Phin lands beside me, and together we move over the top of the Crachan, keeping low.

I see them.

It's almost too many to believe.

It'll be a goddamn bloodbath.

Just then they swarm. From the wood, the surrounding trees, the street. And at the same time, Noah, Luc, Seth, Rhine, and the Ness boys fill the Crachan's courtyard.

Like a medieval war, both sides charge.

Without waiting for Phin, I leap down, draw a blade, and jump in. Just as I land, I'm grabbed, and as curses and screams fill the air, I'm forcefully dragged into the shadows.

Part Nine

CHAOS

We're gonna need a bigger boat.

—Sheriff Martin Brody, Jaws, 1975

Of course I fucking love her. What kind of a dumb-ass question is that?

—Noah Miles, when asked if he loves Riley Poe

A strong, rock-hard biceps is wrapped around my throat, dragging me back into the shadows behind the Crachan. His familiar scent, burned deep into my memory and sensory, hits me in waves. So much that, for a second, I'm powerless to defend myself. Powerless to escape. It's tempting to just let him drag me off and do . . . whatever.

At least it's him. Eligius. And for a split second, we're together.

Eli goes stone-dead still, turns, and looks down at me. He hesitates. In the half shadows, I see his face. Conflict and confusion war in the depths of his red eyes.

I stretch my hand out to graze his jaw. "Eli—"

Oh no, you don't, Riley. Fight. Get away from him. He's not your love right now. He's your enemy. Run. Now. Or all chances of saving him are gone.

Athios's words hit me in the gut; it doesn't take much. I'm not suicidal, or so awash with grief that I don't want to survive in this chaotic world I live in without Eli. The faces of Seth, my

Gullah family, the Duprés, Noah, Rhine—they all flash before me.

I focus, forcing all of my energy to my core, and when it gathers, builds, and then explodes, Eli is thrown back. I don't turn around, and I don't stop to wonder where he was thrown to. I run. Haul ass, straight for the back entrance of the Crachan.

I've got to get the scatha.

Carrine's voice catches my ear. "Go after her, imbecile!"

I know what I've got to do.

When I reach the door, it's partially open and I hurry inside. The lights are out, and darkness and shadows stretch and distort my surroundings in a building I'm already not overly familiar with. I'm in the kitchen, and the sounds of the fight outside waft in from several broken windows. I push the thoughts and visions aside and make my way to the staircase.

I'm not alone.

Eli's right behind me. There's no use in hiding from him. I know he can sense me, smell me, just like I can him. On my way through the hall, I grab an iron poker from the hearth, leap over the sofa, and dash for the stairs. Just as I reach them, my arm is grabbed.

Eli has a tight grip on my wrist.

Without hesitation, I swing the iron poker and clobber him. His head snaps to the side, and his grip loosens just enough for me to break free. I run. Through the darkness, I take comfort in knowing that, no matter how hideous it sounded and looked, that iron poker didn't do anything to my fiancé except stun him for a second.

It's not like I poked him with silver.

I'm running up the corridor to my room when I'm slammed into and I hit the wall. A newling. Female. Face distorted, ragged teeth dropped and snapping at me.

I drop the iron poker, yank a blade from a sheath, and ram it into her heart. As she falls, I leap over her and into my room. Grab my scatha off the bed where Luc left it, and just as I'm slipping the newly packed duffel filled with cartridges over my head, Eli grabs me and yanks me around. His grip is tight. And I've dropped my nonsilver weapon.

He starts to drag me now, back toward the door. Eli's eyes are bloodred, his expression blank. He's wearing a black T-shirt, and his biceps bulge as he yanks me hard. My heart plummets; confusion webs my brain, and part of me wants to scream, wrap my arms around his neck, and kiss him, or hit him, until he wakes the *fuck* up! Recognizes me!

"Eli! Please!" I holler.

For a split second, he hesitates. His grip is still tight, but he stops. Studies me. And confusion flashes in his eyes.

I don't waste time. Instead, I focus my energy. It's happening faster now. I'm gaining more control over my Fallen powers. In the next second, Eli is tossed across the room. I'm stunned at the force and exactness of my powers, but I don't hang around. I head straight for the window and leap out.

At the bottom, I land, crouched, and in the middle of . . . chaos. There's fighting all around me, Ness boys fighting vampires. Blood. Piles of quivering dead newlings. I catch sight of Noah, and Seth and Rhine are close by.

He turns and sees me, then glances up.

Eli lands behind me, and I take off. I head straight for Rhine, and he doesn't even look at me as he reaches into his pocket and throws me the key to his bike. I catch it and keep running, and I jump the last few feet and land, straddling his bike, jam the key in, and hit the engine. Just as Eli nears, I peel out down the drive. No time for a helmet. Eli's on foot, right behind me. So close I can hear his grunts in my ear.

I run over two vamp bodies, and hit another one as he surges toward me; then I skid out into the street and take off. Vehicles are sparse, but still on the road, along with trash cans and plastic recycle bins as I nudge my way through and make it to the bridge. I glance over my shoulder; Eli no longer follows on foot.

But I know he and Carrine will follow me.

It's me she wants.

And I fucking want her.

I hit the A-9 and let the throttle out. I'm heading for Dingwall, Ivy Cottage, and the standing stones. I'm going into the realm.

And I know Carrine and Eli will follow me.

I squint against the frigid Highland wind pelting into my eyes. In my rearview mirror, I see a single headlight. It's growing closer. Faster. I look straight ahead and pray Rhine's bike can outrun the one behind me.

The one carrying Eli and Carrine.

As I fly through Strathpeffer, then Dingwall, I'm pushing the bike to its limit. It's pretty fast, and I'm relieved I don't have to take the time to convince a local cop not to chase me down. Luckily, the cars are few and far between, and by the time I'm heading out of Dingwall and up the steep incline next to the car dealership, there are no cars at all. Ducking my head against the wind, I fly toward Ivy Cottage. At the drive's entrance, I hit the brakes and skid sideways, coming to a stop. Kickstand down, I grab the key, stuff it in my pocket, and take off up the drive on foot. There's a light in the living room of the crofter's house, and I'm hoping he didn't hear or see Rhine's bike. It's dark, and clouds obscure most of the moonlight. But I know where I'm going, and I rush past Ivy Cottage at the top of the hill, jump the sheep's fence by the barn, and tear up the path toward the stones. In the distance behind me, I hear the roar of another motorcycle.

I'm running top speed through dead gorse and heather, the big prickly clumps catching my boots so much that I have to take large leaps to get over them without falling. Higher I climb, and before long, the moon slides out of the clouds, and the silhouettes of the stones rise before me. I stop, looking around me as I reach into my duffel, grab a handful of cartridges, and quickly load the scatha. I snap the lever in place and, without a glance backward, step into the stones.

The air shifts around me; a mist gathers and swirls up, crawling higher and winding around my legs and my torso and obscuring my vision. Then it begins to thin out, before me. Here, time is lost, from the world I just left, and this one. It's unpredictable, and I might as well not hurry. I'll fuck up if I hurry, and this is not the time for a fuckup. What I want is coming. Eventually. And I have patience this time. My head is clear. My will is stronger than it has ever been. And I have control.

I'm facing a slight incline: a hill, with a path walked smooth. I follow it, and notice a black iron gate ahead. As I walk, my fingers tighten around the scatha; my pack is slung over one shoulder. My arms are bare in my leather halter top, and yet the cold doesn't bother me at all. Walking through the gate, I descend stone steps embedded into the cliffside, and at the bottom, a long, barren street. Abandoned cars line the curb on either side, tires flat, windows broken out, doors and trunks open. At the end of the street, another pair of tall black gates. A cemetery. I'm walking down the center of the street, unwilling to get too close to the buildings on either side. Some have doors; others have black, cavernous mouths. No way am I getting close enough to those, so I stay walking straight down the middle of the street. My gaze roves back and forth, up and down, searching. The building has no glass in the windows. No drapes. No lights. The lone *click-clack* of my black leather heeled boots against the paved street makes echoes in the silence, the solitude.

Only then do I see eyes staring at me from the shadowy windows and doorways.

Dozens and dozens of them. Red. Unblinking.

Then music. I hear it, coming from some back room in the building beside me. I glance over, the top-floor window glassless and dark, and the music grows louder. Billy Idol. "White Wedding."

Then the eyes disappear, and a rustling, scratching noise begins, growing louder and louder, and then out of the doors and windows pours dozens and dozens—maybe hundreds—of cats. They crawl atop the abandoned cars and line the streets, and their eyes follow me as I walk, as Billy's voice carries out through the upper window.

Cats? Am I really going to have to blast cats?

They don't set one paw in the street; they stick to the curb. And as I slowly pass them by, they crack open their mouths and smile, their little cat lips pulling back over complete, perfect sets of human teeth.

They're not moving toward me, not rushing me. Not attacking me. So I continue on my way to the large iron cemetery arch at the end of the street.

Then one solitary cat yawns, and its mouth widens to a disproportionate size: a big black jagged, gaping hole that takes up most of its head.

And it screams.

At once, they all stand on their hind legs, straight up, and join in the screaming. They look like some discombobulated Meerkat Manor of the alternative world, and the minute they launch at me, I take off. I run, hesitating to use my cartridges on a bunch of fucking big-mouthed cats.

The first one latches on to my hip, and those human teeth drop long and sharp and sink into my flesh. With my free hand I grab it by the scruff and fling it off, but it's soon replaced by another, and another, and now they're all lunging at me from their curbside perches. It's the first time Billy Idol has ever, ever annoyed me.

I now have hundreds of vampire cats flying through the air and attacking me.

I focus, zero in on them, envision in my head a room filled with cats, and I release my energy. The shock wave rocks them all back, sends them flying against the buildings. I run top speed to the iron gates in front of me. Glancing over my shoulder, I see the cats are dazed, but shaking their heads and watching me. Then they run after me. I hurry.

The moment my feet cross the cemetery's threshold, the cats disappear. I breathe a quick sigh of relief that A: I didn't have to blow a cat away. And B: I still have all of my cartridges.

As I glance around, the cemetery shifts, and tall Celtic crosses bend unnaturally to the side and back, and the marble statues, blackened with age, begin to move, walk, drag themselves toward me like stone zombies. Cemetery. Bad choice, Poe.

Only choice. Consecrated ground. Sanctuary. Better than out in the open, with rabid vamp cats throwing themselves at my throat. I hurry.

Just as I think, *Where the hell is Carrine?* she appears. Slipping from behind a leaning crypt, she emerges. She's wearing clothes similar—no, almost identical—to mine. Tall black boots, leather low-riders, leather halter. Her hair is down, and her eyes are bloodred. Behind her, Eli stands still, watching me. Silent. Silent, but seething in bloodlust. Bloodlust and . . . confusion. He's fighting her. I can tell it, sense it, feel it. I can feel it where I stand. But will he be able to withstand the brunt of her power if she enforces it? Jesus, I don't want to kill my beloved.

"Are you wondering if we just followed you here for the hell of it?" Carrine says to me. She smiles and lifts her hand, pulls Eli's mouth to hers, and traces his lips with her tongue. She looks at me, slightly shaking her head. "Hardly."

I don't speak. I just watch. I know now that Eli is heavily under her spell. He doesn't know what he's doing. And that eases the pain somewhat. My forefinger flips the lever on the scatha, and my palm tightens the grip. I wait. I can't hit Eli with my aim.

Carrine laughs. "You'll hit nothing with that toy, silly girl." With a swipe of her hand, she sends my scatha flying. The force of her power knocks me back several feet, and I slide against the gravel and rock, slamming into a gravestone. I shake my head, dazed, but I stand. Carrine slowly walks toward me, taking long, exaggerated runway model steps.

I jump up, face her. She looks at me, first at the ink at my cheek, then at my dragon tails down my arm. Her gaze lifts to mine. "Pity to waste such a . . . unique shell," she says. "But your blood is much more important. It's something I must have, you see. To add to mine." The smile that stretches over her face chills me. "You canna conceive the power your blood and mine combined will produce. It's almost . . . erotic, the thought of it—"

I swing with my fist and catch her jaw. Her head rocks to the side, and she snaps her gaze back to mine. She smiles, but her face is contorted with hate.

In the next breath, she morphs, and she's ugly as holy fucking hell. Her face shakes and blurs, then elongates; jaws unhinge, and her teeth drop from her bleeding gums in long jagged shanks. Her mouth resembles the cats': disproportionate and taking up a lot of her face space.

With as much energy as I can focus, I turn and roundhouse kick her in the mouth. Carrine spins, and when she is righted, her foot is airborne and catches me in the shoulder. I stumble, and she's lunging toward me, teeth snapping together, coming an inch from my throat. I fall against a crypt and slam her body against it, once, twice. She lets go, and I turn and dive for my scatha. My fingers touch it, but Carrine grabs my ankles and she flings me away from it. I roll, and she hits the ground I just vacated. Leaping up, she faces me. We're both crouched, eyes trained on each other. Slowly, we circle.

"You won't survive me, Riley Poe. I thought I'd never escape that hell Valerian entombed me in." She laughs, but her gaze is locked solid on to mine. "Much to my surprise, he set me free. Thought his power over me was enough to make me obey his commands." She laughs again. "What a foolish, selfish little prick he is."

"What do you know? We finally agree on something," I say.

I stare at Carrine, her lips pulled back into some weird catlike gaping-hole-of-a-mouth specter as an unfamiliar language pours from her lips. A curse? Black magic? I don't know, and I honestly don't give a damn. Forcing all of my energy to the center of my body, I draw a deep breath, pulling the energy from my core to my fingertips. I . . . throw it at her.

And her arms rise, too, and her energy is thrown right the hell back at me.

Together we stand, our energy forces colliding in an electric punch, and I can feel her severe witchpireness. It's strong. Tough as shit.

But she doesn't have a fiancé. A life. A family.

Somewhere deep inside me, it all collides together, and like a tornado it rips from my body. Carrine is flung back, far, and her body crashes against a contorted Celtic cross.

I dive toward the scathe, palm it, and roll to my back. Carrine is in the air, almost upon me.

I fire. Direct hit, right in the heart.

Carrine's scream pierces the air as her body bursts into shards, and by the time the pieces hit the cemetery ground, they've turned to dust. It's like a volcanic ash fallout.

My body is thrown to the ground, and my head hits hard. Stunned and shaken, I take a second or two to realize Eli has moved. He stares down at me now, has me trapped.

For some reason, I'm only worried about Carrine. Not once does it occur to me that Eli would be a danger, regardless of whether he knows what he's doing.

I know it now.

I've misjudged him.

Eligius Dupré, my love, my fiancé, may not be under Carrine's control any longer, but he's in full-blown bloodlust, and he hovers over me now, fully morphed, his face contorted and disjointed. His red gaze focuses on the pulse at my throat. I dive left, and his hand encircles my ankle and yanks me down, my head slamming into the ground. I feel his hand go around my throat, squeezing, lifting me off the ground. For a split second, I'm eye level with him. His bloodlust ones stare hard into my human ones. He doesn't see me, Riley Poe. He sees what he craves, what surges within my still-human veins, and his body is propelled by the desire to have it. My blood. Yet he cocks his head to the side, studying me. Again, hesitating.

Dread fills my insides, even as I slide my hand to the back of my pants and grip the hilt of a silver blade. I ease it out. Without changing expression, Eli's fingers tighten around my throat, and my eyes bulge from the pressure. His other hand covers mine holding the blade, and he squeezes until the pain is too much and I drop it.

He's going to lunge. Sink his teeth into me. Drain me of blood until I'm an empty shell, then throw me aside. I can't move. I'm paralyzed. With fear, dread, and an overwhelming broken heart. My brother's face flashes before me, Preacher's and Estelle's, Nyx's, even my dog Chaz's. I'll never see my loved ones again. . . .

My eyes close. I'm powerless to move him.

I'm going to die by Eli's hands. . . .

Then, unbelievably, he loosens his grip, and I'm free. . . .

My eyes snap open, just in time to see Eli smash into a tree.

Standing before me, Valerian Arcos stares down at me. His face is unmorphed, aristocratic, and beautiful. Perfect. He smiles at me, reaches a hand toward me. "Come to me, my love. At last."

My feet begin to move. Toward him. His full lips pull over perfect white teeth in a victorious smile. "That's right," he croons. "Come here, Riley."

I focus. Concentrate. Imagine my core a fireball of energy.

Valerian merely smiles at me wider. "Stop that, Riley. 'Tis a waste of time. You should know me well enough by now. When I desire something, I get it. Just like I desired Carrine's power to coerce you into killing Dupré," he sighs. "Although I didn't count on him fighting her control so much. Nor her being so rebellious."

I glance at Eli, who is standing now. Shaking off his injury.

"Oh, wait," Valerian says. "You took care of her rather well, my darling. You have quite the power within in. But trust me. I have full Strigoi in my veins. You've got . . . simply a dusting of it. And by the way, your little message to my idiot brother? He always was a weak one. He didn't have the balls to tell my father." He shrugs. "Just so you know."

I stare at him. Hatred pools inside me. Not a feeling I relish, but I can't help it.

"Let's see here. Ah yes. Let me finish this . . . distraction." He glances at Eli. "Shall you do the honors?" Valerian asks me. He grins. "Yes. I think you should. I can't very well be the cause of a vampiric war, can I?"

"Won't work this time, Valerian," I challenge. I grin.

"We shall see." His expression hardens. "Go to him. To Eli. And take your silver and plunge it into his heart. Do it now."

My fireball core is boiling hot. I stand, staring at Valerian. Again, I grin. And I don't move.

"Go now!" he commands.

I feel his will, his strength, trying to penetrate my core; it doesn't. I smile at him. "Go fuck yourself, Arcos."

Valerian's brow pulls into a hideous frown. "Very well. I'll risk a war—"

Everything happens so fast after that.

Valerian's features morph into that of the hideous Strigoi bloodsucker that he is. He lunges at Eli, and I throw my cored energy into my legs and leap at them both. Valerian and Eli are entangled, fighting, jaws snapping, and I wedge between the two and, with all the power I can control, throw Eli as far as I can. His body sails, knocking over tombstone after tombstone like dominoes as he crashes. Only then, once I see Eli on the ground, do I feel the piercing of skin, ripping of artery, and fiery intrusion of Valerian's poisoned toxic fang as it enters me. I turn and look at him, my hand flying to my throat. He snaps back, his face confused, contorted. Filled with agony. I stumble backward, something warm and sticky trickling between my fingers at my throat. Already, my vision begins to blur.

A rumble rises, roars, and vibrates within me as a body flies past and rocks into Valerian. I shake my head to clear my vision. Shock steals my breath.

Victorian Arcos, in one fierce twist, takes the head of his very own brother.

Another roar pulls my attention back to Eli. I'm falling now, stumbling like I've had too much tequila, and I see another figure fighting him. They tangle, twist, and the other figure throws his head back, dreads pulled into a queue, and Noah sinks his jagged fangs into Eli's throat.

I stumble back, horrified, dizzy, and I hit the ground on my backside. My energy is spent. My scatha—I've been clutching it the whole time— drops from my hands. I fall back on the cold cemetery ground and stare skyward. No stars. Just blackness. Oh yeah, I'm in an alternative world. Nothing's real here anyway except the creatures and souls within. . . .

Victorian's flawless face and warm brown eyes stare down at me. His mouth is moving furiously, and he is shouting my name. I can't hear him. But it's my name. He grips my shoulders and shakes me, and he falls to his knees and scoops me up. He must be running with me . . . somewhere. My body begins to convulse, my breath quickens, stops in my lungs, and I can't breathe. I'm clawing at Victorian's shirt, his hair, but he's running fast, his head turned yelling at someone over his shoulder. I can't hear who. His face is drawn tight in fury and concern, but he doesn't look down at me again. I think I see tears streaming down his face. Fear pits my stomach, but I can only stare. Only straight ahead. I grow weak fast, and now my arms fall helpless. I feel like I'm floating again. Where's Noah? *Please, God, please at least let Noah get out*. A black curtain is pulled over my eyes, wrapped around my head until I can't breathe, and I see nothing, hear nothing . . .

Nausea. Ears drumming. Voices. I don't know where I am. I try to get up, can't move my arms.

My legs. I can't even turn my head. Eyes won't open. Pain. My flesh is ripping apart!

"She's moving around too much," a voice says.

"She won't break out of that."

"You said that the last time she broke out of it."

"Shut up and just tighten them."

"You tighten them."

I try to speak. My mouth is frozen, stuck in place, like my lips are sewn together

Finally, I give up. . . .

Pain roars through me, skidding along every nerve and pathway inside my body, and I scream so hard my insides quiver. I still can't see—something's tied around my eyes. I force my core energy to my arms, my legs, and I push so hard with my mind that whatever's holding them down flies off. Curses, shouts, as whatever I'm in rocks back and forth, jolting me forward. I catch myself, and just as my fingers fly to my eyes to remove the blind, a body hits me. We crash to the floor.

Suddenly, I'm overcome by a powerful sense of . . . sexuality. Erotica. Deep-core horniness that makes me scream and grope at the body pinning me down.

"Someone better fucking hurry up over here," the voice on top of me says. "If she gets loose, someone's in trouble."

His breath brushes my lips as he speaks. I reach, wriggle beneath him. Gotta have him . . .

"Hold her still," a voice says.

"I might like her kind of trouble," a new voice comments. Accent . . . funny. Hard to understand. Familiar.

"This is as still as she gets," the voices says on top of me. "Hurry."

A pinprick, and as soon as the sensation has begun to claw at the body hovering over me, it disappears. I settle, ease, and the pain leaves me as I drift into a weightless black cloud of nothingness. . . .

The ebb and flow of waves against the shore pull me out of my deep slumber. The heavy brine of salt and sea life wash over me, and I inhale. Familiar.

"Hey," a voice says gently. "You're back."

I'm on my back, a thick softness below me, and a chilly breeze lifts my hair. I open my eyes and blink rapidly as the light pours in. Finally, my eyes can tolerate the sudden change and I focus on the figure kneeling beside me. His face grows closer, and he reaches out and strokes my cheek. I lift my hand and thread my fingers through his.

"Noah," I say, and my voice comes out croaky and broken. My throat feels as if someone has dragged a handful of thorns across it.

"Shh," he says, and covers my lips with his finger. He leans closer, mercury eyes searching my face. "How ya feeling?"

I look at him. "My whole body aches." My gaze goes beyond Noah's figure, to the lean-to palm roof I'm lying under. Several feet away, the edges of the sea wash up onto the shore. It's late afternoon, and a low sun falls somewhere behind us. "I'm at Da Island?"

Noah nods. "Yeah, darlin', you are."

I stare up at the palms covering my head. Fear chokes me into a panic, and my breath hitches in my throat, quickens. "Noah?" I don't even know what to ask, or what to say. I don't know what's happened.

"What do you remember?" he asks. His hand squeezes mine.

I concentrate. "The realm. Victorian." I squeeze my eyes shut. "Jesus Christ, he killed his brother," I say. Then my eyes flash open and I force myself to sit up. "You," I say on a painful whisper. "Eli— you bit him. Noah, Christ—"

"He's alive," Noah says with a smile. "Fine, no, not yet. Far from it. He's in deep detox. Deeper than you, Riley. Couldn't even keep him on the same island as you. I'm surprised even on the same continent. He's not out of the woods yet. He's . . . in it bad."

I sit back and my brain hurts from trying to sort things out. I push my fingertips to my temples, massaging, trying to force the memories out. "I don't remember anything."

Noah chuckles, and another biting breeze whips through. "Yeah, I guess you don't. Another hell of a plane ride. Had to take two jets. You on one, Eli on the other."

I stare up at the fading sun peeking through

the makeshift roof made of scrub palms and pine limbs. I'm not as settled as I should be, hearing that Eli made it out of the realm. "Tell me everything, Noah," I say. Tears choke my throat and claw behind my eyes, and finally, they escape. "Where's my brother? Preacher? Victorian? Rhine?"

Noah reaches over with a finger and wipes my cheeks. "It's just you and me here, darlin'. We have the island to ourselves. Rhine and the Ness boys are fine. Had to make that young pup return to Inverness. He wanted to come here, watch over you, insisted on flying back with us. He left a couple of weeks ago, and he calls or texts me every day, asking about you. And yes, everyone else is . . . alive." He narrows his eyes. "You sure you're up to this?"

With a gusty sigh, I nod. "Might as well be." Relief washes over me. Rhine and the boys are safe. Everyone is alive.

Noah scoots close, pulls me up in his arms, and settles me against his chest. He pulls the patchwork quilt—one I recognize is made by my Gullah grandma, Estelle—over my legs and waist. "This is going to take all night."

Part Ten

✦━◆━◆━✦

SACRED VOWS

I'm your density. I mean . . . your destiny.

—George McFly to Lorraine Baines,
Back to the Future, 1985

Before this is all over I am probably going to lose my mind. I don't remember ever being so off track and restless. I've got chunks of time missing in my memory, and I can't seem to get a straight answer out of anyone. What I thought was one thing turns out to be something else. What have I become? Something feels different this time, something inside me is different. Almost . . . like I have two people inside me. Or more.

—Riley Poe

"It's what?" I ask, almost jerking out of the comfort of Noah's arms.

"Settle down, wildcat," he says quietly. "It's mid-January."

No longer comforted, I sit up, turn around, and face Noah. He's sitting with his back against the pile of quilts and pillows. "How in the hell can it be mid-January, Noah? We were in Inverness in early November."

"I know."

I blink, awaiting a decent answer.

Where has all the time gone?

Noah rests his forearms against his drawn-up knees and looks at me. "Do you remember everything that happened in the realm?"

I think about it. "I killed Carrine. Then Eli attacked me." I look at him. "Valerian tried to make me kill Eli. But . . ." I think hard, my memories starting to blur. "Victorian showed up. He killed Valerian." Panic rises in my throat. "I saw you . . . bite Eli. Then Vic picked me up and ran. Everything else is a . . . blur."

Noah nods, his gaze locking on to mine. "It's called a cluster fuck, Riley. I had to subdue Eli. He was . . . out-of-control sick. His bloodlust . . ." He shakes his head, and a long dread falls over his shoulder. "It was greater than any I've ever seen before." He looks at me. "Ever."

"What'd you do, Noah?" I ask. My fear has risen and turned to bile. My stomach hurts.

"I gave him my venom. Maybe too much. It was the only thing to do at the time. He was going apeshit crazy in there. It made him calm enough to get him out of the realm and back to the Crachan. I had him in chains by the time Jake and Gabriel showed up. And then, hell. There was you."

I look at him, waiting.

"Jake, Gabriel, and Luc took one jet with Eli, back to Savannah. I grabbed another one with you, Seth, Phin, Rhine, and Arcos. Preacher, his cousin Garr, and Eli's parents were waiting for us at the airport. Preacher accompanied Eli's parents to the other island with Eli. Jake, Gabriel, and Luc went, too. Garr set us up here. Arcos, on another island."

I cock my head, puzzled. "What do you mean?"

Noah shrugs. "Between Preacher and Garr, and Eli's parents, they insisted that if Arcos was going to hang around here, he had to be cleansed. It didn't take long. He was pretty cooperative."

"Where is he now?" I ask.

Noah rubs his chin with his hands. "Lucky for us, Vic killed his own brother, instead of me killing Valerian. He's back in Romania right now, clearing things up with his family."

I notice Noah is telling me everything there is to know about everyone . . . except me.

And that's got me a little worried.

"Why are we here alone?" I ask.

Noah's penetrating, serious silver gaze makes my heart leap. "Noah?"

He sighs. "The bite you took from Valerian Arcos?" He shakes his head. "It wasn't meant for you. It was meant for Eli. To kill him."

I blink, confused. "And?"

"You . . . went through a few changes."

I shake my head. "I've had Arcos venom before, Noah—three times. Why is this different?"

He shrugs. "Arcos venom overload? Don't exactly know yet, Riley. But your DNA may have . . . crossed over."

The air swooshes out of my lungs. "Crossed over? As in full-blown vampire?"

Noah's hand reaches for mine, and he squeezes. "We're not sure yet. You've been detoxed in the most aggressive ways possible. Eli, too. And Victorian. Going on nine weeks now." He shakes his head. "Eli . . . he's not exactly remembering things, Ri." He stares at me. "Last time I saw him, he didn't remember me. He may not remember you."

My heart plummets. I thought all we had to do was get him alive. Detox him. The thought never crossed my mind that Eli wouldn't remember me. His family. His old life. I take a deep breath and push myself to my feet. My legs are wobbly, weak, and Noah's up and beside me. His hand slips under my elbow, and I look up at him. "Why are we here alone?"

"Eli needed all hands, so to speak. Once your detox was complete, and you only needed a guardian, I volunteered. The others are all with Preacher and Garr at the other island. Besides . . ." He gives me a warm smile. "A vow's a vow. I promised Eli I would keep you safe. Remember?"

I lean my head on his shoulder. "Yeah, I do. And I appreciate it." Outside the makeshift lean-to, the waves roll up onto the sand. "I need to walk," I say.

Noah drapes an arm over my shoulders and guides me out. "Then let's walk."

We start out of the lean-to, and I stop, looking up. "Thank you," I say.

Noah flashes a grin—different from the sexy, cocky one he usually portrays. "Anytime." As we walk, he reaches in the pocket of his jeans and pulls out his cell.

"She's awake," he says into the phone, and hangs up.

"Who was that?" I ask. I'm barefoot, and the sand squishes between my toes as we walk along the shoreline. Gulls scream overhead, and sandpipers scurry along the tide, poking their long beaks into the sand. The familiar briny scent washes over me, and I breathe it in. It settles me, comforts me. It's home.

Noah pulls me against him. "You'll see. And by the way . . . I saw what you did with Carrine." Affection and admiration lighten his gaze. "You're sick, you know that, right?"

I give a wan smile. "Yeah."

Noah kisses the top of my head. "We're not giving up on Eli, darlin'. No one's giving up on him. You got that?"

His words comfort me. "I know."

Riley? How are you, love?

Vic . . . I'm fine. How are you?

Ready to leave this drafty old Arcos castle. I just wanted to hear your voice. I'll be along to the States as soon as I can. Please, mind your Gullah brethren. And mind Miles. I beg you.

I will, I will. See ya soon, Vic.

Not soon enough.

A few minutes later, the purr of a boat motor carries across the inlet, and as the sun's setting I see the boat heading toward us. Two dark figures, and a handful of light ones.

The boat pushes up onto shore, and my heart leaps.

"Dere's my girl," Estelle says, her beautiful ebony skin splitting at the mouth in a wide grin, showing off her stark-white teeth. "Somebody git me outta dis ting."

Eli's brother Phin scoops her up, and Estelle squeals like a little girl. He sets her in the sand, and she makes her way to me. I rush into her arms and squeeze her tight.

"Grandma!" I say into her neck. She smells of spices and Dial soap, and it's never smelled so good.

Estelle pats me on the back several times. "Oh, now. Dere, dere, child. Don't go gettin' my dress all wet, right?" She laughs, and the familiar sound goes straight to my soul. "I'm almost too old to be jumpin' from island to island, watchin' out for you young'ns."

"Ri!" Seth says, leaping out of the boat and rushing over to me. Estelle steps back and my baby brother wraps his arms around me and picks me up. "You're okay?" he says into my hair. He pulls back, and is searching me all over, as though he might find a cut or a scratch, or something out of place.

"I'm fine, Seth," I say.

"You wasn't so fine before, girl," Preacher says, ambling up to me with a slight limp. His dark eyes regard me. "You might not be too fine now." He smiles. "But we'll keep ya, dat's right."

I laugh and throw my arms around my surrogate root-doctor grandfather's neck. "Preacher Man," I say against him, then kiss his cheek. "It's been too long."

"You, and that odder Arcos boy," he says.

"Not so bad. But your fiancé? He's been a challenge."

"When can I see him?" I ask.

Preacher's dark face stares back at me. "Soon. Not now."

Phin walks over and pulls me away from Preacher. "'Bout time you woke up," he says, and kisses me. "You scared us all for a while, too."

"Good to see you, too, garçon," I joke.

"We thought you were in a quickening," Phin says, and concern replaces his usual joking gaze. "Freaked me out."

"We still don't know, boy, so watch your neck," Estelle says, and giggles to herself. "Dat girl bites you, it's gonna be bad."

"Who's staying with Eli now?" I ask. We all walk toward the lean-to. Seth and Noah pull out lawn chairs, and we all sit.

"Pa-pa, Jake Andorra, Garr, and Gabriel," Phin says. "Ma *mère* and Josie remained in the city with Nyx."

"It's been quiet," Seth says. "Vic went back home to deal with his family. But he'll be back."

I sit in the sand at the feet of my surrogate grandparents, and let their conversation wash over me. I'm home. I don't know how right I am, but I'm home. There's something missing, a piece of me that feels incomplete, and I know it's Eli. The fear that he won't remember me terrifies me. I guess I could go on in my life—whatever that is now—and carry on, being content that at least, he's alive. But I'm greedy, and I want more than that.

I want *him*.

I'm not too sure how long I can wait to find out if he wants me, too.

Or just wants to kill me.

Preacher decides he's happy with my recovery but wants me and Noah to remain on Da Island a few more days. A thought suddenly comes to me, and I pull from my grandfather's arms and look at him.

"Are his eyes still red?"

Preacher gives a short nod. "They are, yeah." He shakes his head. "Dere's somethin' missin', dat's right. But I don't know what it is yet." He kisses my nose. "We'll figger it out, girl. Don't worry. He's progressin' good enough, I reckon."

After hugs and kisses and tears, everyone leaves me and Noah alone. Seth accompanies Estelle back to Da Plat Eye, where she and Preacher live in the shop's upstairs apartment. Preacher and Phin head back to Eli.

Eli's eyes are still red. And everyone expects me to just sit . . . and wait?

I am Strogoi. I am Dupré. And I am a Fallen.

I can do more than just kick a little ass now.

"I do not like that look in your eye."

Slowly, as I hear the purr of Preacher's boat fade in the distance, I smile at Noah.

He does not smile back.

"Riley," he warns. "Whatever it is you're cookin' in that pretty little head of yours, stop."

I take a step toward him. "Or what?"

His hand eases up, reaches down his shirt, and grasps his satchel of herbs. "Don't make me throw this in the water."

Slowly, I shake my head. "Are you seriously using your sex appeal against me, Noah Miles?" He grins. "Tsk-tsk, you crazy vampire." *Take your sexy backside and go sit in the lean-to. Now.*

Without hesitation, Noah drops his hand from his satchel, turns, and walks into the lean-to. He plops down on the pile of stacked quilts.

And simply sits.

Dusk has taken over the sky, throwing swirls and lines of purple and gray and burnt orange in a canopy overhead. I listen closely to Preacher's boat motor, and gauge the direction. A quick glance at my beach attire—cutoff jeans and a fuchsia Inksomnia T-shirt—and I decide that will do just fine in the chilly winter waters of the Atlantic. I turn my gaze to the end of Da Island, two hundred feet of shoreline and sand, and I launch myself into a full run. Ten feet from the edge I gather my strength and leap, landing thirty feet in a dive. The water rushes over my head, and I kick a few times before surfacing. Taking a deep breath, I turn in the direction of Eli's island.

I swim. Fast and hard.

An old fear rises while I swim, and I laugh it off. Sharks? Hell, I'll punch one in the nose now, no second thought. Within a few minutes, I see the lights strung in front of a lean-to similar to mine, and Preacher's boat is just pulling up onto the sand. I stop, wade in the water, and wait for Preacher and Phin to get out. Then Seth and Estelle leave, cutting across the sound toward Savannah.

I ease toward the other side of the island and climb to shore. Soaking wet, but unaffected by the cold, I creep toward Preacher's camp. Remaining are Gilles, Preacher, Jake, Gabriel, Garr, and Phin.

That's three vampires, two powerful root doctors, and . . . whatever Gabriel is. Plus Eli.

Seven. Against me.

Whatever I am.

I got this.

Through the maritime scrub forest, I make my way to the opposite shore. When I see Preacher and Garr, standing just outside the lean-to, I stop. Everyone except Eli is outside, by the shore. I close my eyes and concentrate. Pushing my energy until it forms a fiery ball in my center. I will it outward, to my fingertips.

And then like some crazy half-cocked inked wizard, I point my hands in their direction.

Everyone take a seat. Do it now.

To my surprise, every single one of them scrambles to find a seat in the sand by the shore.

Look nowhere except out to sea. Ignore me. Ignore Eli. Only stare out to sea. And stay in your seat.

As if on cue, every one of their heads turn toward the water. Since there were only two lawn chairs out, Gilles and Preacher take those. The others plop right down onto the sand. Still as zombies, they stare out.

I smile to myself and make my way to the lean-to.

Palm fronds and pine needles crunch under my bare feet as I push open the quilted doorway and look inside. Eli is lying on a pallet, similar to the one I was on earlier. He looks so peaceful, lying there with his eyes closed, his full, sexy lips soft, slightly parted. His dark hair sweeps over one side of his face, obscuring his eye.

A stick snaps behind me, and I look over my shoulder. A rabbit looks up at me, then hops away, startled. His little white tail flips in the dark.

When I glance back, I gasp.

Eli's gone.

The hair stiffens on my neck, on my arms, and I know before I look, he's behind me. Slowly, I turn.

Bloodred eyes stare down at me. Wordlessly, yet with a gentleness that surprises me, Eli grabs my throat with one hand.

I stare at him.

Then I rear back with my free hand and punch him in the side of the head.

His hand drops from my throat.

My knee goes up—hard—into his groin, and he groans.

I don't wait for a reaction. I take off.

Scrub palms and thick underbrush scrape my legs and feet as I rush through the maritime forest, and Eli's right on my tail. He lunges, grabs my feet, and we both go down.

I turn and kick him in the jaw, and he flies backward. I scramble up on hands and knees and cut a path through the wood. Just as the sandy beach is in my view, I'm tackled. Eli and I hit the ground in a tangled grunt, and I writhe and clobber him with a piece of driftwood I find next to us. He rolls off me and I'm up and running again. I leap, hit the water, and start swimming. The big splash behind me lets me know Eli's not giving up.

Good.

My arms cut the water, my legs scissor fast, and I swim as hard as I can to the next little barrier island in the sound. The shore in sight, I kick into high gear, and before long the sandy bottom settles under my feet and I pull myself up onto shore.

Just as I right myself, I'm hit from behind and fall face-first in the sand. The wind is knocked out of me, and a big body lands full-on atop me. My shoulders are grabbed, and I'm flipped over. My hands are trapped, held above my head.

Eli stares down at me, his face drawn in puzzled fury. Bloodred eyes blazing. Confusion. An inner struggle.

I focus. Stare fearlessly into those eyes. *Eligius, it's me. Riley. Your fiancée. Please remember me. I demand you remember me!*

He cocks his head to the side, studying me hard. His dark eyebrows furrow.

I've missed you, Eli. Come here. Lower. Press your mouth against mine.

Eli hesitates; then slowly, he lowers his head. I brace myself, those venomous teeth inches from my throat.

I'm lost the second Eli's lips press against mine. He doesn't move, doesn't taste. Just . . . lets them be against mine. I inhale, and only then do I notice . . . I can inhale. Air into my lungs. My heart is pounding.

I have a heart.

Eli's scent seeps into me, and yet I keep my eyes fastened on his, so close to me.

Kiss me, Eligius Dupré. Kiss me like you mean it. Kiss me and remember. . . .

Eli's mouth settles, shifts, and nudges mine apart. His tongue brushes against mine and he kisses me. Gentle at first, he explores and tastes. I lose myself, pushing aside the thought that I'm commanding him to do this with my Fallen powers, to kiss me like this, and it's not really Eli, but a puppet. At the moment, I don't care. Couldn't care less, actually. I can make out with an Eli puppet.

All I think about is Eli's body pressing into mine, his fingers entwined with mine, pushing our hands into the sand, and his mouth moving erotically over mine. . . .

"Riley," he whispers against me. His voice is throaty, raspy, and his hands move from mine to hold my head on either side. He rises, looks at me. With those bloodred eyes fastened to mine, he kisses me again. "You don't have to talk me into kissing you, *chère*."

My heart leaps—and at the same time, confusion webs my brain. "Eli?" I dare to breathe his name. I'm scared it's all going to fade away. That he'll morph, grab me, kill me. My heart slams against my ribs, and my breath lodges in my throat.

"It's me," he says, and presses his lips to mine again. "Why'd you run?"

I look at my fiancé, wide-eyed at first, and then I laugh. "Because you . . . chased me!"

Eli's head drops, his hands move down my body, and he's kissing me so deep, so hard, the sand bites into my back, my head. A deepthroated groan escapes his throat, and it rumbles against my chest. "God, woman," he says, almost whispering, "I didn't think I could last another day without you."

I'm kissing him back, and running out of breath doing it. I don't care. "Eli, your eyes," I manage in between kisses. "They're still red."

"I know," he says, tracing my lips with his tongue, then sucking on the bottom one. He rolls, pulls me on top, and I stare down at him, amazed. He grazes my jaw with his thumb. "Preacher says they'll eventually turn back, but for now, I'm stuck with them."

I throw my head back and laugh, and then fall into a long, sexy kiss with my fiancé. "I can't believe we're okay," I breathe. "Eli, I've never been so scared in all my life."

His hands are gripping my thighs, and trails up my back. "Me, too, baby," he admits. He holds my jaw steady, threads his free hand through my hair. "I can't stop looking at you."

I shove my hands into his silky hair and kiss him softly, and he lies still while I explore his mouth. I suck his bottom lip, slowly, then trace his teeth with my tongue. The unshaven scruff on his jaw against my palm turns me on and makes me writhe against him. I slide my hand down his throat, and he runs his hands over my bared thighs and pulls me hard against him and deepens the kiss. My mind goes completely blank as his tongue slowly grazes mine, and his mouth moves erotically over my lips, and everywhere his hands touch makes me burn for him. On fire.

Then he stops.

"Riley." He looks at me as I pull back, out of breath.

"Yeah?" I say.

"Can we get married now?"

The moonlight is dim, only a slice hanging low above the water, and it casts Eli's face into sexy planes and shadows. His teeth gleam white as he grins.

I laugh. "Are you safe?" I inquire. "I mean, you were being guarded by vampires, root doctors, and . . . whatever Gabriel is." I brush his bottom lip with my fingertip. "Are you . . . dangerous?"

"Nah," he says. "They were just taking extra

precautions. I want to get married. Soon. And get off this island." He pulls my bottom harder against him, and I feel his arousal pushing against me. "I want you, every day." He nuzzles me.

Suddenly, my eyes fill with tears. "Eli," I say, and the thoughts of the recent past are choking me, making me hyperventilate. "Eli, oh my God, I thought you were dead." I shake my head. "In Edinburgh. It was the most pain I've ever experienced. Then, with Carrine—"

"Ri, I'm . . . so sorry," he says, and wipes away my tears. "In all of what's happened, I remember two things. One." He holds up one finger. "The hell I was stuck in after I left you at Waverly in Edinburgh." He closes his eyes briefly, as if pushing aside horrifying memories. "Two, you, head-to-toe leather, the scatha, dragging me and Victorian Arcos down a gravelly street by our wrists." He shakes his head. "I wasn't able to speak, but I saw you, and all I could think was *That's my woman. She's dared an alternative Hell, and has rescued me.*" A smile tugs at his lips. "I've always thought you were badass, Riley, but Jesus."

I sniff, and smile. "I'd die for you."

"If I could, I'd die for you, too," he answers me, and pulls me close. "I don't remember what I did while in Inverness—only what Miles has told me. I have flashes, though—of you, trying to get through to me. And you did. Even if for a split second, I remembered." His lips move over mine, frantic, desperate, and every fear he's ever had, I feel, and I drink him in. He raises his head. "I'm sorry. For all the hell I've put you through. I have a pain inside that won't stop, and I know it's from the things I've done. I tried hard to fight it, not to drink human blood. I tried hard as hell."

With my knuckles, I graze his jaw. The contempt and self-loathing I see in the depths of his red eyes nearly choke me. I can't imagine his suffering. I look at him hard, long. "Yet look at us now." I smile. "We survived all of that. And we're here, together." I kiss him. "Forever. And this is the last time you need ever mention apologies, Eli. You were not you. A freaking witchpire had you under her dark control." I narrow my eyes. "I kicked her ass to Hell, by the way."

One side of his sexy mouth lifts in a half grin. "So I've been told."

For a few moments, we're silent, just drinking each other in.

"When?" Eli breathes against my mouth. "You. Me. Nuptials." His fingers lace through mine, and his brow lifts. "Where's your engagement ring?"

"April," I answer. "Best time of year in Savannah for a wedding. And I left it in Savannah, safe with your mom, so it wouldn't get lost."

Eli breaks the kiss. "We'll have to remedy that, first thing. And April? That's . . . weeks away."

I grin, start to rise. "I know."

"Whoa," he says, and fastens his hands at my hips. "Where are you going, *ma chère*?"

"Well," I say, and trust me when I say it, it is *not* easy, "we have to save something sacred for our wedding night." I leap off him and stand, leaving Eli lying in the sand. "From now until our wedding night, consider yourself celibate."

Eli's mouth drops open. It makes his red eyes even more menacing. "What?" He leaps up, grasps my shoulders. "Ri, we've had . . . tons of sex!"

I grin. "Yeah, I remember. Every single time. A lot of it nasty." I rise and brush my lips across his. "And now you'll have to savor those memories until we're married."

"Okay, I changed my mind," he says. "We don't have to get married yet."

I laugh and lace my fingers through his. "Too late. Won't work."

Eli's face draws into a mask of pure agony. He pushes his hands through his tangled wet hair. "Oh, Jesus Christ. I'm going to die."

I laugh. "You're not going to die, Eli. Besides," I say, experiencing a bit of agony myself, "it'll be worth it. Trust me."

Eli's red eye peeks from between his fingers. "That alone makes it worth it."

I laugh, and my fiancé pulls me into his embrace. He holds me, our bodies still soaked from our swim, and his chin rests on top of my head. "Are we going to be okay, Eli?" I ask. Uncertainty clouds my joy, and a worry starts in the pit of my stomach. "Are you going to be okay?"

"I've never felt more alive," he whispers. "The one thing that was lacking in my detox was you." He grasps both sides of my face with his hands and stares at me. "I don't remember much, except the pain. But the one thing I do remember is thinking, *What am I missing? Something's not right, something is supposed to be here, and it's not.*" He smiles, and the moonlight glances off his jaw. He's so sexy it hurts. "You. I felt empty, dead without you."

Love and contentment spread through me, and I realize now that, no matter what else happens, we can handle it. We'll be okay. I frown then, staring up at him. "Swear to God, Eli. If those creepy red eyes of yours aren't changed back to that engaging cerulean blue by the wedding, you have to get contacts."

He kisses me then, and I fall into his embrace. After the kiss starts to get heated, I pull back and peck him on the jaw. "Do you remember the first time we were together?"

Eli cocks a dark eyebrow. "*Together* together?"

I laugh. "Yes. That."

He lowers his head and brushes his lips to mine. "Every last detail."

I breathe him in, and the memory of it rocks me. . . .

The brush of his tongue against mine, his skin, my skin, bare and moving together. His hand caressing every inch of me, his mouth making love to mine. The way he completely filled me, rocked me to my core, and made me all but crawl with need. I couldn't get enough. . . .

It takes me a few seconds to breathe, and when I do, my eyes flutter open and stare into Eli's bloodred ones.

A grin lifts his mouth. "Damn, Poe."

Strangely enough, I feel a blush creep up my neck. "What?"

"I saw that," he says. "It's like we . . . watched. Us. Together."

My eyes widen. "You saw that?"

Eli's deep laugh cracks the night. "Yeah. I damn sure did."

My mouth goes dry at the memory. "Maybe we can negotiate the celibacy."

Lacing his fingers through mine, Eli pulls me to the water. "I don't think so, Poe. You called it. Now let's go free up all the folks you mind-whammied." He kisses me one last time. "We've got a wedding to plan."

Even as we both dive into the chilled Atlantic water, my mind can't wrap around the fact that Eli is okay, he recognizes me, and we'll be getting married in a handful of weeks. As we swim together through the darkness, I realize Eli is more than my fiancé. Way more than the best sex I've ever had or ever will have.

He's my other half. My mate.

For as long as I live.

Epilogue

NUPTIALS

Unorthodox doesn't even cover it.

And I say this with all the love and affection I have in my heart.

This is one fucked-up life I have.

I wouldn't have it any other way.

I'm staring out of my balcony, over River Street and at the Savannah River. It's been weeks since I awoke on the little barrier island with Noah, and then zapped him and, Jesus, even old Preacher Man, into a zombielike state, all so I could get my fiancé alone. Just to see if he'd remember me.

Oh, remember he did.

I almost beat the hell out of him. He wasn't so gentle with me, either. I kinda dug it, too.

In the distance, the *clop-clop* of a horse pulling a carriage makes his way through the moss-draped oaks of Savannah's historic district. The brine off the river is refreshing, slightly pungent. Perfect. The sun is shining. There's a slight chill in the air. And not a mosquito in sight. How perfect is that?

Today's April seventh. My wedding day. I can barely wrap my brain around it.

And I'm marrying a two-hundred-plus-year-old vampire.

That's not as hard to grasp as one might think.

"Oh. My. God!" My door flies open, and my

best friend, Nyx, rushes into my apartment. I've set the living room up as a getting-ready bridal suite, with a long full-length oak mirror in one corner. I'm standing in front of it now, and Nyx sashays up behind me. She slips her arms around my middle and hugs my bare back.

"You are beautiful, Riley!" she exclaims, looking over my shoulder at my reflection in the mirror. "I've missed you so much. I was so scared you wouldn't come home."

I smile at Nyxinnia Foster. She and Josie, Eli's little sister, are my bridesmaids, and we'd gone shopping together. I'd let them choose their dresses, and they'd done a jam-up job.

Fuchsia silk, above the knee, with a haltered top, and a narrow black velvet strip just under the breast. Solid black wedge shoes. Black velvet chokers. Their bouquets are faded green hydrangea and calla lily. Both have their hair down and swept to the side with a black velvet clip. "You look beautiful yourself, Ms. Foster."

Nyx slips her hand over my shoulder and wiggles her ring finger, where a beautiful platinum engagement ring holds a fairly impressive cluster of sparkling diamonds. She grins. "Not Foster for long," she sighs. "We'll actually be sisters, Ri. Isn't that exciting?"

Eli's brother, Luc, had asked Nyx to marry him. She'd said yes.

I couldn't be happier.

I pull her gently to me and kiss her cheek. "Always sisters."

A tap at the door sounds, and we both jump, then burst into giggles. Phin and Luc both stick their heads in the door. "Everybody decent?"

"Never!" Nyx and I both holler out.

"Yeah, well, that's a— Whoa." Phin lets out a low whistle. "Damn."

I laugh. "Perv." My gaze moves to Eli's other brother, Luc.

His eyes are bugged out as he inspects Nyx. "You two are the most gorgeous creatures I've ever seen. In. My. Life." He walks over to Nyx and pulls her into a quick embrace and a kiss, then moves over to me. "Sister, I am speechless," he says, and studies me. "Eli is going to freak. You're breathtaking."

"I hope so," I say, and I'm surprised to find myself nervous.

"I'm freaking," Phin says with a grin.

"Bro, watch it—that's my sister you're freaking over," my brother says, entering. His eyes light up when he sees me, and he hurries over to pull me into a gentle hug. "Mom would've loved being here, you know? You look amazing. But . . . this feels so weird, Ri," he says against my hair. "You, getting married? Almost like I'm losing you or something."

I pull back and look at my baby brother. "I'll always be here," I assure him. "Always together, me and you. I promise. Despite Rhine and the Ness Boys asking you to join them in Inverness."

Seth grins. "I haven't said no to that yet."

I return the smile. After what had gone down

in Inverness, Rhine had asked Seth to join the
Ness Boys. As in live there, with them at the Crachan, to keep Inverness and the Highlands safe.
After Carrine's reign of terror, there's no telling
how many newbloods are roaming the glen. It
wouldn't surprise me at all if Seth accepted, too,
no matter that he's hesitating. Might be good for
him, although he'd probably have to take Eli's
little sister, Josie. Now that I think about it, she'd
also be quite an asset to the Ness Boys. Knowing
Rhine, it's probably his master cunning scheme
of getting me back to Scotland. "I know you
haven't, but if you do, it's totally okay." I step
back and admire. "You guys look fabuloso," I
say. The guys are decked out in black tuxes and
Luc and Phin each sport a fuchsia bow tie. Luc's
dark blond hair brushes his tux collar. Phin's
dark blond buzz cut makes him look simply
badass. Both have blue eyes that sparkle. My
brother? When did he grow up into such a handsome guy?

"Heard all that," Phin says, reading my mind.
He looks at Seth. "She thinks you're cute."

I mock-glare at Phin.

Luc looks down at Nyx. "Ready, love?"

"Maybe I should wed Riley, instead of Eli,"
Phin says, rubbing his jaw with a knuckle. He
winks at me. "He's so damn old."

I shake my head. "Please take him out of
here," I tell Nyx.

She gives me a kiss on the cheek and links her
arms between both brothers. "See ya out there,"

Nyx says sweetly. "I can't wait! Come on, Seth Poe. You, too."

My brother gives me a sweet, wide smile. Words aren't needed. I'll always remember that smile of his, on this day. My wedding day.

Just as they step out the door, Noah walks in. He looks at me, and I grin.

"God Almighty, woman. You just killed me," he says, and walks to me. "No, wait. I'm dying now." He places a hand over his heart. "I'm serious, Ri. It actually hurts."

"Cut it out," I say, and twirl in a circle. "Too much?" I ask.

"Are you kidding?" he says, and shakes his head as he studies me from head to toe. "Dupré, that lucky fuck. He better thank me later that I didn't bite him a little longer."

"Noah!" I exclaim.

His mercury eyes dance with merriment. "Kidding. Sort of."

He walks over to me and stares at me through the mirror. "You're beautiful, Riley Poe."

I look at my reflection. I admit, I do feel like an inked and slightly unconventional version of Cinderella. My hair is a messy updo, with fuchsia tendrils swirling down toward my collarbone. My dress is pretty simple, A-line, antique white, with a layer of fine lace overlay, strapless, backless—almost obscenely so. I turn in the mirror, inspecting my inked dragon that goes up my back and down my arm.

"I want to do just one thing before I put you

on the back of Eli's bike and drive you to your wedding," he says, and turns me around to face him. He's wearing a black tux, just like Luc's and Phin's, complete with a fuchsia bow tie. So very handsome. With my white strappy heels on, I'm just about eye to eye with him.

"What's that?" I ask.

Gently, he takes my face in his hands, turns my head to the side, and presses his mouth against mine.

And kisses me. I kiss him back.

It's not a short kiss.

But it's not perverted and obscene, either. I'm a little stunned.

And I'll never, ever forget it.

He pulls back, and his eyes are softened. He smiles. "I will always love you, Riley," he admits. "And I'll always regret the day Eli met you first. But . . ." He pulls me into a hug. "I am satisfied just loving you as a friend. And I will always, forever be here for you. No matter what."

I smile, adjust a loose dread that has escaped the velvet tie at the nape of his neck. "I'm the luckiest girl alive," I admit. "To have you, Eli, and so many others. I'll always love you, too, Noah. You'll always be more than a friend to me."

His mercury eyes sparkle. "Really?"

I laugh. "I'm trying to be serious. And yes, I mean it, but not in a nasty, sex way. I do love you." I kiss him quickly on the lips. "But I can only be in love with one. And it's always been Eli."

A slow smile cracks his beautiful face in two.

"I know. And I know what you mean." He inclines his head toward the door. "Ready, gorgeous?"

I take a deep breath and ease it out. "Absolutely."

We head to the door, and he hands me my bouquet. "I told Eli I was gonna do that, by the way."

I smile at him. My feelings are deep for Noah, and I don't know what I'd do without him. We've been through a lot. "What'd he say?" I ask.

Noah grins and holds the door open for me. "Last chance."

I shake my head, Noah hands me my shades, and I slip them on. I inhale a lungful of Savannah springtime air, hike up my dress, and let Noah help me onto the back of Eli's Martin Brother's Silverback. White silk streamers and tin cans are tied all over the back and fenders, and trail behind us as we ignore the helmet law and move through the streets of Savannah. I slide my arms around Noah's waist and hold on, and smile at the passersby on the sidewalks as we make our way to Forsythe Park. Azaleas and wisteria are in full bloom, and honestly, it couldn't be a more perfect day.

If only my mom could be here to see it.

We get to Forsythe. Noah pulls into a space, and parks. He helps me off and tucks my hand in the crook of his arm as we make our way to the fountain.

The invited crowd of loved ones is way too large

for an indoor church wedding. Outdoors was the only way to go, and I'd chosen the fountain because, well, it's beautiful, and my mom had always loved it. God, how I miss her on this day.

"She's watching you, love," Noah says in a quiet voice. "She sees."

Yeah, Noah Miles is one sweet man. I pray he finds a woman one day who deserves him. Luckily, I'll be around long enough to ensure that. I pull him closer. "Thanks."

He walks me to a large moss-draped tree, where Preacher awaits me. His white smile nearly blinds me as Noah hands me to my surrogate grandfather.

"I'll see ya up there," Noah says with a wink, and disappears up the walk.

Preacher tucks my hand into his large ebony one. Callused, familiar, and loving. "You are a painted beauty, girl, dat's right," he says with love. "Me and your grandmudder are so proud of you. Dat boy"—he inclines his head toward the front, where Eli awaits—"he loves you in de same way I love Estelle. The forever kind." He gives a single nod. "Dat's all I want for my baby girl."

"I love you," I say, my voice choked.

Preacher kisses me on the cheek. "I know dat."

I suppress a laugh.

"You gonna take dem tings off your pretty face?"

I slip off my shades and ease them into the pocket of Preacher's black tux. "Thanks," I say.

He grins and faces forward.

The music starts up.

It's not your conventional wedding.

Rhine, Tate, Gerry, and Pete are playing my wedding march.

Rhine wrote it himself. It's the first time I've heard it.

It's nearly breaking my heart.

"Dat's a fine boy, too, dat Rhine," Preacher informs me quietly. "Good boy. Nice voice, dat's right. Your grandmudder ordered his CD on Amazon. Plays it all da time, she does."

I look at my grandfather and laugh. Lord help the world, Estelle has discovered the Internet.

Through the crowd, I see Rhine with his bass, and I have to agree. He's a great guy.

Ahead, a small line starts to move toward the fountain, where Garr, also an ordained minister, awaits us. Noah is Eli's best man, and the pair stand at the fountain, on Garr's left. But Noah is standing in just the right position, so I don't have a good look at Eli yet. My insides ping with nerves. Ahead of me, Nyx and Luc make their way up an aisle covered in dogwood blooms. Guests are seated in white wooden folding chairs on either side of the fountain.

They're filled to the gills with people I love.

Next, Phin grasps his sister's arm and they head up the aisle. He returns for his mother, Elise, who is stunning in a champagne silk gown with a diamond choker. Gilles follows behind them. Luc returns and escorts Estelle down the aisle then, but not before she turns, her eyes wide, and a big grin stretches across her aged ebony face. She's wearing a soft light dove gray dress that shimmers in the sunlight. It reminds me of Noah's eyes. She's my beautiful Gullah grandmother, and she kisses me, then heads up the aisle.

I glance out over the crowd gathered before me, and I'm in absolute awe of my life and all who is in it.

First, my baby brother, who sits on the front row. This whole thing started when he and his silly friends inadvertently set the Arcos brothers free of their graves. What would have happened if they hadn't done that?

I shudder at the thought.

All things happen for a reason. I'm so totally convinced of that.

Next to my brother, of all souls, is Victorian Arcos. One of the entombed devils, who turned out not to be such a devil after all. He smiles at me, and I'm surprised he's behaving so well. Not once since our last mind convo has he entered my thoughts. I think Eli must have had a talk with him.

Gabriel and Sydney are here, Lucien and Ginger. Jake Andorra, and he has a date, which makes me slightly curious. Victorian Arcos is next to Jake's date. My WUP family. Perfect. They'd settled the wolf war in the Highlands, by the way.

And then all of my lovely Gullah family.

Jack and Tuba, Preacher's nephews, flanked

by big Zetty the Tibetan, are nearly taking up a row all themselves. Preacher's family. Garr's family, and several of Noah's Charleston crew have gathered.

It's all pretty fantastic.

Werewoves. Gullah. Humans. Vampires.

And whatever Gabriel is.

I am not there, Riley, but I can see you. I'm envious of Eli, and I'll always love you. I'm here to watch over you. All you have to do is call me.

Thanks, Athios. Because of you, this is possible. I'll never forget it.

I'll never forget you, my love. And Miles is right, by the way. Your mother is here. She sees. Her happiness for you makes her light brighter.

Tell her I love and miss her so much, Athios.

She knows.

My eyes mist with tears. My mother's watching. Of course she's an angel. She was in life. Why would she be anything less in death? A joy fills me, and I know it's her.

Thank you, Athios. What do you know? My own guardian angel.

My eyes drift to the other side of the guests.

The side that is nearly taken up by the absolute largest men I've ever seen in my life. Tristan de Barre of Dreadmoor Keep, his wife and brood, along with Jason, Gawan, and Ellie, and all of their children, have crossed the Pond to attend the nups. Tristan's men have come as well, and let me tell you, it's an impressive bunch of once-medieval fellas.

To think of all the lives that have been lived. Lost. Relived.

Shocks me to the core.

"Time to go, baby girl," Preacher whispers to me.

Rhine starts a new tune—another he's written—and Preacher and I start up the dogwood-petal-strewn aisle.

My eyes are fixed now on only one soul. My breath leaves me.

His eyes are mostly back to that beautiful cerulean color I love. But there are still flecks of red embedded in them that may never go away. I'd decided that it's him, and I wanted all of him. No contacts needed. Our gazes are locked as I make my way toward him. The look on his face reveals much. Jaw muscle flexing, and he's fighting a smile, but soon loses that fight as his beautiful lips stretch into a wide grin.

I think he's freaked.

He meets me and Preacher in the front of the fountain. Preacher kisses me and places my hand in Eli's. Then he joins them together and sits beside his wife.

"I can't stop shaking," Eli whispers in my ear as we face Garr.

My heart leaps.

Garr goes through the typical ceremony, and I hear every single word he says. Through sickness and in health. Yes, yes, of course. For as long as you both shall live? Is there any other choice? Longer than that, maybe? His words register, and

Eli and I both answer. Inside, though, I'm a quiver of nerves. My wedding day. To Eligius Dupré.

How did I get so lucky?

"You wish to say your own vows, dat's right?" Garr asks.

Eli nods and turns me to face him. He holds my hands and slips a platinum band over my ring finger. It nestles next to the engagement ring he'd given me, before Edinburgh. It feels right, like it's belonged there all along, and my breath hitches. "All my life, I've waited for you, Riley Poe. You're everything I could ever want, no matter how many lifetimes we live. You make me full, complete, and I'll spend every single day making sure you never regret marrying me."

My heart is in my throat, and I swallow past it. Eli's words sink to my core. Love makes my nerves tingle. My eyes meet his, and I hold his gaze. My heart flutters. "I worked hard to pull out of the dregs that were once my life," I say, and I ease the wide platinum matching band over Eli's ring finger. My hands are shaking. The sun beams overhead but is filtered through the canopy of live oaks. Dapples of sun light on Eli's face, and just looking at him I feel my heart melting. His mouth lifts on one side, fighting a grin. "But to love you is the easiest thing I've ever done. I'll love you till the day I die, Eligius Dupré. You're the best thing that's ever happened to me. You're my life."

I hear Nyx sniffling behind me, and I fight my own tears.

"Well, den," Garr says. He's dressed in a dark gray tux and a slick hat to match. "I think you two belong togedder, forever. In the eyes of God, and all dese folk, I pronounce you wife and husband, for as long as you both exist." Garr grins at Eli. "Well, den, kiss her, boy!"

My whole body is humming with love and excitement as Eli grasps my face with both of his hands and presses his mouth to mine. It's a sweet, long, sleight-of-tongue kiss, and I melt into him. He pulls back and looks down at me, and the love in his mostly blue eyes takes my breath away. He smiles. I smile back.

You're mine, he says.

Nuh-uh, you're mine, I correct.

"Mr. and Mrs. Eligius Dupré, all hitched and legal!" Garr hollers.

Someone in the crowd whistles, and I know without looking it's Tristan. The sound pierces the air and rivals that of a screeching falcon. The crowd roars then, clapping and rising to their feet. Eli takes my hand and we make our way right into the center of them all, and we stand there forever greeting, hugging, and rejoicing.

"My God, woman," a deep voice rumbles at my ear. "I thought you were a vision wearing a battle helm and yielding a broadsword." I turn and look up—way up—into the strange blue eyes of Tristan de Barre. "But I fancy this dress, for sure!"

I throw my arms around Tristan, and for the first time, meet his lovely wife, Andi. In turn, I hug all of the Dragonhawk knights, Gawan of Conwyk and his wife, Ellie, and all of their children combined. It's like a small army. Eli shakes their hands, and they're none satisfied with that. They pull him, too, into a tight bear hug.

It's a day of hugging I'll not soon forget.

"You did well, gel," Gawan's strangely accented voice says in my ear. "You're a strong-willed lass—that's for sure. No one else woulda survived that realm, save you."

I grasp his large hands in mine. "We wouldn't be here if it not for you, Gawan. Thank you."

Gawan holds my gaze for a moment, and together we share a silent understanding. He nods, then joins his family.

"Well," a familiar voice sounds off to my left. "I guess this means you two need paid vacay."

I turn and throw my arms around Jake Andorra's neck, and he hugs me tightly. Then he slaps Eli on the back. "Good to see you, Dupré. You both look fitter than ever. Can you two wrap up your honeymoon so we can get back to work? I hear there're unexplained ghostly slayings in an Irish asylum. Could use your help."

Eli and I pass a look.

And grin.

Jake walks off, shaking his head.

We greet the WUP team, Ginger and Lucian, as well as Gabriel and Sydney, and I'm thankful for all of the eclectic souls in my life.

Including the one I'm now married to.

My brother hugs me close and kisses my cheek.

"You're the prettiest bride I've ever seen, Ri," he says. Still the sweetest kid ever. "I love you."

"I love you, too, bro," I tell him. I'll later let him know what Athios told me about our mother.

"How about me?"

I turn and, without hesitation, throw my arms around Victorian Arcos. He's handsome, velvety black hair still pulled into a queue, and looking positively polished in an Armani tux. "Slick threads," I say. "I'm glad to see you."

"And I, you," he answers. Then sighs. "I suppose this is the end?"

I lift an eyebrow. Vic and I had spoken on the phone after he'd settled things with his family. I owe him my life. He'd sacrificed so much. I couldn't imagine, well, life without him. I smile. "Never the end, my friend. But yes. I'm married now. Your chances with me are officially over."

"I suspected as much."

Eli laughs and claps Vic on the shoulder. "Don't sweat it, old boy. You'll find someone. I've no doubt."

No one like her.

I smile at Victorian for slipping that one past Eli, and kiss him on the cheek.

"So this is the lucky one," an accented voice says at my side. I turn and find Rhine grinning. He sticks his hand out to shake Eli's. "I almost stole her from you, ya know."

Eli's grin is genuine. "Almost," he says. "Thank you for watching after her. She's not stopped talking about you. Quite impressive."

Rhine leans over and brushes a kiss across my lips. "Anytime," he says. His green eyes flash with mischief. He shakes his head and walks over to talk to his band.

"So, here we all are, full circle," Noah says. He drapes an arm over my shoulder. "Now what?"

Eli grins and shoves Noah's arm off me. "Now we honeymoon. For a long time. Alone."

Noah's brow furrows. "I was afraid of that."

I laugh and lay my head against his chest. "You're overwhelming, Miles," I say. "It's almost like I have two husbands."

When I glance at Noah, his eyes are twinkling.

"Don't even think it," Eli warns.

"He kissed me before we came here today," I tattle.

"She kissed me back," Noah adds.

"But I get to take her home," Eli says, looking down at me. "Now?"

"No, not now, silly boy," Eli's mother, Elise, says at his elbow. She kisses me and hugs her son. "We've got a huge reception planned. You've got to go to that first."

"That's right," Nyx says at my other side. Luc is beside her, and Phin won't stop staring at me, grinning. Their youngest sibling, Josie, is holding Seth's hand.

"How long will you guys be gone?" Josie asks me. "I haven't hardly been able to catch up with you, Ri."

"I know," I answer, then look at her brother.

My husband.

"Two weeks, shorty," Eli tells his sister. "Then I'll share."

"Can I have your word on that?" Phin asks, grinning. "My new sister here is supposed to ink me when you get home."

"Phin's letting me design it, too," Josie says. "Wait till you see it!"

"My new daughter," Gilles says, stepping close and hugging his wife. "You're simply stunning, *chère*." He lifts my hand and kisses it, and I'm briefly reminded of the first time I met him. It brings a smile to my face. He grins in return. "I'm ever so glad to have you and Seth in our little family."

"I am, too," I say, smiling.

"Let's eat!" Seth cries. "I'm starving!"

The whole party moves to the Dupré family home for a reception. Eli and I do all of the traditional things a wedding party does: cut the cake, sans squashing it in each other's faces; the toast. The throwing of the bouquet, and the flinging of the garter, which Phin catches with a grin. A photographer who's been taking pictures the whole time smiles to herself, apparently proud of her work.

I'm just glad vampires really can be seen in photos.

Rhine and his band play, and we dance. We eat. We party. I share a dance with, God Almighty, everyone. Rhine, Noah, Victorian, Gabriel, Lucian, Jake, Tristan, Gawan. Jason, and every single one of the Dragonhawk knights. Gilles, Preacher, and Garr. By the time I've danced with the last of my Gullah family, I am thinking I will pass out.

Luckily, Preacher had slipped me a little root doctor concoction before my wedding, to prevent me from falling out in a narcoleptic coma. Jesus, that would've been a disaster. Me. Asleep. On my wedding night. As it is, I'm wide awake. Anxious. Elated.

Filled to the rim with a joy I can't even begin to explain.

More hugging, more kissing, and more memories are made. I truly am a lucky girl.

"If we don't get out of here within the next five minutes I'm going to maul you here in front of everyone," Eli whispers into my ear. I look at him, and his eyes shine. "I mean it."

I grin.

I believe him. "Well, let's go, Mr. Dupré."

Eli grins. "As you wish, Mrs. Dupré."

Yes. We're that annoying couple who relishes calling each other by their newly married name. I love it. I can't say it enough.

"This way," Noah suddenly says at my shoulder. He grins down at me. "I must love the hell out of you both. Assisting in your honeymoon getaway." He shakes his head. "What have I become?"

"The best friend a man could ask for," Eli says, and hugs him. "Lead the way, my good man."

We weave through the back of the house, and

outside, Eli's Silverback awaits. Cans and streamers sill hang behind it. Noah helps me onto the back.

"I'll take care of everything until you get back," he tells Eli. Then leans over and kisses me. "I love you, Mrs. Dupré. See ya."

"Love you, too, Mr. Miles."

Noah grins and waves us away.

I hold on to Eli's waist, and I have absolutely no idea where we're going. He told no one—except Rhine and the band, who'd helped him get whatever he's gotten ready ready. He pulls the Silverback up to the landing on River Street and helps me off. Wordlessly, he takes me down to the dock and helps me onto a small boat. Without saying one word, he pulls me against him and starts the engine. We take off into the harbor.

A half hour later, and ahead, through the darkness, one of the small barrier islands is awash in moonlight. On the beach, a fire flickers. Eli runs the boat up onto the sand, jumps out, and lifts me up. He carries me to a lean-to, sits me on my feet.

Not any old run-of-the-mill lean-to.

Our wedding night lean-to. He steps through the gauzy white material of a doorway and looks back at me.

In his eyes shine possession, fierce longing, and something way deeper than I've ever seen before in those blue depths. "Come in here," he says, and grasps my hand, pulls me inside. I follow.

His eyes are trained on mine. "Stand still."

I do as he says.

Slowly, Eli's deft fingers move over my skin to the tiny buttons at the lower back of my gown. Loosening each one, he pushes my gown off my shoulders, his lips falling against my skin. My eyes close as his fingers trail down each hip, and he helps me step out of my dress. He removes my shoes. When he stands, I take off his tux jacket. Push his suspenders off his shoulders. Unbutton his shirt. When my hands move to his belt, air hisses from his lips. I slowly push his slacks over his muscular hips, and I'm not surprised to see he's gone to his wedding commando-style. He grins, kicks off his socks and shoes, and scoops me up and lowers his head. Full lips brush over mine, and he kisses me until we reach the massive pallet of quilts thrown together for our wedding bed. He follows me down.

My body involuntarily shakes.

He comes to me then, close; his body brushes mine, his fingers ease over my bare shoulders, across my collarbone, down the front where my strapless bra clasps between my breasts. He releases it, eases it down, and I wince. With a gentleness that no longer surprises me, he pushes the silky material off my body and drops it to the ground.

Inside, I'm dying.

"I know, baby," he says, reading my mind. He slips his fingers through the waistband of my panties and eases them off. "I'm going to fix that."

My heart leaps.

"Close your eyes," he whispers. I do.

Eli's mouth moves over my skin, tasting erotic samples of each rib, over my abdomen, each breast. I can feel the heat building inside me. It's been so long. I reach for him.

"No, don't do that," he whispers. "Stay with me, Riley."

I sigh. "I'm trying."

His seductive mouth against my skin makes my nerves leap. "Try harder."

Eli's hands glide over my shoulders, down my arms, intertwine his fingers with mine, and draw me close. His hard body presses close to me; his lips seek the top of my shoulder, my throat, my ear, my jaw, and slide to my mouth. In a slow, erotic kiss, his tongue grazes mine, his teeth scrape my lips and capture the bottom one, and he suckles gently.

Inside, I grow heavy with desire; my knees weaken, and I lift my hips; his breath catches in his throat; he captures my hands in his hands and lowers them.

"Not yet, Riley," he says, his voice strained, his French accent thick. I move my hands to his chest, trail the muscles there, his breath brushing against my ear. "You touch me, I explode. Just . . . be still."

"Then don't kiss me like that," I insist.

I feel his smile against my skin. "No promises there."

I sigh.

"Turn around," he says against my cheek.

I do, and he pushes my hair over one shoulder and moves his mouth over my skin. It takes even more control not to touch Eli.

There's a hot, sexy, naked vampire in the marriage bed with me.

Eli chuckles, reading my thoughts. I think of nothing but Eli, his touch, and the craving he stirs within me. His hands glide over my body, every inch passed makes my eyes roll back in bliss; I want him everywhere, inside, out, and I never, ever want him to leave again.

His hands move over my hips, encircle my stomach, and pull my body against his. I feel his muscles pressing into my spine, his hardness pressing against the small of my back. His arms tighten around me, his mouth at my jaw. "I swear, I'll never leave you again," he whispers, his voice strained, somewhat painful. "I'm yours forever."

I turn in his arms and lock my gaze on his. His dark hair falls across his eyes, and I reach up and push it aside, graze his jaw, run my thumb over his sexy lips. "Promise?"

His mouth seeks mine. "I promise," he whispers, his tongue tasting mine.

I push him back. "Good. Now *you* be still."

A small smile tilts his mouth. "Yes, ma'am."

I lose myself in his drugging kiss; my hands glide over the muscles in his back, over his tight ass, over his hips. The feel of his tongue against mine, his teeth scraping my lips, makes me hot, wet, crazy. Blind with need, I move my hands over the cut ridges of his abdomen, lower, and grasp his hardness. He gasps in my mouth, groans deep, kisses me deeper.

"Jesus, Riley," he says, pained. "Control's slipping." His hands are roaming all over me.

"Don't care," I mutter against his throat, my hands stroking him. "Need you," I pant, pressing my body to his. *"Now, Eli."*

Without words, he moves over me, sinks his hard length in until Eli fills me completely. My head drops back, drugged, weightless. Eli's mouth tastes my skin; his tongue teases the hardened, sensitive peaks of my breasts, first one, then the other. With his fingers digging into my hips, he moves, the feel of his hardness sliding inside me making me crazy high. His mouth caresses me, makes love to me.

"Eli," I gasp, and hold on, our rhythms matching, and somewhere deep within me, an intense orgasm begins like a faraway storm. We move together, fast, out of control, until the storm grows in strength and finally crashes, wave after wave of climax claiming us both; I lose my breath, spasms rack my body. Eli holds me close; his mouth presses to my throat. The world tilts still; Eli's lovemaking has that effect on me. I can do nothing more than hold on to him.

Through the darkness, Eli's eyes search mine. Slowly, he lowers his head, captures my mouth, and kisses me. Now his control has returned and he uses it to savor my lips, my tongue, to speak to me with just his mouth: actions that speak volumes over any words he could have whispered to me.

Until he *does*.

Eli pulls me close against him, my head resting on his chest, his arms completely around me, holding me to his body. He pulls back, just enough so I can see his face. With his fingers, he finds my wedding ring. Caresses it.

Serious, cerulean eyes with tiny flecks of bloodred bore into mine. "I love you, Riley Poe Dupré." He brushes a thumb over my lips. "If I could, I'd die for you. Don't forget that." He kisses me then, slowly, erotically, then looks at me again. "*Ever.*"

I pull his mouth back to mine and kiss him until I'm breathless. "You're mine forever, Eligius Dupré."

He smiles against my mouth and pulls me closer. "Not long enough, but it'll do for now."

Elle Jasper

BLACK FALLEN
The Dark Ink Chronicles

Tattoo artist Riley and her vampire fiancé Eli Dupré, of the Worldwide Unexplained Phenomena team, are sent to Edinburgh, Scotland, where they must take down a powerful and evil trio of fallen angels.

"The most...enticing and unique paranormal world [we've] read in years."
—Romance Junkies

Also available in the series:
Afterlight
Everdark
Eventide

Available wherever books are sold or at
penguin.com

facebook.com/ProjectParanormalBooks